SOMETHING
TO TALK ABOUT

SOMETHING
TO TALK ABOUT

Meryl Wilsner

JOVE
NEW YORK

A JOVE BOOK
Published by Berkley
An imprint of Penguin Random House LLC
penguinrandomhouse.com

Library of Congress Cataloging-in-Publication Data

Names: Wilsner, Meryl, author.
Title: Something to talk about / Meryl Wilsner.
Description: First edition. | New York: Jove, [2020]
Identifiers: LCCN 2019052279 (print) | LCCN 2019052280 (ebook) |
ISBN 9780593102527 (trade paperback) | ISBN 9780593102534 (ebook)
Subjects: GSAFD: Love stories.
Classification: LCC PS3623.I577777 S66 2020 (print) |
LCC PS3623.I577777 (ebook) | DDC 813/.6—dc23
LC record available at https://lccn.loc.gov/2019052279
LC ebook record available at https://lccn.loc.gov/2019052280

First Edition: May 2020

Printed in the United States of America
1 3 5 7 9 10 8 6 4 2

Cover design and illustration by Vi-An Nguyen
Book design by Alison Cnockaert

To Brooke,
who makes me feel bigger than words

1

EMMA

*J*O JONES IN THE RUNNING FOR SILVER GIG, THE HEADLINE on the screen said. Right beneath that, in italics, it read, *But should she be?*

Emma huffed as she scrolled through the article for the fifth time. She didn't normally spend her mornings reading gossip columns about her boss, but earlier that week, Jo had had a meeting with the studio producing the next Agent Silver movie. As her assistant, Emma knew which appointments were on Jo's schedule but not what happened within them. She wanted to know how the meeting had gone.

The article didn't clear that up for her. Jo was on the short list, at least, but was apparently a terrible choice. No experience writing a movie, certainly not an action flick. It was like they forgot she was the showrunner of TV's top drama five years running. Sure, *Innocents* didn't have explosions or fight scenes—except that one time in season 2—but it was *good*. It was quality television. Jo had the Emmys to prove it.

Not good enough for this columnist, though. He didn't come out and *say* it was because Jo was a Chinese American woman.

Instead the article was filled with worries about too soft a touch and a concern she would somehow miss the truly American essence of Silver. Emma rolled her eyes. Jo was born and freaking raised here.

Emma wasn't going to tell Jo about the column. While it might be good for Jo to know what people were saying about her, it would also be an unnecessary distraction that did nothing but hurt her feelings. Emma wouldn't bother her with it. Jo had more important things to do with her time anyway.

The click-clack of Jo's heels came from the hallway, and Emma quickly closed the browser tab. She stood, tucking her long hair behind her ears. By the time Jo rounded the corner, Emma was ready with her coffee and a smile.

"Thanks," Jo said, taking the latte without breaking stride. That didn't bode well for the day. Neither did her ponytail, high and tight enough to look severe. "Clear the afternoon for the both of us."

Emma stopped analyzing Jo's hairstyle choices and grabbed her tablet off her desk. "Sure, boss," she said, pulling up Jo's schedule as she followed her into her office. Most of the afternoon was blocked off for writing. All Emma had to cancel was a check-in with an assistant producer. "What do we got?"

"Dress fitting."

Emma stopped in front of Jo's desk and looked up at her. She tilted her head, confused. "You need me at a dress fitting?"

"Given that it's *your* dress fitting"—Jo took a sip of her coffee—"that would be ideal."

She set her purse on her glass-top desk, her long black ponytail swinging as she leaned over to take her laptop out of the bag.

"Excuse me?"

"You're coming to the SAG Awards with me on Sunday," Jo said. She sat behind her desk. "You'll need a dress."

Working for Jo, Emma was used to expecting the unexpected. In her nine months as Jo's assistant, she'd dealt with paparazzi and hate mail, overnight shoots and fans who'd loved Jo since she first appeared on their TV screens almost three decades ago at thirteen years old. Emma went to events with Jo, too, but those events were usually studio parties or advance screenings. They were things Jo needed her at for work-related purposes. They weren't the *SAG Awards*.

"I'm coming to the SAG Awards with you?" Emma's voice was higher pitched than she'd like it to be.

Jo arched an eyebrow at her. "Is that not what I said?"

Emma nodded once. "Um. Why?"

"I don't want to talk about that damn movie," Jo said, fluttering her hand like it wasn't all that important.

So much for keeping Jo's focus off the Agent Silver rumors.

Maybe Emma shouldn't push it, but Jo always told her to ask questions if she didn't understand something. "And I'm helping with that how?"

"You can cut in if anyone tries to talk about it," Jo said. "You'll be a buffer."

Right. That seemed reasonable. Emma had been a buffer for Jo on multiple occasions, though never at an awards show with a red carpet and a bunch of famous people. But if that was what it took to be good at her job, she'd do it.

Emma had liked her three years as a production assistant in the props department.

Being Jo's assistant was better.

Sure, there was getting coffee and picking up dry cleaning, but there was also scheduling meetings with TV's top players and mitigating problems, smoothing over ego issues. Emma helped Jo assemble production teams, had to know everyone's personality to figure out who'd work well together. She had her hand in every pot. The only thing she wasn't involved in was the script writing, which was fine with her.

Emma liked knowing how the whole thing worked. She knew every part of the machinery of the show. Five years ago she had basically flunked out of film school, and look where she was now.

Getting asked to accompany her boss to the SAG Awards.

Maybe this was the next step in her career. An opportunity to network, to make connections that would help her when she eventually moved on from this job. She'd rather watch the SAGs in her pajamas on her sister's couch, but she could go with Jo. It would be fine.

"Okay. I'm coming to the SAG Awards with you."

Jo looked up at her, intent. "You're not going to fangirl out over some actor and embarrass me, are you?"

"No, Ms. Jones," Emma said immediately. "Of course not."

"Even if you see Lucy Liu?"

The eyebrow pop accompanying the comment told Emma that Jo was teasing. Normally, Emma might joke back, but her mind wasn't working quickly enough this morning.

"Even then."

"Good," Jo said. "We're leaving for the fitting at one."

She opened her laptop. It was a dismissal, and Emma knew it was, but it took her a moment to leave Jo's office anyway.

So. Emma was going to the SAG Awards. With Jo. In two days. Okay. That was normal.

She wrote an email to the assistant producer about the canceled meeting, but her mind stayed mostly on the awards, the dress fitting. She shot a text to her sister to invite her over that night. She had a feeling she'd need to talk.

Then she put her phone away and got to work.

JO LED HER PURPOSEFULLY through the store. It was an appointment-only boutique. When Emma had used Jo's name on the phone that morning, the shop's completely booked afternoon had suddenly opened up. Emma kept her eyes straight ahead as they walked, didn't want to look as obviously out of place as she felt. Some of the clothes must cost more than two months' rent.

She followed Jo to a staging area of sorts in the back of the store. There were three mirrors with a small platform in front of them. A couch sat off to the side, and dresses were displayed on hangers hooked at various heights on the opposite wall. In front of them stood a tall Black woman, her box braids in a bun on top of her head. She grinned as the other two approached.

"Jo Jones, as I live and breathe," the woman said, stooping considerably to drop kisses on Jo's cheeks.

"Victoria," Jo said with a smile. "How have you been? How was the wedding?"

"Beautiful," Victoria said. "Everything was perfect, even the gift that was too expensive from someone who has never met my son."

Jo dipped her head slightly in acknowledgment.

"Enough talk, though," Victoria said. "I know you've got your mind on the clothes."

Jo didn't disagree. "This is Emma," she said.

Victoria shook Emma's hand, looking her up and down. "Jo said you were a tall brunette, but, girl, you are so much more."

"Thanks?" Emma said. It came out like a question.

"Can I get you a drink?" Victoria asked. "Champagne? Wine? Water?"

Emma had never been to a clothing store that offered you a drink. She declined. Jo raised the stainless steel tumbler she carried everywhere—Emma knew from refilling it that it was generally either coffee or water.

"Okay then, let's get to the dresses," Victoria said. "I have some already picked out, but we don't have to stick with them if you want something different."

They all turned to look at the gowns hanging on the wall. Emma swallowed. They were fancier than anything she'd ever worn. There was a black gown that was skimpy on top but princess-poufy on the bottom, a mermaid-style dress as bright red as Jo's lipstick, an empire-waisted strapless gown the color of café au lait, and a white dress with flowing fabric and huge, multicolored flowers painted along one side.

Jo made a noise of displeasure.

"I specifically said no—" She stopped. "V, the black dress is not the style I requested."

"Have a little fun, Jo. Let the girl decide for herself." Victoria turned to Emma. "You like this one, sweetie?"

Emma glanced at Jo, then looked back at the dress. "They're all beautiful."

"C'mon, try it on first." Victoria ushered Emma over toward the dressing room and hung the hanger of the black dress on a metal hook. "You're gonna look great. Call for me if you need any help getting into it."

Victoria closed the door behind her.

Emma breathed. She twisted her hair into a quick bun and used the hair tie on her wrist to secure it.

Okay. So. Dress number one. She first put it on without taking her bra off, but that wasn't going to work. The bra came off. The dress was way more low cut than she was comfortable with. She looked good, sure, but she was basically dressing for a work event, and this was in no way appropriate.

She reached for the zipper to change back into her regular clothes without even showing Jo and Victoria, but there was a knock on the door before she could.

"Need help, honey?" Victoria asked.

"No," Emma said. "No, I'm—good."

She couldn't get away with not showing them, she guessed. She had to squeeze the bottom of the princess-style gown to fit through the dressing room door. Victoria oohed with obvious delight and directed Emma over to the mirrors. Jo, seated on the sofa, looked up from her phone and immediately looked back down. Emma wanted to put a hand over her chest. She felt way too exposed.

"What do you think?" Victoria asked.

Emma looked at herself in the three mirrors Victoria had put her in front of.

"It's, um, a little low cut for me?" Emma swallowed. "Not that there's anything wrong with low-cut dresses. They're not *bad* or anything. It's just not my style, you know? I'm just—I'm not—"

Victoria laughed. "Fine, Jo, you were right. Higher necklines only."

Emma looked at Jo in the mirror. Still looking at her phone, she raised one hand in acknowledgment. "I'm always right, V."

Victoria rolled her eyes at Emma, still chuckling. "Okay, let's get you into the next one," she said, thrusting the red dress at her. "And I just thought of another one you might like—I'll be right back."

She disappeared, and Emma headed back into the dressing

room. As Emma tried to unzip herself, she caught sight of the price tag on the dress. She opened the dressing room door without thinking.

"*Jo,*" she hissed, and normally she didn't call her boss by her first name, but these were desperate times.

The distress must have been obvious in Emma's tone; Jo was beside her in half a moment.

"What?"

"This dress is *five thousand dollars,*" Emma whispered. She didn't want Victoria or any other employee to realize Emma wasn't rich enough to even try on these clothes.

Jo rolled her eyes. "No wonder Victoria pulled it for you. Trying to up her commission, apparently."

"I cannot afford this," Emma said.

"Well, you're not buying it anyway. And it didn't suit you."

It didn't, but Jo's words made Emma fidget for some reason. She straightened up, had a few inches on Jo regardless of her boss's ever-present heels. "Right. It didn't look good on me."

Jo's lips pressed into a thin line. "You're not usually one to fish for compliments, Ms. Kaplan," Jo said, though Emma hadn't meant to fish for anything. "And you're the one who said it was too low cut."

But Jo did, too, apparently. Told Victoria beforehand it wasn't right. Emma was grateful that her boss knew her well enough to know she wouldn't be comfortable at a work thing in a dress like that. Not that she'd be comfortable anywhere in any style of dress that cost *five thousand dollars.*

"I can't afford something a quarter of this price," Emma said. "I know this place is expensive, but surely there's something cheaper."

"As I said, you're not paying for it." Jo turned and walked back to the sofa, sitting down again and pulling up her phone.

Emma flushed with understanding.

"No, Ms. Jones," she said. "That's too much."

Jo looked up, raising both eyebrows at Emma. "Do you have another way to get an appropriate outfit for the SAG Awards? Please, Emma, I pay you well but not that well. Bryce Dallas Howard may like Neiman Marcus off-the-rack gowns for events but that doesn't mean I'll let my assistant be seen in one."

Jo stood out against the cream-colored couch. Black hair, blacker clothes. Emma wondered what her SAGs dress was like. Jo's everyday style tended toward grayscale. Simple, no nonsense. At events, though, she was a revelation. People still talked about her light blue strapless ball gown with pockets from the Emmys years ago. Emma was going to have to find something outstanding to fit in with Jo on the red carpet.

"Why are you still in that?" Victoria asked, returning with a royal-blue dress draped over her arm. The color was so spectacular, Emma's hands itched to reach for it.

"Can't get the zipper," Emma said.

"You couldn't help the girl out?" Victoria grumbled at Jo. She hung the blue dress by the others and came over to unzip Emma.

"I want that one," Emma said, pointing to the blue gown. Now that it was hung, she could see it fully, high boatneck all the way to the slight train where it was longer in the back.

"You can try it after the red," Victoria said.

Emma didn't look away from the blue one. "But I *love* it."

Victoria laughed at her but switched the dresses.

Just taking the gown off its hanger made Emma love it more. The material was soft and smooth, cool against her fingers. The back was mostly open, with a thick X of fabric crisscrossing it. The zipper was hidden in the side, and she could get it herself. The fit felt perfect. Emma ran her hands over her hips and couldn't help but smile.

When she came out of the dressing room door, Victoria shrieked with delight and Jo stared. She just stared at her, blinking a few times, and Emma felt powerful. Her smile grew.

"Oh, baby, that's it," Victoria said. "And I haven't even seen the back, turn around, turn around."

Emma chuckled. "Let me get in front of the mirrors first."

It looked as good as it felt. Emma beamed at her reflection. She turned her back to the mirror, and that was even better. It was more skin than she'd usually show, but she didn't mind since it wasn't cleavage. She took her hair out of the bun to fall in messy waves past her shoulders.

Victoria whistled. "What do you think?"

"I love it," Emma said.

"Jo?"

Emma looked at Jo in the mirror. Her boss was watching her, eyes unblinking in a way Emma wasn't sure was good or bad. Jo glanced at Victoria instead.

"She'll need heels."

Emma held in a sigh. She wanted Jo's opinion on the dress. Jo was right, though—the fabric pooled on the floor. Emma would trip over it without heels.

"It's pretty damn good, though, right?" Victoria pressed, but Jo stayed noncommittal.

"As long as Emma's comfortable."

"You're hopeless," Victoria said. To Emma, she added, "What size? I'll go find you heels. Don't change into a new dress yet."

"I don't need to try on another one," Emma said. "I want this one."

Victoria nodded. "Shoe size?"

"Nine," Emma said, and Victoria slipped away.

In her haste to get into the dress, Emma had forgotten to check the price. She found the tag. Twenty-five hundred dollars. Cheap, comparatively. It was still a ridiculous amount of money for her boss to be spending on her. Jo *had* a ridiculous amount of money, though, and she could do with it as she pleased. Emma had no reason to turn down a fancy dress. She'd already admitted she wanted this one.

"It's too much," she said anyway. "For you to buy a dress for me when I'll only wear it for one night."

Jo looked up at her. "It's nothing," she said. "I'm inviting you, Emma. I'm not going to make you pay to come."

"Jo, I—" Emma sighed.

She wanted the dress. She wasn't even that nervous about having to go to the awards anymore. This dress fitting went better than she expected; maybe the awards would, too. But the idea of Jo spending $2,500 on her put this weight in her stomach she didn't like.

"Do you not want to go?" Jo asked quietly, not quite looking at Emma.

Emma answered with no hesitation, probably out of habit of making things easier for Jo. "No, I do, I just—"

"It's settled then," Jo said. "This dress, yes? It's beautiful."

Emma nodded, smiling. "Yeah, boss."

THEY BOUGHT THE DRESS—AFTER Emma snapped a few pictures of herself in the mirrors—plus a pair of heels Emma would have to practice walking in all weekend. It was barely halfway through the afternoon, but Jo directed Chloe, her driver, to drop Emma off at her car in the parking garage.

"Ms. Jones, they're still shooting. Don't you want me on set?"

"I think I can survive a few hours," Jo said. "Especially since

I'm monopolizing your Sunday. The suite you booked for me to prep? Come by between ten and eleven. Hair, makeup, jewelry— everything will be taken care of. We'll have your dress there, so you don't have to worry about it all weekend."

Emma hadn't even thought about getting ready. She chewed on her bottom lip and nodded at Jo.

"I've got the Producers Guild Awards tomorrow," Jo said, though of course Emma already knew that. "I'm not doing the red carpet there, and I thought the SAGs would be more—" She paused. "*Fun* for you. We'll be sitting with the cast, of course, so you won't feel too out of your element."

Because being dressed in a $2,500 gown with hair, makeup, and jewelry, all paid for by her boss, would apparently be offset because she was sitting by people she knew. Really, the PGAs would be better for Emma, both in relation to networking and in relation to not having to walk on a red carpet. But Jo needed her at the SAGs, so she'd go to the SAGs.

"Sounds good," Emma said quietly. "I'll see you then."

She thanked Chloe and, for the first time in years, drove home while they were still filming.

She texted her sister again, told Avery to come over when she closed the bakery, and to bring Cassius, the snuggliest of Avery's three rottweilers.

"YOU KNOW YOU'RE GOING to make Billie and Roz jealous if you only ask for Cassius," Avery said as she arrived.

"I'll take them all to the dog park next weekend to make up for it," Emma said, petting Cassius before hugging her sister.

Avery gave the best hugs. She always said it was because she was fat and had some cushion to her, and Emma didn't exactly disagree, but she thought it also had something to do with how much love Avery put into her hugs.

"How was your day?" Emma asked.

"Good," Avery said. She dropped her keys on the table by the door. "Bakery was busy. Twins have been wild. I'm glad I'm not in charge of them tonight. Are we ordering food?"

"Thai's on its way," Emma said.

"From that one place?"

"From that one place."

"I love you."

"I know," Emma said, settling onto her sofa. She patted the seat next to her. "Maybe this means you'll let me snuggle with Cassius on my couch?"

Avery shook her head. "Cash is literally never going to be allowed on the furniture."

"He's literally allowed on it whenever I dogsit," Emma muttered.

"What?"

"Oh, nothing," she said with fake nonchalance, laughing when Avery narrowed her eyes.

"Whatever." Avery plopped herself down next to Emma and took off the bandana she always wore at the bakery. She scrubbed her fingers through her shoulder-length brown hair. "What's up? Are we still doing the SAGs at my house Sunday? Dylan is under strict instructions that he's in charge of the kids for the evening."

Emma laughed nervously. Of course her sister led with that.

"About that . . . ," Emma said. Avery tilted her head at her, and Emma decided to rip the Band-Aid off. "Jo needs a buffer so people won't talk to her about Agent Silver—I don't know if you saw that gossip column about how apparently she's not good enough to write it or *whatever*"—Emma rolled her eyes—"but she needs a buffer. So she's taking me to the ceremony."

"The ceremony?"

"The SAG Awards ceremony."

Avery blinked. "You're going to the SAG Awards?"

Emma nodded.

"That's awesome!"

"I guess?"

"C'mon, Em," Avery said. "That's going to be really cool. It's a little weird your boss is taking you when, like—hasn't she not taken a date to an awards thing since she was a teenager?"

Emma went red immediately. "Oh my God, Avery, I'm not her *date.*"

"You know what I mean," Avery said, leveling Emma with a stare. "But also, like—that's how it's going to look."

"Just because she takes a woman means everyone is going to suddenly decide she's gay? Anyone who actually knows who I am is going to know I'm her assistant. And no one else is going to care."

"If you say so." Avery shrugged. Her eyes widened. "What are you even going to *wear*?"

Emma cringed, because she still felt like Jo buying her the dress was too much, and she was sure her sister would, too. "Um. A dress. I got it today."

"You got a dress for the SAGs today? What, after work? It's barely past six."

"No," Emma said. "This afternoon."

"Jo let you take the afternoon off to get a dress?"

"Not exactly." Emma sighed. She might as well just say it. "Jo and I went to a dress fitting, and she bought me a dress."

Avery stared at her sister. Emma tried not to make excuses, knew Jo could do whatever she wanted with her money. And Jo was right, anyway; it would be rude to invite Emma and then make her pay.

"I've got pictures of it," Emma said, reaching for her phone on the coffee table. "She's taking care of bringing it to the suite where we're getting ready and stuff so I don't have to worry about it."

"You're getting ready together, too?"

"Yeah," Emma said, more lightly than she felt. "She always gets ready in a suite. It makes sense for me to, too. I mean, I don't know how to do my hair or anything for something like this."

"Dude," Avery said. "She wants to wife you."

"What?"

"She totally wants to wife you," Avery said. She ticked items off on her fingers as she listed them. "Buying you fancy things, spending time with you outside of work, showing you off in public."

Emma grabbed a throw pillow and made it worth its name, hitting her sister in the face with it. "That's ridiculous!"

"Is it, though?"

"Yes!" Emma exclaimed. "My boss does not want to *wife* me. She's probably not even queer."

"Just because she's not out doesn't mean—"

"Whatever." Emma rolled her eyes. "We're talking about the SAGs, not speculating about Jo's sexuality. She invited me so she doesn't have to deal with people asking her about the movie."

"Maybe she shouldn't be doing the movie if she doesn't want to deal with people asking her about it."

"Hey!" Emma snapped, still sensitive about the article claiming Jo wasn't good enough for Agent Silver. "We don't even know if she *is* doing the movie, anyway."

Cassius put his head in Emma's lap, seemingly distressed by

the raised voices. Emma set her phone down again to scratch behind his ears. She could tell her face was flushed.

"You'd totally let her wife you," Avery said. "What with your crush on her and all."

Emma gave up, sliding onto the floor to fully cuddle with Cassius. He immediately put half his body weight on her.

"I do not have a crush on her," she said.

"Em, you basically had a shrine to her on your wall as a kid."

"I had pictures of inspiring women!" Emma said. "Maya Angelou was on that wall, too. You think I have a crush on Maya Angelou?"

Avery shrugged. "I have a brain crush on Maya Angelou."

"How does your husband feel about that?"

"He has a brain crush on her, too—why do you think I married him?"

"Look, yes," Emma said, "I think Jo is amazing and brilliant, but it's, like, a mentor crush. Not an actual crush. Like how I felt about Professor Allister in college."

"Or"—Avery drew out the word—"you have a thing for older women."

"I do *not.*"

Avery made a face like she totally didn't believe her. Emma rubbed Cash's stomach.

"Your mom's a jerk, did you know that?"

"Let me see the dress," Avery said. "I promise I'll stop teasing you for your crush on your boss."

"Your mom doesn't get to see my dress, does she?" Emma said to Cassius. "Nope, because she's a big—hey!"

Avery had reached over and plucked Emma's phone from where she'd left it on the couch.

"Em." Her eyes were wide as she looked at the phone. "*Em.*"

Emma put her chin on top of Cassius's head and tried not to blush. "It's pretty good, yeah?"

"Emma, you look *amazing*," Avery said. "Oh my God, am I going to see you on TV? Are you going to, like, do the red carpet and all?"

"Oh no, they wouldn't show me," Emma said. "They're only going to show stars and stuff, obviously."

"Yeah, but if they show Jo, you'd be next to her! I could see you."

Emma's throat went tight at the possibility of all those cameras on her. She thought of her inhalers—one in her purse, one next to her bed—and wondered if she could bring one with her. But she didn't have a clutch or anything to carry. How was she going to bring things? What did one even bring to the SAG Awards? She was so not prepared for this.

"Hey," Avery said. "It'll be fine." She rubbed a hand along Emma's arm. "The only time they'd show you would be, like, as Jo's arriving, right? The celebs all go down a fancy red carpet to get their pictures taken, and the people who go with them are only there if they're famous. Or, like, someone's mom and so it's cute. You'll go some other way that they send the plebeians."

Emma rolled her eyes at her sister, though she appreciated Avery distracting her.

"I'm less of a plebeian than you, at least," she said. "Given you'll probably be in a onesie on your couch."

"Touché."

Even if there were cameras on her, it would be okay. Hollywood was all about who you knew. Granted, knowing Jo Jones would be pretty damn helpful when it came to moving on from being an assistant, but the exposure Emma would get from a high-profile event like the SAGs couldn't hurt. She'd be fine.

2

EMMA

EMMA STOOD IN THE HALLWAY IN FRONT OF THE SUITE DOOR for ten minutes. She knocked at exactly 10:30 a.m.

The door opened right away. A short man with dark hair, close cropped on the sides and long on top, stood behind it. He grinned and gestured her inside.

"Are you the infamous Emma?" he asked.

"Emma, yes. Infamous, not so much," Emma said.

The man led her into the living room area. The suite was huge—it even had an upstairs. On one side, there was a spiral staircase Emma didn't trust her clumsy self to climb. Behind the staircase was a closed door that Emma assumed led to a bedroom. The other side of the room opened to a dining area. The living room itself had floor-to-ceiling windows, two couches, an overstuffed chair, a full-sized piano—God knows why—and a chaise near one of the windows, where Jo sat serenely as someone did her nails. She was a picture of luxury in a pink silk robe. She smiled at Emma from across the room. Emma waved, then dropped her hand to her side, wondering how dumb it looked.

"Jo's never had someone else for us to style; you're infamous," the man who let her in said. "I'm Jaden, by the way. I work with Kelli, who I think you know."

Emma only knew Kelli from phone calls setting up appointments. She did Jo's makeup for events where there would be media.

"That's me," a woman said. She stood at a table covered with makeup products. "Nice to put a face to the name."

Emma smiled. "You, too."

Kelli was much older than Emma had expected. She sounded so young on the phone, but crow's feet peeked through her flawless face of makeup.

"As soon as Mai finishes touching up Jo's nails, it's your turn," Jaden said. "Do you know how you want to wear your hair?"

"Um," Emma said. She had googled hairstyles all day yesterday but kind of figured the stylist would have something picked out for her. "I like it down?"

"I can work with that."

Emma felt a bit like a doll then. Jaden played with her hair—over this shoulder then over that shoulder then half-up, half-down—inspecting her with each adjustment. Kelli brought over makeup palettes, holding each up to Emma's face to figure out what worked best with her coloring. Someone appeared with a glass of water. They disappeared before she could get their name. Emma trusted these people—Jo always looked great at events—but she'd never been primped like this before.

It settled down eventually. Mai came over to do her nails while Kelli worked on Jo's makeup. Emma let Mai pick the color of her polish. She stayed mostly silent throughout, only speaking when spoken to. She wanted to tell Jo she was robbed at the Producers Guild Awards last night, but she didn't know how to bring it up.

"I thought you said she was talkative," Kelli said, and Emma looked over at her.

"She usually is." It was the first time Jo had spoken since Emma arrived.

"She said you'd probably talk our ears off," Kelli told Emma.

"Whatever happened to beautician-client privilege?" Jo asked.

Kelli rolled her eyes at Jo. "It's not that you have to talk," she said to Emma. "But you don't have to be afraid to, either."

"I'm not afraid to talk," Emma said, thrown by the idea of Jo discussing her with other people. "Nor am I particularly talkative?"

Keeping her eyes closed as Kelli applied shadow, Jo waved a hand at Emma. "You always have a gaggle of PAs around you."

"Because I'm *friendly,*" Emma said. She made her voice go sweet. "And if they want to complain about their overbearing boss—"

"Watch it," Jo said, but there was no heat behind it.

"I listen," Emma continued. "And by being friendly, I get things done. You catch more bees with honey, you know."

Jo rolled her eyes and Kelli tutted at her. "You want me to stab you in the eye with this brush? No? Then keep still."

It was more fun after that. Emma seemed to have won the stylists over. Jo was relaxed, easygoing. She wasn't terrible at work or anything, but she was always focused and serious, and Emma wasn't used to seeing her so laid-back. Emma tried to stay relaxed, too, though whenever she let her mind stray to the ceremony later, and the red carpet beforehand, her pulse spiked a bit.

To keep herself calm, she asked the stylists questions. Kelli had been doing Jo's makeup for events for more than twenty years. Mai's mother did Jo's nails for the first Emmys she ever went to, back when she was *fourteen.* That was the year Emma was born.

Lunch arrived as Emma's nails were finishing drying. Mai made her let everyone else get a plate before she was allowed to, just in case.

Emma salivated over the spread while she waited. It was a variety of appetizers. There was toothpick caprese salad and spring rolls and three different types of bruschetta.

"Is that seriously pigs in a blanket?" Kelli said as she loaded her plate. "Jo, are you losing your refined taste?"

"I love pigs in a blanket!" Emma said.

"I believe they're technically cows in a blanket," Jo said. "They're kosher."

"Sweet!" Emma said, even though she didn't keep kosher. She would've eaten them anyway, but it was nice Jo took it into consideration.

Kelli smirked and Emma shrugged at her. Pigs in a blanket were delicious, kosher or not, refined or not.

When Emma finally was allowed to get her plate, she piled it high, couldn't say no to anything she saw. There wasn't enough room. She would have to come back for dessert.

"You know, Ms. Jones," she said, "not to advocate nepotism or anything—but my sister owns a bakery. Next time you need mini cupcakes."

"Does she now?" Jo asked. She had zero pigs in a blanket on her plate.

"Yep," Emma said. "Floured Up, over in WeHo."

"Talk to craft services tomorrow," Jo said. "See if we can't get her some business."

Emma grinned around the bite of spring roll in her mouth.

JADEN DID EMMA'S HAIR after lunch. He talked the whole time. When he broke for a moment to find some product in his bag, Emma glanced over at Jo, who was getting her toenails done.

"And you said *I* was going to talk their ears off?"

Everyone laughed, except Jaden, who either didn't hear or at least didn't seem to mind. Once he'd found the product, he was back to explaining this fight his sister had with his mom earlier in the week.

After hair came makeup. On a normal day, Emma wore a swipe of mascara and lip balm, maybe concealer if she had an especially bad pimple. She was a little afraid of Kelli and her menagerie of liquids and powders and brushes. But Kelli was gentle, and she explained everything she was going to do before she did it, like she could tell Emma needed to know what was going on.

Kelli worked on her eyes, and Emma was surprised at how comfortable she felt, here in a suite with her boss and all these stylists, getting ready for an awards show. She had her inhaler in her purse—and she still wasn't sure how she was supposed to carry anything to the ceremony—but she wasn't feeling anxious for the time being, so maybe she wouldn't even need it.

Kelli finished brushing something onto Emma's lids. "Open," she said.

Emma opened her eyes. She opened her eyes and saw Jo across the room, in nothing but Spanx and a bra. Emma immediately closed her eyes again. Kelli cleared her throat.

"Open."

Emma opened them again, studiously *not* looking at Jo. All of her comfort disappeared. She was glad for the layers of foundation and whatever else Kelli had already put on her cheeks—maybe the way Emma blushed wasn't noticeable. Kelli seemed too focused on Emma's eyes to care much.

It wasn't that Emma saw anything she shouldn't. She would've seen more had Jo been in a swimsuit. It was just—it was a lot of skin. And it wasn't that Avery was right, because she wasn't. Emma did not have a crush on Jo. But Jo *was* an objectively beautiful woman, all creamy skin and surprisingly long legs for such a petite person. So Emma was a little flustered, was all. She was glad when Kelli told her to close her eyes again.

By the time Kelli finished, Jo was nowhere to be seen. Emma breathed a sigh of relief.

"Your dress is in that bedroom," Kelli said, gesturing to the door on the right. "I'll bring in jewelry choices when Jo's picked hers."

Emma hadn't considered jewelry. She didn't consider it much then, either. She simply went to get dressed. It wasn't until she was adjusting the zipper and Kelli and Jaden came in with a box that Emma realized just what "jewelry" entailed.

"It's Martin Katz on loan," Kelli said.

Emma stared at the open box. She couldn't do anything else. There must have been tens, maybe hundreds of thousands of dollars of diamonds. Emma almost sat down on the edge of the bed. She was grateful she hadn't put her heels on yet.

"I . . . ," she said, and couldn't come up with anything else.

Jaden reached right into the box of diamonds and picked out a bracelet. "Girl, wear this," he said. "You don't need a necklace with that high neckline. Let's find you some earrings, too."

Emma looked at the bracelet he held out to her. It was strand after strand of small diamonds. Jaden shook it in her direction, but she just stared, slack jawed.

Kelli took pity on her and reached for the bracelet. "First red-carpet jitters is all," she said, fastening it around Emma's wrist.

It wasn't red-carpet jitters—first or otherwise. This had more to do with the fact that the bracelet probably cost more than her entire wardrobe, all the clothes she owned put together. What if she lost it? What if a diamond fell out? She could be a buffer. She could be good at her job. But she couldn't possibly wear this.

And then Jaden held up earrings, little dangling teardrops.

"Yes or yes?" he said.

"You guys, I can't—" Emma started.

"You can," Kelli said gently. "Put them on."

"We did not spend hours making you up so you can get scared of some rocks and not look perfect, babe," Jaden said.

Put that way, it was easier for Emma to wear the earrings. She had to—it would be rude to not look her best after everyone worked hard to make her look good. She focused on that rather than on how much the jewelry must cost.

And she did look good. Once she had the earrings in, she slipped on her heels and checked out the full-length mirror. She had been a little afraid, before this, about fitting in. She had been afraid she'd look obviously out of place with all the glamorous celebrities on the red carpet. But she looked the part, her hair in perfect chestnut waves over one shoulder. The bracelet balanced her look from the opposite wrist, and the earrings sparkled. She looked like she belonged.

"You guys did a great job," she said.

"We did," Kelli said. "Also, you're just pretty."

Emma smiled and rolled her eyes.

They went back out to the living room of the suite, and there was Jo, no longer in Spanx and a bra. Now she was in her dress, and that was *worse*.

She looked like a princess—no, like a queen. Absolutely gorgeous.

Emma hadn't seen Jo's dress in advance, and she was bowled over by how lovely it was. It was yellow, beautifully bright, daffodil yellow. There was still a lot of skin, with the off-the-shoulder sweetheart neckline and Jo's hair in a side updo. Strands of diamonds cascaded around Jo's neck and over her collarbones. The ball gown bottom half of the dress fell just past her knees, and she was barefoot for now, but Emma was sure there was a pair of her signature four-inch heels somewhere nearby.

"Ms. Jones," Emma said, no longer concerned at all with how she herself looked. "You look beautiful."

Jo smiled, acknowledging the compliment with a nod. "Your clutch is on the table by the door," she said. "It's already stocked with hand sanitizer, makeup for touch-ups, and tampons, just in case."

"You're a lifesaver," Emma said. "I had no idea how I was going to bring anything."

Emma headed over to move her inhaler and phone from her purse to the clutch. Jo clearing her throat made her pause.

"You look nice," Jo said.

Emma's face warmed. She looked at the floor, smiling. "Right. Thanks. Will we be leaving soon?"

"Yes, but there's no rush," Jo said. "If we show up late enough, we can hopefully slip inside fairly quickly."

Emma nodded like she had any idea how to slip inside a Hollywood awards ceremony.

THE RIDE OVER WAS interminably long until suddenly it wasn't, and they arrived.

Emma stepped out of the car—carefully, because she was in a long dress and heels that still felt a little too high for her, even after the practice in her kitchen. She stepped out of the car, and there were already cameras. People were shouting. She didn't know where to look, didn't know where to go.

Jo was at her side then, a tight-lipped smile and only a glance in Emma's direction.

"What are you waiting for?" Jo said. "Move."

She was as straightforward as ever, because this was normal for her. Emma, meanwhile, didn't actually move that much, just stepped aside to let Jo lead the way. It was part deferential assistant behavior and part "I have no idea what I'm doing" behavior.

Emma had grown so comfortable in the suite. The relaxed atmosphere made it feel more like a spa day than preparing for an awards show. But this—this was wild. Watching on TV didn't capture how many people were actually there. People directing traffic, people directing *foot* traffic, people taking pictures with really expensive cameras, fans taking pictures with their phones from afar. There was a tent full of people, and Jo's publicist popped out to greet them. Amir gave Emma a cursory hello before focusing on Jo, who made it clear she wasn't doing any interviews. Emma just tried not to trip over her feet. It was loud and busy and she would really rather be on Avery's couch.

She didn't need anyone else to know that, though. She needed to look like she belonged here, because she would, one day. She tried to keep a small smile on her face as she followed Jo.

Of course, then she didn't get to follow Jo anymore. Because Avery was right about the red carpet—Emma was sent one way, away from the photographers, while Jo went down the other, posing every few feet. The show was set to start in twenty minutes, so the carpet was emptying out and Jo moved quickly. Emma held Jo's clutch and shuffled along, never getting ahead of her boss. Everyone focused on the famous people, not on all the boring people who came with them. Emma wasn't in the spotlight anymore, and her heels were easier without as much pressure to be perfectly graceful in them.

She wasn't quite calm, though, because while she had promised Jo she wouldn't fangirl out over anyone—well, she wasn't fangirling.

She wasn't. But Annabeth Pierce was two people ahead of Jo on the red carpet, and Emma might have been fawning a little. She'd loved all of Annabeth's movies since her breakout a little over five years ago. Her dress was this sleek white gown with a sparkling pattern in the front. Emma barely paid attention to Jo until Annabeth finished the red carpet and headed for the door to the theater.

When she finally did look back at her boss, Emma narrowed her eyes. Jo looked stiff. Uncomfortable. Her smile was fake. Not the "I'm getting my picture taken and being forced to smile" fake, but the "if I smile through this, maybe it will end sooner" fake. Her cheeks were tight and her eyes wider than usual, like she was actively trying not to furrow her brow.

Emma heard a voice from somewhere in the crowd. She wasn't sure if it was a photographer or a fan, couldn't tell where exactly it was coming from as the person shouted about Agent Silver. Another voice then, asking if Jo was worried that backlash had begun before anything was even official. Jo moved toward the last posing area on the red carpet, and people kept yelling.

This was what Emma was there for, right? She was supposed to be a buffer, was supposed to be keeping people from asking about Agent Silver. Jo put her hand on her hip and looked more like she was grimacing than smiling.

Emma moved without thinking. She maneuvered herself to the real red carpet, the red carpet where the celebrities were. Jo didn't notice Emma until she was barely three feet away, suddenly unsure what her next move should be.

Jo's smile remained tight. "What are you doing here?" she asked through her teeth.

Emma took a step closer. "I'm supposed to be a buffer."

It was then that she registered how many cameras were pointed in her direction. People were still yelling at them, asking her name, telling them to smile. Emma needed exposure, but this was too much. Her throat went tight. She stepped backward, ready to flee to the safety of the other path, but Jo wrapped a hand around her wrist and held her in place.

"Just smile for a second and let them take a picture," Jo said. "Don't be weird."

Emma tried *really hard* to smile like a normal person. "Don't let me fall on my face. I don't know how to walk in these heels."

"Right, of course," Jo said. "You're an Amazon."

Emma stiffened, and Jo tightened her grip on her wrist.

"I only meant you're tall," she amended. "Compared to me? Of course you're an Amazon."

Someone appeared and fixed the train of Emma's dress, disappeared just as quickly.

"Anyway," Jo said. "The Amazons were mythological women warriors, so really it's a compliment."

Emma smiled, a real smile, without even thinking about it. "Didn't they kill all men who entered their lands?"

Jo slid her a glance, smirking slightly. "See? Definitely a compliment."

Emma giggled, and Jo grinned, and then just like that, they were ushered on. Jo let go of Emma's wrist and placed her hand gently on her lower back instead, directing her toward the theater. Emma had survived the red carpet. She had even forgotten she was there for a moment. She tried to think of neither the number of pictures that now existed of her nor the gentle stroke of Jo's thumb against the skin of her back.

Emma's phone buzzed inside her clutch. She wondered if Avery had seen pictures of her already, if she showed up in the red-carpet coverage.

"Shall we?" Jo said, gesturing toward the doors.

Emma put her phone on do not disturb and followed Jo into the building.

3

JO

A PHONE CALL FROM HER PUBLICIST BEFORE JO ARRIVED at the studio was never a good sign. She rolled up the privacy window between her and Chloe, then answered the phone.

"Good morning, Amir."

"Yes, right, good morning," her publicist said. He didn't bother with small talk, which Jo appreciated. "Have you seen the response to your red-carpet stunt?"

Jo bristled. "I wasn't aware I had pulled any kind of stunt."

"People think you and your assistant are dating."

Jo couldn't help a short laugh.

"I'm not joking," Amir said. "We have to get ahead of this."

"Amir." Jo tried to keep the incredulity out of her voice. He was only trying to do his job. "There's nothing to get ahead of."

"This rumor is going to get legs," Amir said. "And we don't need to give anyone any ammunition when it comes to reasons you shouldn't be involved with Agent Silver."

He never bullshitted her, she had to give him that. Amir didn't sugarcoat his opinion.

"I don't comment on my love life," Jo said. "And I'll be officially announced as writer and producer of Agent Silver on Thursday—that'll be enough to make them forget about whatever this is."

"Since you aren't actually dating your assistant"—he said it with less certainty than Jo would've hoped—"this isn't technically your love life. A short denial, nothing special."

"I know Judy stressed that there would be no such denials before she handed you the reins here."

Judy had been Jo's publicist since she was thirteen. Not commenting on her love life began because no teenager needs that kind of public scrutiny. Jo grew up, but the no comment policy stuck. Nothing changed when Judy retired two years ago.

"Ms. Jones, you do not need any more bad press at this moment," Amir said. "A short statement would be an easy fix."

Amir obviously couldn't see her, but Jo shook her head anyway.

"A short statement after almost thirty years of never commenting would not be an easy fix," she said. "You know better than that."

Amir sighed. Jo could only assume it was because she was right.

"Perhaps Emma could—"

"Do not involve Emma in this," Jo said.

"She's already involved. And most of what's being written isn't particularly complimentary."

Jo's fingers twitched. The thought of Emma being disparaged in the media made her consider letting Amir make a statement.

"Leave it be," she said instead. "It'll pass."

Amir sighed again, but he didn't fight her. They said their goodbyes as Chloe pulled up to the studio.

From the look on Emma's face as she stood by her desk with Jo's coffee in hand, she'd seen the rumors. Jo made a split-second decision to pretend she herself hadn't.

"Thank you," she said, taking her coffee.

Emma followed her into her office, which wasn't unusual. She often gave Jo a rundown of the schedule for the day first thing. But today, as Jo put her bag down and hung up her jacket, Emma simply stood there, twisting her fingers together.

"Did you need something?" Jo asked.

"Um," Emma said. "Ms. Jones." She paused. "Have you by any chance seen TMZ this morning?"

"I have not," Jo told her honestly.

"There's—well." Emma took a deep breath. "There's some speculation. About why you took me to the ceremony last night."

"Oh?"

Jo was being unfair. She should've made this easy on Emma. But she rather enjoyed watching her work her way through something.

Emma seemed to decide that the direct route was best. She dropped her hands to her sides and stood tall.

"They think we're in a relationship," she said.

Jo pressed her lips together. "How novel," she said. "This is perhaps the first time two women seen together weren't labeled gal pals."

Emma offered a tight smile. If this were anything else, she would joke with Jo about it, her goofy grin coming easily.

"What are we going to do?" she asked.

"What are we going to do?" Jo parroted back at her.

Emma flailed more than shrugged. "How are we going to deal with this?"

Jo told Emma what she told Amir. "I've never once commented on my love life," she said. "I'm not about to start now."

Emma looked like a goldfish, her mouth opening and closing but nothing coming out.

Jo opened her computer and logged on. Perhaps she should actually read what people were saying.

"Jo, I—" Emma started. "Ms. Jones. It's inappropriate. That people should think this. About either of us."

Jo fluttered a hand. "If I got upset every time people thought I was sleeping with someone I shouldn't, I'd be a lot less well-adjusted. Let it pass. They'll move on eventually."

"They've found my Instagram," Emma said. "I've gained *nine thousand* followers since last night."

Jo couldn't help but chuckle at that. "Enjoy your newfound stardom."

"I don't *want* to enjoy any stardom," Emma snapped. "I don't want to be known as the girl sleeping with her boss! We *have* to say something about this."

Jo looked away from her computer before getting to TMZ. She leveled a stare at Emma.

"I have not once, in almost three decades in this business, commented on my love life," she said. "I will not be starting now just because you're embarrassed to be associated with me in this manner. Is that why you didn't want to stand near me on the red carpet?"

Jo hadn't meant to ask, had figured it was Emma's nerves that made her freeze up. But as soon as the question was out of Jo's mouth, Emma blushed and tripped over herself to refute the accusation. Better to distract Emma from her discomfort than let her descend into panic.

"No, of course not, Ms. Jones," she said. "I—"

"You what, Ms. Kaplan?"

"Jo." Emma swallowed. "You're an amazing woman. I'm just— I'm not used to being in the spotlight."

Jo was the level of famous that people tended to tell her whatever she wanted to hear. It was probably worse with her employees, but for some reason she couldn't help but believe Emma when she complimented her. Emma seemed genuine with everyone, but especially with Jo. It was ridiculous. She was probably just good at her job, at making her boss happy. Jo didn't let herself dwell on the thought.

"You'll be fine," Jo said. "They'll forget about it within a week if we don't comment." She finally looked at the article on her computer and sucked in a breath at the photo. "Well. They certainly got a good picture, didn't they?"

Emma came around Jo's desk to look at it with her. It was a completely normal action, and yet it set Jo on edge. She rolled her eyes at herself.

"Yeah," Emma said quietly. "It's quite the photo. Must have been when you called me an Amazon."

It wasn't the moment Jo called Emma an Amazon so much as the moment after it, when they were laughing together. Jo's fingers were wrapped tightly around Emma's wrist, and Emma leaned toward her slightly, looking right at her instead of at any of the cameras. Emma's nose scrunched up with her smile, and Jo was grinning, too, staring right back at her. They looked like there was no one else in the world. Jo remembered it all happening, but hadn't realized they had looked quite so . . . well. She understood why this rumor got off the ground so quickly.

"Wearing matching jewelry didn't exactly help," Jo said.

Emma took a step back. "We wore matching jewelry?"

"Your bracelet and my necklace were part of a set, but I thought it was too much to wear both."

Emma paced to the other side of Jo's desk. She blinked a few times, then looked at Jo. "Why'd you let me wear it?"

Jo considered. "You looked nice."

Emma looked at the floor, her cheeks flushing. It was the truth—she had looked beautiful. But Jo also knew Emma wasn't exactly comfortable with the whole thing. She hadn't wanted to exacerbate that by making her change the jewelry she'd picked.

"Perhaps you should make your social media private," Jo said.

Emma nodded. "Yeah. Already done."

"Right. Well." Jo closed the tab and Emma straightened up. "I'll be writing all morning. No calls unless it's an emergency."

"Yes, boss," Emma said. She headed for her own desk. "Door closed?" she asked over her shoulder.

Jo hesitated. "Yes, please."

She always wrote with the door closed. No distractions. She didn't know what made her hesitate today. Emma didn't need Jo watching over her. The rumors were meaningless; they weren't going to affect Emma's workday. Even if they did, Emma could handle it. She'd handled everything that came with the job, thus far. Jo didn't need to worry about her.

The door closed behind Emma. Jo knew she should get to writing, but she opened her browser again anyway. She wouldn't normally read the gossip columns, but for some reason, she was interested.

She and Emma were apparently dating, which was all Amir let her know that morning. None of the sites reporting on it seemed to be able to decide when they'd moved beyond the boss-assistant relationship. Some claimed they'd been dating from the start. Many had collected pictures of the two of them, on set or at studio events, as though Emma standing near Jo was evidence of a relationship. The red-carpet picture was the most prominent, though, no matter what site Jo visited. She understood why. Looking at it, even she was almost convinced there was something there.

She allowed herself ten minutes of perusing the internet before closing it all and opening her script document. She was almost finished with the first draft of the finale. She laced her fingers together and stretched her arms in front of her, palms out. Time to get to work.

JO WAS BEGINNING TO get into the groove of writing when her cell phone rang. The caller ID made her roll her eyes affectionately. She should have expected this.

"Hello?"

"You want to tell me what's going on?"

"Nice to talk to you, too, Ev."

Evelyn scoffed. "Oh, don't pretend like you bother with niceties when you call me."

True. Jo had a tendency to start phone calls with her best friend with *you won't believe what this fucking idiot did*—Evelyn had always been her favorite person to complain to.

"Nothing is *going on*," Jo said, leaning back in her chair.

"Nothing is going on? But you took someone to an awards show? And that someone happened to be your assistant? And not the frumpy assistant I expected—she fit in just fine on the red carpet."

"Yes, well, I bought the dress for her, didn't I?"

"Are you serious?"

Jo almost paused at the incredulity in Evelyn's voice, but better not to give an inch. "Of course," she said. "You think I was going to trust her to find one herself? Or make her buy a dress she'll likely only wear once?"

"How else could you have fixed that problem?" Evelyn said. She *hmm*ed. "Let me think. Oh, I know! You could have not invited her. Then she wouldn't have needed a dress that she would only wear once."

"You're just jealous I've never taken you to an awards show," Jo said.

Evelyn laughed. "I haven't wanted to go to an awards show with you since we were teenagers."

Evelyn and Jo had grown up together in LA's Chinatown. Evelyn was the only person outside of Jo's family who didn't treat her any differently after she got famous. Younger people acted like celebrity made Jo suddenly special; older people in their community tutted over Jo taking a stage name, as though it were her fault Hollywood didn't want Jo Cheung. When Jo told Evelyn she landed her breakout role, Ev said, "Cool," and kept dealing cards for big two.

Jo glanced at the closed door. She was sure Emma had heard plenty of her phone conversations—raised voices with the network or, worse, with her father. Jo spoke quietly.

"I didn't want to deal with the rumors about Agent Silver," she said. "About whether or not I could hack it in film. I didn't want to talk to anyone. I needed a buffer. Emma filled that role well."

Evelyn let Jo's rare moment of vulnerability slide. "You admitting you took the girl as a buffer isn't helping your case," she said. "You brought her so you didn't have to deal with people you don't like. Ergo, she is not in the category of people you don't like."

"Yes, Evelyn, I like my assistant. That's not some 'gotcha' situation."

"Oh God," Evelyn said. "I know you haven't accidentally texted me when you meant to text her in a while. But if you start sexting, please make sure you find the right contact in your phone first."

"For fuck's sake." Jo rubbed the bridge of her nose.

Evelyn had a point about the accidental texts, though. It happened more often than Jo would like, generally when she'd taken her contacts out and wasn't looking closely at her phone. Emma and Evelyn were next to each other in Jo's contact list.

"She looked gorgeous, Jo," Evelyn said.

"I'm not going to deny that," Jo said. It would be a lie. Emma had already looked good when she arrived at the suite the day before. Jo's prep team didn't need to help much. "She's twenty-seven years old and looks like she could be goddamn Wonder Woman. And yes, I enjoy her company over that of obnoxious, self-important actors, especially at a night designed to celebrate their self-importance. The rest is so-called journalists speculating about things to get clicks."

Evelyn was quiet for a moment, and Jo considered that maybe she'd convinced her.

Instead, Evelyn said, "When you give in to the inevitable way you guys were looking at each other, will you call me?"

"Do you want me to ever call you before then," Jo asked, "or would you rather never hear from me again?"

Evelyn hung up without responding. Jo went back to her script.

INNOCENTS CENTERED ON A group of lawyers working to exonerate the wrongly convicted. It was Jo's second TV show, even more successful than the first. As they approached the fifth-season finale, Jo was ready to move on. She loved her characters, but she knew them by this point. There wasn't as much to explore, weren't as many new ways for Jo to challenge herself.

So she turned to an action franchise with six decades of history; Agent Silver wasn't like anything she'd done before. The announcement of Jo as writer was scheduled for Thursday, but the whispers about how people expected her to fail were already everywhere. Jo would never admit to being nervous, especially because *terrified* might be the more appropriate adjective. But she couldn't get better unless she pushed her limits.

Jo imagined leaving *Innocents* would feel like what parents experience when their children go off to college. Her baby, suddenly grown up and not under her roof anymore. She'd already delegated a lot of her show-running duties to her co–executive producer, Chantal. Jo trusted her. She knew Chantal was more than capable of running the day-to-day.

Plus, Jo liked the way she was always prepared to step back when Jo showed up on set. Chantal ran things while Jo was away and offered to hand over the reins in her presence. Today, she nodded at Jo, her corkscrew curls bouncing. Jo waved her off. She wanted to watch a bit, clear her head from all the words jumbled inside it.

Emma stood beside her, working on something on her tablet. Normally, Emma's presence on set was filled with hellos from PAs. Today, acknowledgment of her was noticeably subdued. Before Jo could give it much thought, Chantal called for a five-minute break while they adjusted lighting, and Tate, one of the leading actors, headed her way.

"You got that finale script for us yet?" he asked.

Jo managed not to roll her eyes at him. As an actor, he wouldn't get the script for weeks, after it went through revisions and rewrites, but he always liked to meddle.

"I'm surprised I get any writing done," Jo said breezily. "What with how much Emma and I are apparently fooling around in my office."

Tate laughed, big and booming, and the crew joined in, albeit less enthusiastically. Jo smirked. Emma was the color of a tomato.

"You take your time with that," Tate said, his white-toothed grin standing out against his hickory skin. He glanced at Emma and chuckled. "You okay there, Emma?"

"I hate you," Emma told him. Then: "Ms. Jones, let me get you a refill."

She took the tumbler right out of Jo's hand and marched off. Jo didn't bother to point out that it was still mostly full.

"Go easy on her," Tate said.

"She can handle it," Jo said, fluttering a hand like she wasn't worried about how this all might affect Emma. "Your break's almost up."

It had barely been a minute, but Jo didn't want to deal with him anymore.

"Yours, too," he said, then left her alone.

Jo tried to be unobtrusive on set. People were working, and she was only there to clear her head. But she could feel eyes on her, darting away when she looked back. At least some of these people believed the rumors, which was unfortunate. Not worth doing anything about, but unfortunate nonetheless.

Emma hadn't returned with her promised refill, and loath as Jo was to admit it, Tate was right; she had to get back to writing. She headed to her office. Emma would figure out where she went.

But Emma didn't have to figure anything out, because she was sitting at her own desk when Jo got back.

"Your refill, Ms. Jones," she said, offering the tumbler without making eye contact.

Jo took the cup and decided she needed to face this head-on.

"I apologize if I made you uncomfortable," she said. "The rumors are something that needed to be addressed without being taken seriously. Tate provided me an easy opportunity."

"It's fine," Emma said.

Jo could have left it at that, but she was the one who got Emma into this mess.

"If it upset you, it's not. I won't joke about it again."

Emma stared at the papers on her desk. "Thank you."

"It really will just go away," Jo said. "It always does."

Emma didn't look up. Jo was pretty sure she didn't believe her.

"Did you at least have a good time?" Jo asked. "Since you have to deal with all of this, I hope you at least had fun."

"I did," Emma said, finally making eye contact. Her smile was soft.

"Good. I'm glad I took you."

She was. She had thought—both before asking Emma and after—that maybe she shouldn't.

Jo's mom had accompanied her to every awards show of her career until the cancer diagnosis. Jo skipped the red carpets when she was twenty, watching from the hospital instead. Her mom was gone before Jo turned twenty-one. Jo hadn't taken anyone to an awards show since. Her brother was younger and busy, and her father was too uninterested to bother.

Jo had known the press would make something of her taking Emma, but she had to—she was hideously bored of awards by this point. While she was proud of the work she put out, proud of the work everyone did on her show, awards were too often political, too rarely went to the right people. Ceremonies were an excuse for everyone to schmooze and drink and celebrate themselves. Even before the speculation about Agent Silver, Jo had considered asking Emma. Her assistant's company was a lot better than that of any of the drunk schmoozers.

"Why did . . . ," Emma started. She looked down, then back up at Jo. "Why did you take me? I mean, I know I was supposed to be a buffer for Agent Silver stuff, but besides the red carpet, no one even asked you about it. And we know how well my intervening on the red carpet worked out."

Jo sighed. "Because I was sick of getting hit on by people who thought since I was alone I was interested." It was true enough. Without a date, she had no way to avoid conversations with people she didn't want to talk to. She rubbed her temples. "I expected the story to be 'Jo Jones is so obsessed with work she brought her assistant to an awards show,' not 'Jo Jones is dating her assistant.'"

"You knew there'd be a story?" Emma asked.

"There's always a story."

Jo had dealt with the press, with journalists and people who shouldn't be allowed to call themselves journalists, since she was a teenager. She should've known better.

"If anyone makes you uncomfortable, let me know, yes?" Jo said. "I'll have it taken care of."

Emma half rolled her eyes. "Sure, boss," she said. "But I'm fine."

"Any inquiries go to Amir," Jo said. "All comments, even no-comment comments, need to come from my publicist."

"Of course," Emma said. "But why would *I* get inquiries anyway?"

"Just in case."

If Emma hadn't realized that reporters might find her phone number, might find out where she lived, Jo wasn't going to put the idea in her head. She truly did believe this rumor would pass quickly enough that Emma would never be bothered.

THE NEXT MORNING, THOUGH, reporters had discovered the phone number at Emma's desk. Jo told her to turn off the ringer. Anyone who truly needed her had other ways of getting in touch.

Emma was harried, having been caught off guard by calls that morning.

"I really don't understand why we can't just say this isn't true," she said.

Jo sipped her coffee and remembered when Emma first started as her assistant, how afraid she had been of speaking out of turn.

"What if I want to date someone, but they think I'm dating *you*?"

Jo rolled her eyes. "If a man doesn't believe you when you tell him the rumors aren't true, he's not worth your time."

"I didn't say a *man*," Emma snapped, and Jo blinked at her. Emma colored slightly. "I mean—maybe a man. But not necessarily."

Jo nodded once. "Regardless. Anyone interested in you should trust you. Besides," she said, shifting away from the subject of Emma's sexuality, "a comment is going to make this story *bigger*, not make it go away. Like I said, I haven't discussed my love life in almost thirty years in Hollywood. To say something now would make this time seem somehow different, which isn't going to make reporters stop calling."

Emma scowled.

"Not commenting will make them stop calling," Jo said. "Any comment leads to clarifying questions, leads to requests for more. When they know you're never going to say anything, they eventually leave you alone."

Jo was right, whether Emma wanted to believe her or not.

"I've been in this business as long as you've been alive, Emma."

That got Emma to sigh and tell Jo her schedule, apparently done with discussing the rumors.

JO'S BROTHER CALLED HER when she was eating lunch.

"Jo Jo, have you been keeping secrets?"

"You know I hate that nickname, *Vinny*," Jo said. "And no, I have not."

Vincent laughed. "Really? Because it seems like you're dating!"

"Don't believe everything you read."

"Yeah, yeah," he chuckled. "I was just hopeful. Thought you had finally found someone who'd put up with you."

"She does put up with me," Jo said.

"Maybe you *should* be dating her."

Jo didn't dignify that by addressing it. "These rumors have done wonders for my social life," she said instead. "Evelyn yesterday, today my little brother. I probably have a call from Father to look forward to."

"Nope," Vincent said. "He'll call me for the details later."

"Of course."

Jo was glad. She last spoke to her father at Christmas, and she'd prefer not to again until next Christmas. She didn't want to deal with her father's disapproval, even over something fictional.

"How are the boys?"

Her nephews were five and nine and were some of her favorite people in the world. She'd never wanted kids herself, but she adored her brother's. Even when she was busy, she found time for their baseball games and birthday parties and anywhere else they might want her.

Vincent told her all about them, and Jo let her lunch run long.

THE RUMORS TRULY WERE great for Jo's social life. Evelyn called again that evening. Again, she didn't lead with hello.

"You made *Us Weekly*."

"At this point in my life, I don't think being in a magazine deserves a congratulatory phone call," Jo said. She dropped her silverware from dinner into its rack in the dishwasher.

"You and your *girlfriend* made *Us Weekly*," Evelyn clarified. "It's gold." She began to read over the phone. " 'No best-dressed list would be complete without the it couple of the week: Jo Jones and Emma Kaplan.' In parens they write, 'Her assistant! Shh!' They say she's your assistant with an exclamation mark, but then they say 'shh' like readers aren't supposed to talk about it."

"Do you really need to read this to me?"

"Absolutely," Evelyn said. She went on, "Blah blah blah, what designers you're wearing. Then: 'We can hardly believe the way these two look at each other! Even on the red carpet they're too busy being enthralled with each other to bother looking at the cameras.' "

Jo considered hanging up on her. She started the dishwasher.

" 'Jo keeps her fingers around Emma's wrist like she can't bear to let her out of reach,' " Evelyn continued. " 'Though it doesn't look like there's much chance of that—the way Emma leans closer.' "

"Can we *please* stop this?"

Evelyn laughed.

"I hate you," Jo said.

"You hate *Us Weekly*," Evelyn said. "I'm just the messenger."

"Taking joy in rubbing this in my face doesn't count as being the messenger," Jo said. She poured herself a glass of red wine, certain she'd need it if this conversation continued.

"You know, you should probably hate yourself, actually."

"Oh, thanks for that," Jo said. "Really good advice, best friend."

"Aiyah, what were you *thinking*?" Evelyn asked. "You go over twenty years without taking someone to an awards show, and then you bring your assistant. This would have been a big deal even if you'd kept your hands off her."

Jo rubbed the bridge of her nose. "I thought I'd get more of the 'Jo Jones is obsessed with work' story," she said. She'd told Emma this already, and it was the truth. "I didn't think they'd get a picture of us like that."

"How in the world did they?"

Jo sighed. "Emma decided me inviting her as a buffer meant she had to barge onto the red carpet when people yelled questions about Agent Silver."

"Did you train her as a guard dog, or did she come that way?"

"Don't call my assistant a dog."

Evelyn laughed. "You know that only explains why she was next to you. It still doesn't explain the picture. The way you're holding her wrist? The way you're looking at each other?"

"She almost fled," Jo said. "With all the cameras on her. I held her in place and I made her laugh to calm her down. It wasn't anything more."

She was there. She knew it wasn't anything more. But a copy of the picture sat in the top right drawer of Jo's desk. She kept looking at it; she didn't know why.

Eventually, Evelyn said, "It will die down at some point."

"I know," Jo said.

"How's Emma dealing with it?"

Jo chuffed out a laugh. "By coming out to me."

"What?"

Jo relayed the story, much to Evelyn's delight.

"I'm surprised they haven't found evidence of relationships she's had with other women," Evelyn said. "Surely that'd be gossip fodder."

"Don't even suggest that," Jo said. "These rumors are going away, not stirring up more shit for us."

"Right, of course. I won't jinx it." Evelyn paused. "Though, given that she's bisexual, maybe you should take a hint from these rumors and make a move on Wonder Woman."

"It's inappropriate to even joke about that." Jo couldn't keep the edge out of her voice. "And you should know that, *Attorney* Yu."

"But you like her, and you don't like many people."

"I do like her," Jo said. "Emma is smart and capable and kind and *my employee*. Liking her doesn't mean anything. I like you, too. Most of the time anyway."

Evelyn laughed at her and finally let the subject drop.

4

JO

J O CALLED AN ALL-HANDS MEETING THURSDAY AFTER LUNCH. Emma walked beside her to the soundstage, uncharacteristically quiet. Jo could've told her about Agent Silver before everyone else, but she hadn't. Chantal knew, given that she would be taking over *Innocents* when Jo moved on, but other than that, the news was held close.

Jo kept the announcement quick. This wasn't going to affect her work on *Innocents* for months yet, no reason to drag anything out.

"I'm going to be writing and producing the next Agent Silver movie," she said.

Tate hollered, and everyone else joined in with a short round of applause interspersed with shouts of congratulations. Jo caught Emma's eye—she was beaming.

"Don't get too excited," Jo said. "You're not rid of me yet. The schedule isn't set in stone, but I should still be here until at least the middle of next season. Nothing will immediately change. I'm only telling you now because you deserve to hear it from me rather than the press. And so you can extend your congratulations to

Chantal, as well, who will be fully taking over the show when I leave."

Jo was the one to lead this round of applause. Then she sent everyone back to work.

There was pep in Emma's step now as she walked with Jo back to her office. When Jo got back behind her desk, Emma still stood in the open door, hugging her tablet and grinning.

"Boss."

A smile slipped over Jo's face. "Emma."

"Boss," Emma said again. "You're really gonna write it!"

"I really am."

"That's—" Emma threw her arms to her sides and went up on her tiptoes. She looked like a kid on Christmas morning. "That's awesome."

Jo couldn't help but laugh. "It's not terrible, is it?"

"I'm so excited to see what you do with Silver," Emma said. "You know, when I was a kid, I went through a phase where I read all the companion novels for the Silver movies. I went as Clara Hayes, from *Silver Sunset*, for Halloween three years in a row." Her cheeks went a little pink. "I might have been a bit obsessed. And with you writing it, I'll probably get obsessed again."

It was Jo's turn to blush, just slightly. "I appreciate the enthusiasm," she said. "But you know we also have to talk about how this affects you."

Emma did her typical confused head tilt. "Me?"

"What job do you want after this?" Jo asked.

"What?" Emma took a step back.

"I always help put my assistants on the right career track," Jo said. "I don't know exactly how soon I'm moving on from *Innocents*, or how soon you'd like to move on, but it's something we should discuss."

"Boss, I—" Emma swallowed. "I like my job."

"I didn't say you didn't."

"I just—I'm not sure of the next step yet."

Usually by this point in Jo's working relationship with her assistant, she'd know exactly what said assistant wanted to do with their career. Her assistants generally couldn't help but talk about their goals, as they used their position as a jumping-off point. Jo understood, and didn't mind, but it was pleasant with Emma, how she seemed to care more about doing this job than getting the next one. Whatever Emma wanted to do, if she put half as much work into it as she put into being Jo's assistant, she'd thrive.

"Think on it," Jo said.

Emma nodded once. The conversation clearly took her by surprise. Her beaming pride had turned to wide-eyed anxiety. It was adorable, actually, how fully she seemed to feel everything. Jo had perfected her poker face long ago. Emma was refreshingly different from most people in the business with the way her feelings were always scrawled across her face.

OVER THE WEEKEND, MOST coverage of the announcement of Jo's work on Agent Silver was positive. On Monday, though, Jo and Emma left the studio in step with each other on the way to an off-site meeting, and cameras flashed in their faces. Emma took a step toward Jo and put one arm up in front of her. It was Emma's usual protective stance in a crowd, whether it be fans or paparazzi, but Jo knew the tabloids would run with it. Nothing to be done about that—they obviously got the shot as the flashes continued.

It was much like the red carpet. Emma was there as some kind of buffer as the paparazzi shouted questions about Agent Silver at

Jo. This time, though, plenty of the questions were about Emma, as well.

"Any comment on the suggestion you got involved with action movies and your assistant because you're terrified of getting older?"

Jo rolled her eyes behind her sunglasses.

"Was the Agent Silver announcement timed to distract from the scandal with your assistant?"

When Jo and Emma were only a few feet from the car at the curb, close enough to safety that Emma's arm had dropped back to her side, one paparazzo asked, "What do you say to reports that you're, and I'm quoting a source here, 'a midlife crisis of a person in love with your assistant'?"

Emma's feet stumbled, but Jo caught her at the elbow and pulled her forward.

"No reactions, Ms. Kaplan," she muttered.

They got into the car without further incident.

Emma waited until they pulled away from the studio to fish gape at Jo.

"He—they—he was *quoting a source* that said that about you?"

Jo shrugged. "That source could be a tourist on Rodeo Drive for all we know. It's nothing to worry about."

"But how can they just *say* that stuff?"

Jo looked at her. Emma breathed through her mouth, cheeks flushed.

"You've dealt with paparazzi before," Jo said. "Why are they bothering you now?"

"Normally we deal with them because they *like* you, not because they're being dicks to you!" Emma huffed, clearly affronted.

Jo tried not to chuckle. "You hardly need to defend my honor."

Emma didn't immediately reply. She turned to look out the window and folded her hands in her lap. Quietly, she said, "Well, it deserves defending."

EVELYN CALLED TO TEASE again that night. Jo suspected she had an alert set for Jo and Emma's names together. It was annoying, a bit, but it was the most regularly Jo had talked to her best friend in years, so she didn't mind.

She overthought, though. The next day on set, Jo went to lead Emma back toward her office, but froze halfway there.

This was normal, right? To gently guide Emma with a hand at her back? Jo had never thought about it before, never worried about it, but now they were in front of the crew, and Jo swore some of Emma's PA friends were watching them.

Emma tilted her head at Jo. Jo rolled her eyes at herself and pressed her hand into Emma's lower back, directed her toward the hallway to their offices.

It was obnoxious, the way she overanalyzed their every interaction now. Jo worried she was crossing a line, doing something inappropriate. Then she worried she was pulling back, allowing the rumors to affect how she behaved. She wanted to be able to focus on *work*. They were getting down to the end of filming for the season, and Jo was working on the Agent Silver script. She didn't need any distractions.

But the rumors *were* distracting. Every snide article, blind item, tweet—all of them made Jo want to break something. They made Emma even madder.

"I get why you didn't want to say anything about us dating." She backtracked. "Or—not dating, I mean. Like the fact that we're not dating. I get not talking about that. But this is ridiculous! The idea that you're going through some midlife crisis and that's why you want to do Agent Silver! When you know it's just sexism and racism—God forbid a woman write an established male character. What if she gives him feelings that aren't punching and having sex?"

Emma had brought Jo a midmorning coffee and stayed in her office to rant.

"Who can imagine why Jo Jones might be interested in a movie?" Emma continued. "Oh, I don't know, she's already conquered television—maybe she wants to challenge herself to do something new. Something you'll be great at, by the way. Literally everyone who has ever worked with you knows you're going to be great at this, and there's just these strangers on the internet saying—saying—casting *aspersions* on your talent!"

Jo pressed her lips together so she wouldn't laugh. Emma's indignation was charming. Jo didn't even want to break anything anymore.

"How can you just not say anything when they're writing stuff like this?" Emma asked. "Acting like you can't do this?"

"The people who matter know I can," Jo said. She hoped it was true.

Emma looked at her for a moment. "Right," she said. Then: "I have work to do."

She marched out of Jo's office. Jo didn't think anything of it. She wished she had. Could have saved herself some trouble.

Three days later, Chantal knocked on the doorjamb of Jo's open office door after lunch.

"Come in," Jo said, tossing her sandwich wrapper into the trash.

Chantal shut the door behind her. They didn't have anything scheduled, which meant this must be bad news. Jo didn't ask. She knew Chantal wouldn't beat around the bush.

"There's an article on Celeb Online," Chantal said. "With quotes from your employees about how great you are."

"I know."

Amir had called Jo that morning, congratulating her on the relaxation of her no-comment policy. The article featured five current and two former employees, unnamed, all extolling Jo's virtues. All certain she'd make an amazing Agent Silver movie. The smile in Amir's voice had stayed even after she told him she had nothing to do with the article.

"Did you know there's a follow-up?" Chantal asked.

Jo had been waiting for the other shoe to drop.

"About how Emma was the one who arranged the first article," Chantal continued. "Thought you might want a heads-up."

Amir certainly wouldn't think the article was a good idea now. Jo scrubbed a hand through her hair.

"What was she thinking?" She said it more to herself than to Chantal, but Chantal answered.

"When she asked me, I reminded her no one is supposed to talk to the media."

Jo looked up at her. Chantal's arms were crossed.

"She asked you?"

Chantal gave a nod.

"You could've told me then."

"I thought I had talked her out of it," she said. "And I'm not trying to be in your business. I only know about the second article because I overheard some PAs talking about it."

Jo sighed. Emma meant well, organizing the article, but she really should have known better. They didn't need to give the tabloids any ammunition. Emma couldn't be talking to reporters about how great Jo was—even if that thought made Jo warm inside.

Chantal was still standing in front of Jo's desk, arms crossed, scrutinizing her.

"Say what you want to say," Jo said.

Chantal's arms dropped to her sides. "When have I not said what I wanted to say to you?"

It was true. On Jo's first show, Chantal had regularly contradicted Jo's ideas. Most people thought they hated each other, but Jo cherished having another perspective, someone who wasn't afraid to tell her when she was wrong. Now, more than a decade later, *Innocents* was the only program on network TV with two women of color at the helm. Jo and Chantal got to this point by not bullshitting each other.

Still, Jo pressed. "You have thoughts?"

Chantal shrugged one shoulder. "If I believed the shit they're writing, maybe I'd have thoughts, but I know you better than that."

Jo let out a relieved breath. At least she still had Chantal on her side.

"Send her in, will you?"

Chantal nodded and left, leaving the door open behind her so Jo could hear her tell Emma that Jo wanted to see her.

Emma hovered at the door like she didn't want to come in.

"Chantal said you needed something?"

"Come in," Jo said. "Door open."

She didn't need anyone thinking she and Emma were holed up in her office doing who knows what.

Emma stood with her hands twined in front of her, looking at the floor. She already knew what this was about, then.

"What were you thinking?" Jo had expected to be angry, but her voice was filled only with disappointment.

Emma sighed. "I thought—" she started. "They're not even

giving you a chance—just saying you're not good enough, with nothing to back it up. It seemed so easy to debunk. I knew everyone who ever worked for you or with you or near you would know you could do this. Phil's—you know Phil in props? His old roommate is a journalist. It seemed like a simple solution."

"And how exactly did it get out that you organized it?"

"I don't know!" There was the slightest whine in her voice. Jo tried not to find it endearing. "I was discreet! All I did was kick-start the process by asking some people if they'd be willing to do it. I'm not even one of the ones quoted in the article! I never spoke to the reporter directly. He shouldn't have known I was the one to organize it."

That made Jo pause.

If Emma hadn't talked to the reporter herself, where did the second article come from?

Jo wanted to interrogate her, ask who all knew she was the one who arranged the article, but Emma looked like a dog with its tail between its legs.

"So you not only conspired with other employees behind my back to violate the no-media agreement, you knew your involvement was a bad idea."

Emma's head hung. "Chantal said it was a bad idea, too," she said. "I'm sorry. I should've listened."

This gave the press more to throw at Jo. Not only was she a "midlife crisis of a person in love with her assistant," she couldn't even fight her own battles. How was she ever supposed to run an Agent Silver movie if she couldn't keep her employees from talking to reporters?

"You should've," Jo agreed. "The rumors of our supposed relationship will drag on now. As will the belief that I can't do my job."

Emma huffed at that. "You *can*," she said. "That was the point!"

"As I told you, the people who matter know I can," Jo said. "I've got a contract already signed with the people who matter. All you've done is make them second-guess themselves."

Emma's eyebrows knit together, her mouth turning down.

"I'm so sorry, boss," she said. "I promise nothing like this will happen ever again."

Jo had already known that from the dejected way Emma had walked into her office. It made her want to comfort her assistant when she was supposed to be dressing her down. Emma's earnest belief in her meant a lot, actually, even if it didn't manifest itself well.

She considered telling Emma that her indiscretion wouldn't have been such a problem if it weren't for a bigger issue: that second article. If Emma didn't talk to the reporter herself, there was a leak. A real leak, not just her assistant trying to make her look good. That was something Jo was going to have to deal with at some point.

Emma didn't need to know that, though. It would only serve to make her feel more guilty, and she obviously felt guilty enough.

"I do appreciate it, you know," Jo found herself saying. "How you think I'll do a good job with the movie."

It felt heavier than she meant it.

"I *know* you will, boss," Emma said.

Maybe Jo should've had her close the door after all.

AS EXPECTED, EMMA'S MISGUIDED attempt to help had hurt instead. The rumors swirled harder, the articles taking on a cruel edge. The network scheduled a phone call with Jo the next week. She knew it wasn't going to be good news, and indeed, they opened the conversation with "We wanted to touch base regarding these rumors."

While one of the execs droned on, Jo muted her side of the call. "Emma!"

Her door was closed, but Emma came right in.

"Yes, boss?"

Jo pointed to the phone, where the guy was doing everything he could to avoid saying the word *lesbian*. "This concerns you," Jo said. "If you're interested in listening in."

"It all seems a little inappropriate," said John or Dave or whatever his name was; Jo could not for the life of her remember. "An assistant and a showrunner."

Emma's eyes widened. She sat down on the couch.

Jo held her finger to her lips, then unmuted the phone. "I agree it would be inappropriate were there anything between us. But there's not."

"Why don't you just say that?"

"I've never commented on my love life," Jo said for what felt like the fortieth time. "To do so now would be tacky. And offensive, as this is the first time a prolonged rumor has concerned me and a woman."

Jo considered flat-out calling them homophobic, but the hint should work well enough. Emma pressed her lips together, her palms resting flat on her thighs.

"Is the rumor affecting our ratings?" Jo asked like she didn't know the answer. It might be affecting her personal reputation, but the show was doing well, averaging two-tenths higher than last year.

"Well, no, but—"

As Josh or Dan continued about the potential issues that could come up, Jo rolled her eyes at Emma, who gave a rueful smile.

"Perhaps you could go out with someone else," Jake said. "Pick a guy, pick a restaurant, and—"

"I know you did not just tell me I should be seen out with a man in order to quell rumors about a relationship with a woman," Jo said. "Rumors that are having zero effect on our ratings and advertisers."

The line was silent for a moment.

Someone else spoke up. "No, Jo, what I think Don meant—"

"Great," Jo cut him off again. "If you'll excuse me, I've got a lot to get done here. Do keep in touch if the rumors ever actually cause any issues?"

"Right. Thanks."

Jo *mm-hmm*ed, and ended the call.

She leaned her elbows against her desk and held her head in her hands.

"I'm going to fucking kill him," she said.

Emma made a noise that sounded like she was hiding a laugh. "Boss . . ."

"The fucking *nerve*."

"You've always said the network execs were idiots," Emma said.

Jo lifted her head to level Emma with a look. "And yet they've never been as bad as that was."

Emma shrugged. "They're worried about their reputation. It's not a big deal."

"Their reputation?" Jo stared at her. "He was being a homophobic asshole. I don't give a fuck what he was worried about."

Emma gave a small nod.

"If anyone should be worried about their reputation, it's *you*," Jo said. "You're the one everyone thinks is sleeping with her boss."

Emma blushed, but Jo was serious. Emma had said she didn't

know what the next step in her career was, but they'd figure that out, and what then? What would happen when Emma was ready to move on from *Innocents*? How much stock would other potential employers put in these rumors? How would they affect the importance of Jo's recommendation letter?

"I suppose I *can* be seen with someone else," she said.

"No."

Jo blinked at Emma, whose cheeks were still flushed pink.

"I just mean—" Emma started. Took a breath. "That network guy was wrong to suggest that. And you definitely don't have to do it for my benefit."

"It would be simple," Jo said. "Go out to dinner with someone once or twice so the paparazzi move on."

"If you already have dinner plans, of course that's fine," Emma said. She rubbed her hands along her thighs. "But my so-called simple solution to people claiming you'd be bad for Agent Silver is what made the network call to begin with. It doesn't always work out the way you expect."

Jo conceded the point.

"Regardless, you don't have to go out of your way on my behalf," Emma said. "The rumors aren't that much a of a problem at this point."

Her smile was stiff. Jo smiled back gently.

"I did have to have a fun phone call with my mom at the beginning," Emma said. "Typical Jewish mother thrilled at the idea that her kid has a significant other. She completely approved, and was actually a little disappointed when I told her it was just a rumor."

Jo chuckled, like she knew Emma wanted her to, and tried not to think about how she hadn't met a girl's parents since she was in her early twenties. She hadn't dated enough since then, too famous and just closeted enough to not bother much.

"If you're sure," Jo said.

"Certain."

They looked at each other for a moment. Emma took a breath.

"I want to apologize again, boss," she said. "I thought I knew what I was doing—with the article. I obviously didn't. I just—" She broke eye contact. "I hate what they're saying about you. When everyone who knows you knows you're going to be great."

"How can anyone know that? I've never done this before. I don't even know if I can."

Emma's eyes snapped back up. "Jo," she said quietly.

Jo didn't mean to admit any of that. She hadn't even told Evelyn about her nerves. She waved her hand dismissively.

"It's nothing," she said. "A little self-doubt is all."

"That's . . ." Emma trailed off, then geared up again. "That's understandable—we all doubt ourselves sometimes, especially with something as new as this, and especially when you have the press and the network breathing down your neck. But you're going to be fine. You're so goddamn talented—excuse my French—there's no way you're not going to be awesome at this, just like everything else you've done."

Jo's chest fluttered. Emma's unwavering belief felt strong enough for the both of them. It was so new from what most people were writing about her.

"When I need the reminder . . ." Jo paused, not sure she could actually bring herself to ask for help like this. "You won't let me forget?" she said eventually.

"Never," Emma vowed.

Jo believed her.

"Do you have work you can do in here?" Jo asked.

"Sure, boss," Emma said. "Let me go grab it."

Emma disappeared, returned with her tablet. She gave Jo a

smile and then sat back down on the couch, her focus entirely on her work.

She was used to it by now, Jo supposed. It wasn't often that Jo asked Emma to work in her office—only when things got incredibly frustrating, when Jo lost the thread of plot or couldn't get the right tone of dialogue. That was where she was at the moment, brain too busy to figure out the last-minute edits to the finale script. She had thought she was done with it, but there was this one scene that didn't quite work, and she hadn't been able to fix it.

Jo wasn't sure what it was, exactly, about Emma in her office that helped her. She thought perhaps it was Emma's sturdiness. Emma was steadfast. To have Emma there, silently accomplishing things—it made Jo's troubles seem irrelevant. There were no excuses. Just do the work.

And Jo did.

THE GLAAD MEDIA AWARDS in early April were Jo's first public event since the SAGs. She wouldn't be bringing Emma, obviously. She considered getting Evelyn to fly out from New York, but then Jo would be labeled a lesbian *and* a slut, probably, so it wouldn't have been the best choice.

The GLAADs weren't as bad as other awards shows. They weren't considered as prestigious, which helped, Jo thought. Made them more bearable. But it was more than that—being in a room with so many young, open, *proud* people, it made Jo's heart ache a little, in a good way. She still wasn't publicly out—no matter what gossip magazines said about Emma and her. She wrote queer people into her shows and she let people speculate, but, as her publicist kept reminding everyone, she had never commented on her love life. She'd considered it once, when she was nineteen. She came out to her parents first.

Her mom told her to think of her career. Her father told her they were never going to speak of it again.

And so she hadn't, not really. She was, for the most part, okay with that. But then she went to the GLAAD awards and saw young women holding hands, and her heart ached.

Regardless, she'd be going alone.

Except for the rumors, the SAGs were the best awards show Jo had been to in years. Prep went smoothly, they arrived late enough that she skipped interviews, and the food was delicious. Emma hadn't simply been a buffer—she had been entertaining in and of herself. And Jo hadn't ended the evening exhausted and longing for sleep; she'd ended it smiling as they dropped Emma off at her apartment building.

Jo wanted the GLAADs to be similar, wanted to enjoy them. But everything reminded her of the SAGs. As Kelli and Mai put her together, as she walked the red carpet, Jo thought of Emma. It didn't help that both her prep team in the suite and the photographers at the event kept asking after Jo's "girlfriend."

She tried to let it roll off her, tried to keep a smile on her face. With no buffer, she had to talk to anyone who came by, but it was fine—it was; she swore the GLAADs were better than other ceremonies. Tonight they simply took more mental energy than she had.

And then, when Jo was almost at her breaking point, when she wanted to go home, *Innocents* won for Outstanding Drama Series, and she had a speech to give.

The whole cast came onstage with her. Jo accepted the award and stepped up to the microphone, everyone still hugging behind her.

She had a speech planned. They'd won this three years running now; she came prepared. She had a list of people to thank.

She didn't.

"This is my favorite awards show," she said instead. "This is the award I will always be proudest to win. I write fiction, but these are real stories. These are important stories."

These are our stories, she thought but did not say as people applauded. This wasn't about her, not really.

"There are plenty of people who work on our show who I could thank, but I want to thank *you*," Jo said. "Thank all of you, for being so strong in the face of a world that sometimes seems like it would rather you not exist. Thank you for being proud in the face of people who think you should be ashamed. Thank you for being here, in this world. For surviving. You are an inspiration."

Everyone congratulated her again as they left the stage together, hugs and high fives and big grins. Jo wished Emma were there.

5

EMMA

"CONGRATULATIONS ON THE WIN," EMMA SAID AS SHE handed Jo her coffee the Monday following the GLAADs.

"Thanks," Jo said. "Is everything on track for Friday?"

Emma had never seen Jo do anything with a compliment except brush it off. She followed Jo into her office.

"Everything is set for Friday, yes," Emma said. "Except for the last-minute RSVPs who I am going to make grovel before telling them they can still come."

That got Jo to smirk slightly as she sat at her desk and opened her laptop.

"Would you like to see a list of songs for karaoke?" Emma asked. "So you can practice in advance?"

Jo chuckled. "Good try."

Karaoke was Emma's favorite part of every wrap party, but Jo never sang.

"I have a new duet partner this year," Emma said. "You won't want to miss it."

"You're bringing a date?" Jo said, looking up at Emma, her brow furrowed.

"I am!" Emma said. "My sister's coming early to drop off the desserts from her bakery, and then she'll change and come back as my date slash singing partner."

The wrinkles in Jo's forehead smoothed. Emma wondered if Jo thought she was bringing a *date* date—not that it would have quelled the rumors: What happened at wrap parties stayed at wrap parties. Part of planning the party was ensuring there would be no paparazzi anywhere near it. That was kind of a necessity when you had an open bar and no call time in the morning.

"Are you bringing anyone?" Emma asked.

"Have I ever?"

Emma smiled. "There's a chance that in years past I may have been too busy with karaoke to notice your date situation."

In years past, wrap parties were easier. She was a props assistant then, had no responsibility for the party. She just got to show up and get drunk and sing. This year, even with the added responsibility, she was looking forward to the week. It would be quieter, less stressful after weeks of rewrites and reshoots and struggling to get everything perfect for the finale.

"I don't bring dates to wrap parties and I don't partake in karaoke," Jo said.

"Has anyone ever told you you're not very much fun?" Emma teased.

"I'll have you know, my five-year-old nephew told me I was the *coolest.*"

"Oh, well then," Emma laughed. "You'll never hear me disagree with a five-year-old."

"They are your peers, aren't they?" Jo asked, an eyebrow arched and the corners of her mouth quirked up.

"You really want to start age jokes, boss?"

Jo laughed and waved her off. Emma returned to her desk with a smile on her face.

THE RESTAURANT THEY'D RENTED out for the wrap party was a rooftop bar, strung up with twinkle lights. Karaoke was inside, and most of the mingling was outside, under a night sky dulled by light pollution.

Emma had to make sure everything was in place: food, drinks, security, entertainment. It was the first wrap party she'd ever planned. She wanted it to be perfect. Avery eventually pulled her away from explaining ticket taking to the bouncers for the third time.

"They know what they're doing," Avery said. "Let's get you a drink or three."

Emma stayed stressed until her sister put a gimlet in her hand.

Emma loved wrap parties. Everyone intermingled—big-name actors and location assistants alike, coming together and having a good time. She sought out her old crew. She'd worked in the props department for three years before Jo handpicked her as her assistant. She missed the people. Even though she still saw them around, it wasn't the same as being one of them. Phil was her best friend from back then, and he still was, when she got the chance to hang out with him. He let her set her drink down before he scooped her into a hug that lifted her off her feet.

"How's life?" he asked. He held his arm up against hers, his skin bronze comparatively. "Remember when we used to compete to see who got the tannest? Outdoor shoots and driving golf carts all over the lot? And now look at you, whitey."

Emma laughed. "That's what I get for being holed up at the studio all the time now."

"Speaking of"—Phil dropped his voice to a conspiratorial whisper—"how's sleeping with the enemy?"

Emma rolled her eyes. "I am neither sleeping with Jo nor is she the enemy. What did she ever do to you anyway?"

"Defending your girlfriend, how cute."

She glared at him. "Come on, Phil."

Avery butted in. "You know it'd be less fun to tease you if you didn't get so upset about it every time."

"It's a reasonable thing to get upset about," Emma said, her voice louder than she'd like it to be. She lowered it. "I don't want anyone thinking that I am the type to sleep my way into a job, and I don't want anyone thinking Jo is the type to take advantage of her employees."

"It doesn't count as taking advantage if you're super into it, does it?" Phil said.

"Good point," Avery said.

Emma sighed. "I regret ever introducing the two of you."

She didn't, though, because even if they made fun of her, Phil and Avery also plied her with drinks and made her laugh harder than she had in months. She dragged them both to karaoke to do backup for their props manager, Aly, then spent half the song unable to sing because she was cracking up at Phil's outrageous dancing.

Afterward, the three of them crowded around a high-top table outside and shared cheesy breadsticks.

"Where's your girlfriend?" Phil asked. "Don't you think she'd want some?"

Avery snorted.

"Look," Emma said sharply. "There's like—there's a leak, or something, okay? Like remember when I organized that article about how Jo was gonna do great on Silver and then there was a follow-up about how I organized it?"

Phil was a part of that whole thing, and Emma had relayed the story to Avery in detail, so they both nodded.

"Jo didn't say anything about it but, like, obviously someone had to leak that, right? Because I wasn't even the one who talked to the reporter, so like. Someone had to."

Phil and Avery stared at her with no response.

"So I'm saying don't call her my girlfriend!" Emma said. "What if the leak overhears?"

"Babe," Phil said. "Everyone here is definitely too drunk to bother eavesdropping about whether or not you're sleeping with your boss."

"Whatever," Emma scoffed. "Get me another drink."

LATER IN THE NIGHT, Avery was putting their names in to sing, and Emma had lost track of Phil. She wandered outside to look for him and spotted Jo and Chantal standing at a high table in the corner of the roof. She grinned and headed over.

"Ms. Jones, I've signed you up to sing 'Love Is a Battlefield,'" Emma said as she approached. "I think you're up after Holly."

Emma hadn't, of course. She liked teasing Jo, but she didn't want her boss to kill her. Jo offered a smile and a roll of her eyes. Emma couldn't help but giggle. She knew she was tipsy. Perhaps more than tipsy.

Chantal cleared her throat. "I'm going to get another drink," she said.

Emma wanted to tell her she didn't have to go. Emma liked to think everyone on set knew she and Jo weren't together. They should've known. But then something happened like Phil made fun of her for sleeping with the enemy or Chantal excused herself when Emma came over.

Jo sighed. "Ms. Kaplan," she said. "Enjoying yourself?"

"I am. Are you?"

Emma wasn't asking to be polite; she wanted to know.

"Wrap parties are always enjoyable," Jo hedged.

Emma's smile turned into a frown. "Ms. Jones."

"I think you get to call me Jo at a party," Jo said, like she hadn't just called Emma Ms. Kaplan.

"Boss," Emma said instead. "I was really proud you—or well, we, like, the show—won the GLAAD award. I didn't really say anything but I was. And your speech was really wonderful. But also, like—" She looked at her drink, rattled the ice around in her glass. She didn't know exactly what she wanted to say, but kept talking anyway. "My sister said you looked great and you did but—you didn't look all that happy. And it's probably stupid but I thought about the SAG Awards and I kind of wished I was there at the GLAADs. I thought maybe I could make you smile, is all. Sometimes I don't think you smile enough."

Jo blinked. Emma felt stupid. She didn't think she explained herself well.

"I just mean—" Emma furrowed her brow. "It's basically my job to make you happy."

Jo did something between a scoff and a sigh, and Emma didn't understand it at all.

"Whatever," Emma said. "I just want you to be happy, and if I am sometimes the one who makes you that way, great."

That felt too heavy. God, especially with the rumors, what was Emma thinking, coming over and saying this to Jo? She tried to power through like it wasn't awkward.

"I can probably make you laugh, actually," she said. "My sister and I are doing 'A Whole New World' from *Aladdin* next on karaoke. You should come watch."

"Have you done the proper warm-ups?" Jo's voice was overly serious.

"If singing backup while Aly rocked 'Build Me Up Buttercup' counts as warm-ups."

That, at least, got Jo to smile. Emma took a sip of her drink to hide her grin.

"You know I appreciate everything you do, Emma," Jo said. "That award belongs to you, too—I wouldn't get half as much done without you."

Emma shrugged it off. "Sure you would."

"I wouldn't," Jo insisted.

She held eye contact for a moment before glancing over Emma's shoulder.

"I believe your sister is trying to get your attention," she said. "It must be your time to sing."

"Right," Emma said. She turned to go, then turned back. "You really should come watch. Better than the original, I swear."

Avery was on the other side of the rooftop. She could have walked over, but apparently she'd rather try to get Emma's attention like an idiot, waving her arms around. Emma planned to tease her for it, but Avery teased her first.

"How's your *girlfriend*?" Avery asked, dragging out the word.

Emma smacked her on the arm. "Seriously, could you not do that? Especially *here*. God, what did I tell you about this? I do *not* need people thinking you're serious."

Avery rubbed the place on her arm Emma hit. "Somebody's touchy."

"Somebody's *annoying*," Emma grumbled. "You don't even know if she's interested in women anyway. She's probably straight and definitely isn't my girlfriend."

Avery leveled her with a look.

"No straight person writes queer characters as well as Jo Jones."

"Maybe she's got a lot of gay friends!"

Avery gave an exaggerated roll of her eyes. "No straight woman would've watched you walk away from that conversation the way she did."

Emma could feel her face go red. "I said shut *up*. God, some of the crew already believe the rumors."

She didn't wonder how Jo looked at her. It didn't matter. Jo was—Jo was her maybe straight boss, and Emma didn't have a crush on her anyway.

"I'll make it up to you," Avery said, "by singing Aladdin's part."

Emma gasped. "You never let me sing Jasmine's part!"

"A one-time offer."

Emma squealed and threw her arms around her sister.

When Emma sang about an endless diamond sky, she spotted Jo, at the back of the crowd, just inside the door from outside. She was smiling.

Emma really loved wrap parties.

LATER, EMMA TRACED PATTERNS onto a tablecloth as the last of the partygoers filtered out. Avery was—somewhat drunkenly—directing one of her employees in the collection of Floured Up's platters. Avery's chocolate Guinness cupcakes had been such a hit that Emma no longer felt bad about using her position as wrap party planner to give her sister business.

Emma watched Gina, one of the lead actresses, give Jo a hug

before getting on the elevator. Emma and Jo were officially the only members of the cast and crew left. It was probably time to go. Emma bumped the table as she got up, but managed to catch her cup before it spewed its contents everywhere. At least no one was left to witness her clumsiness.

She made her way over to Jo, who still stood by the elevators.

"Do you always stay until the end of the party?"

"Honestly, no." Jo's eyes crinkled with her smile. "But this was an exceptional party. It must have had an excellent planner."

Emma giggled. It had been a successful night. She hoped everyone else agreed.

"I meant what I said earlier, Emma," Jo said. "I wouldn't be here without you."

Emma scuffed her shoe along the ground and bit her lip. "You would. You just probably wouldn't be as entertained. I mean what other assistant is going to pull off 'A Whole New World' that well?"

"That's true." Jo's smile was tender. "You have a beautiful voice."

If Emma weren't already red from the alcohol, she'd be red from the compliment.

"You ready to go?" Avery appeared at Emma's shoulder.

Emma nodded. Avery pushed the elevator button, and Emma looked back to Jo, who was still smiling at her.

"Good night, Emma."

"Good night."

Emma stepped in for a hug. A half a beat, then Jo slid her arms around Emma's waist. Emma breathed her in. Jo wore the same perfume, every day, just a dash of it. She smelled fresh—like clean sheets or snowfall or something.

Emma turned her head to press a quick goodbye kiss to Jo's cheek. Jo was pulling back from the hug at the same time, and Emma misjudged the distance. She didn't realize what was happening until she suddenly suddenly suddenly knew exactly what was happening. Her mouth was on Jo's. Just the corner, just a little, but unmistakably there. Emma jerked away quickly enough to lose her balance. She took a stumbling step before catching herself, straightening up. Jo's face was—*stricken* wasn't quite the right word, but it was close.

"I'm—" If she said she was sorry, she was addressing it, and addressing it made it real and it couldn't be real. She could not have just *kissed* her *boss*. So instead she said, "See you Monday!" much too loudly, and fled—except she couldn't flee, because she had to wait for the elevator to arrive.

Emma listened to Avery and Jo say good night while she stared unblinkingly at the silver elevator doors. Jo didn't sound upset. Emma could tell by her tone of voice she was smiling. So maybe kissing her wasn't the worst thing in the world?

Fuck.

Fuck fuck fuck.

It was definitely the worst thing in the world. It could not have just happened. Emma could not be that drunk. She wanted to die.

The elevator dinged and the doors opened. Emma did not look back at Jo. She did not look at her sister, getting on the elevator behind her. She pushed the button for the first floor, kept her finger on it even after it lit up. She didn't breathe until the doors closed.

It had been dark on the roof—maybe Avery hadn't seen. No one else was close enough to have noticed at all, probably, and it was just event staff at this point anyway. But Emma wasn't worried about anyone else. She was only worried about Avery beside her, suspiciously silent until she took a breath like she was gearing up for something. Emma cringed in advance.

"So I don't get why you spent the beginning of the party lecturing me and Phil about not calling Jo your girlfriend when at the end of the party you literally kissed her goodbye."

"Noooooo." Emma slumped backward against the wall of the elevator. "I didn't mean to!"

"You kissed her! Right on her fucking mouth!" Avery only swore when she was drunk.

"I didn't mean to!" Emma said again, loud enough that Jo might have been able to hear, now five floors away. "I just meant to kiss her cheek!"

"That's still a fucking weird thing to do to *your boss*!"

Emma realized that now. Realized a lot of things now. Like that she should have stopped three gin and tonics ago.

"I'm *drunk* and she smelled good and she said such nice things about me tonight and I love wrap parties and it was an *accident*, okay? Can we please forget about it? It doesn't mean anything!"

"It means you're super gay for your boss, just like everyone has been saying."

"I hate you."

It did *not* mean that. It meant Emma was drunk and dumb and had bad depth perception. It meant she was embarrassed as all hell and would probably have to deal with some awkward lecture from Jo on Monday about appropriate behavior in the workplace.

"We're not done talking about this," Avery said as she put Emma in a Lyft.

Emma didn't bother saying bye. Her driver was silent, thankfully. She sat in the back seat in a stew of embarrassment and disbelief. What was she supposed to do now? What did one do after accidentally kissing their boss? She could apologize. Should, probably. But it seemed like the much less mortifying solution was just to ignore it.

Yes, an apology would be nice. She didn't want to do things

that were inappropriate or made Jo uncomfortable. But maybe apologizing would make Jo uncomfortable—bringing it back up and having to address it. The best apology was changed behavior, and it was already never going to happen again. Emma didn't want to kiss Jo. Jo knew that, even if the rest of the world— including Emma's own sister—thought otherwise. Emma would just be professional. That would be her apology.

She drank two full glasses of water before climbing into bed. She didn't think about Jo's lips once.

THE SUN WAS TOO bright. Emma pulled her pillow over her face. Her head pounded, not horribly, but enough that she regretted drinking so much. Then she remembered saying goodbye to Jo, and her stomach rolled. Her hangover wasn't bad enough to make her nauseated but her embarrassment sure was.

She'd kissed Jo.

She'd kissed. Jo.

She threw the covers off and got up. It was fine. It had to be fine. There was not another option. She was meeting Jo for lunch Monday to talk about her career path. The rest of the cast and crew were off until late summer when they started filming the next season. Since Emma worked for Jo, she had a job year-round, but she had a week off after the wrap party. Except for lunch on Monday. She was supposed to tell Jo what she wanted to do with her life.

Unless the wrap party changed things.

Maybe instead of asking Emma what career she wanted, Jo would ask her why she thought she could kiss her. Maybe Emma would be fired. But Emma remembered Jo's voice saying bye to Avery. She sounded normal. Not fake normal like when she was actually upset—Emma had worked with her long enough to know when she was pretending like that. And she wasn't. She was fine. So this whole thing had to be fine. It was an accident. Accidents happened. People made mistakes. Jo knew that. She gave people second chances. She wasn't going to fire her. Emma was almost certain.

Running tended to help Emma clear her head. She could work out problems as her feet hit the ground. She liked to coordinate the difficulty of her runs with the difficulty of her problems.

On Saturday, she ran at Griffith Park.

She ran *up*. West Observatory Trail. From the start to the observatory was only about a mile, but the elevation change had her breathing hard early. Her feet sent up clouds of dust with every stride.

She wasn't worried about the accidental kiss. No. That was going to be fine. She'd decided. And if she believed enough, it had to be true.

The problem she was working out instead was what she wanted to do.

Which—

She knew what she wanted to do.

Or did she? How could she be sure? What if she started on the path she thought she wanted, only to be wrong? She liked her job now. It was good. Interesting. She was good at it. She didn't quite see why she couldn't stay on as Jo's assistant when Jo moved to Agent Silver. Maybe not *forever*, or anything, but at least for another year or two. She was still getting her footing. By her third year as props PA, she had everything figured out forward, backward, and sideways. Why couldn't she do the same thing as Jo's assistant?

Because she knew what she wanted to do.

She should have gotten out here earlier, before the tourists and the sun. Only April, but it was hot enough for sweat to drip down her forehead and pool at the base of her back.

Even if she was right about where she wanted to end up, she didn't know how to get there. The path she expected to take didn't work; she'd dropped out of film school. Maybe that had been a bad time in her life or maybe she just wasn't good enough. Regardless, there wasn't any sort of map plotted out for her now. Not any particular next step. Emma latched onto the metaphor as she ran. She could make a misstep, lose her footing, roll her ankle. She could get a cramp halfway through and have to pull up. Or worse, she could not have it in her. She worried about that most as she pushed herself up the incline. She already failed once. What if she got another chance and still couldn't do it? What if she never made it to the top? She could get lost somewhere in the middle. Veer off the poorly marked path.

She was almost to the observatory on top of the hill. The water in her CamelBak was cool and refreshing. She wished she could pour it over her face. Hopefully she wasn't sweating her sunscreen off. She kept going.

Tourists crowded the observatory parking lot. Cars packed in side by side while others circled like they were going to somehow get lucky and find an empty spot. Emma walked, hands on her hips, letting herself catch her breath. She tried to avoid interrupting anyone's photos—of the city, the Hollywood Sign, each other.

She found a spot without people in it and stopped to stretch a little.

The Hollywood Sign sat on the hillside in front of her.

"I want to be a director."

She hadn't said it out loud since she left film school. Had barely even let herself think it.

It was terrifying.

None of the problems she considered on her way up were solved. Nothing was for certain. She could be wrong, could get stuck, could not have enough to get there.

But she knew what she wanted to do.

ON MONDAY, EMMA ARRIVED at the restaurant for lunch before Jo did. No matter how many times over the weekend she had told herself everything was going to be fine, her whole body felt like a coiled spring, like a bolt screwed in too tight. She squeezed her purse against her side and took a step up the sidewalk away from the restaurant when a black car pulled up to the curb.

Emma pressed her lips together as Jo got out. She was still considering fleeing.

Then Jo smiled in greeting. Her regular, happy-to-see-you, not-at-all-stressed smile, and Emma felt like she could breathe again.

"Good to see you survived your hangover," Jo teased gently.

Emma grimaced. Apparently they were going to address the kiss—the *accidental* kiss—right off the bat.

But instead, Jo said, "Let's get a table. I'm starving."

Okay then. One problem down. Or ignored, anyway. Emma didn't care about the specifics. Now she just had to get through the career talk.

She might have spoken her dream out loud to herself, but she stayed quiet as they were led to an outdoor table. And as they ordered, and as the waiter brought her a lemonade and Jo a sparkling water. Jo talked sparingly, about the wrap party, about how work in the summer would be easier on them.

She let Emma be quiet until their food arrived, and then she said, "So what do you want to do?"

Emma had ordered a steak salad. She stuffed a hunk of meat in her mouth instead of answering. "Hmm?"

Jo smiled. "I need to know what kind of recommendation letter I should write you." She stabbed a bite of her Caesar salad. "What job do you want next?"

Emma wanted to direct.

But that was too scary to say out loud. It was a big dream. There were too many ways to fail.

Emma shrugged, noncommittal.

"You're too good for this, Emma. Too smart."

Emma didn't like that, Jo making it seem like her job wasn't important enough.

"I like my job, Ms. Jones," she said.

"Ms. Kaplan." Jo's voice snapped around the *K*. "I'm not letting you stagnate as my assistant. It's nonnegotiable."

Emma felt like she was failing a test. She knew what she wanted to do, long-term, didn't she? But she didn't know how to get there.

"My sister always knew she wanted to have her own bakery," she said. "She got an Easy-Bake oven as a kid but graduated pretty quickly to the regular one. She's always been really good at it and has always known it was what she wanted to do."

Jo probably thought this was a weird segue, but it made sense. It was the only way Emma knew to describe it. Jo wasn't interrupting, though. She looked interested in learning more.

"I wanted something like that," Emma said. "I still want it. To be that sure of something. To know what I want to do and know I'm going to be successful at it. I wish I could tell you exactly what I want to do next. Wish I knew my path the way Avery always has."

Emma paused. She wanted Jo to say something, to fill in the

silence, but Jo just kept looking at her, eyes open and kind, forcing Emma to work this out herself.

"I like my job," Emma said. "This job. And I'm good at it. What if I'm not good at whatever I move on to? What if I don't like it?"

"If you don't like it, you'll do something else," Jo said. "If you're not good at it, you'll learn. You're brilliant, Emma. You hit the ground running in this job, picked everything up easily."

Jo sounded so certain. Emma wished she could believe her. She took another bite of her salad. She wished she could trust herself.

"Things I think I'm sure of, I can still mess up," she said. "I was certain putting together that article about how great you'd be for Agent Silver was going to be a *good* thing. And it was awful!"

Jo didn't disagree because she couldn't. Emma was right about that.

"So who's to say I'm not just as wrong about this?"

"You can't get anywhere without risk, Emma."

Right. Emma knew that. It didn't make it any less terrifying. She stared at her lemonade. The melting ice shifted in the glass.

"I dropped out of film school, you know?" she said.

"I do." Jo's voice was quiet.

"I was—it was dumb." Emma ran her finger along the condensation on the outside of her glass. "I tell people I flunked out, like it wasn't a choice, but I dropped out. It was hard, and I wasn't very good, and so I gave up."

"You were young, were you not?"

Emma tried to look at Jo, didn't quite make it to her face, focusing instead on the wide neck of her top, the line of her collarbone. Finally, she took a breath, brought her eyes to Jo's.

"I want to direct."

A slow smile spread across Jo's face. Emma felt it, warm in her chest.

"You want to direct," Jo said.

Emma fought the desire to break eye contact, to take her statement back.

"I do."

"Okay." Jo went into business mode. "I wouldn't think you have the credits for the Directors Guild yet, do you?"

Emma shook her head. "I'm close."

"So you'll keep working with me, keep working with *Innocents.*" Jo's eyes darted around as she brainstormed. "We could make you an associate producer—*yes.* Midseason I'll probably be moving to Agent Silver. You'll move to associate producer then, finishing up your days so you can join the guild. Before the move, you'll interview and find your replacement as my assistant. What do you think?"

She thought it sounded great, and she told Jo as much. Jo grinned at her.

This meant Emma got to stay with a show she loved, with a cast and crew she adored. And she'd have the days to join the Directors Guild by the end of the season so she could start working her way up. There was a slight pang at the thought of Jo moving on without her, but otherwise, associate producer was the best of both worlds: She was taking a step forward in her career without moving too far out of her comfort zone.

"You really think I can do it?" Emma had to ask.

Jo caught her hand on top of the table and squeezed it. "I think you can do anything, Emma."

AFTER LUNCH, EMMA HEADED to Avery's. Her week off coincided perfectly with Passover. Emma always tried to go home for it, but sometimes her schedule was too busy. This year, she piled Cassius,

Rosalind, and Billie into her car. Avery and her husband, Dylan, had their car loaded with their ten-year-old twins. Emma avoided any significant looks Avery sent her way as they packed the cars.

It had been days since the wrap party, but staying up so late and drinking so much took a toll Emma was still recovering from. She refused to admit it may have been related to an emotional conversation at lunch. Her throat was a little scratchy from how loud she sang along to Gina's karaoke of Brandi Carlile. She resorted to a large iced chai as she followed her sister's family up the coast.

Their parents still lived in the house where Emma and Avery grew up. Emma was grateful for it, grateful it was only a few hours' drive before she could bask in the comforts and nostalgia of home. Their parents were waiting on the front porch when they arrived, and were greeted first by the dogs barreling up to say hello.

There was a lot of hugging then, and Emma enjoyed the warm strength of her father's arms around her for all of two seconds before:

"You didn't bring your girlfriend?"

"Really?" Emma groaned. "I can't even make it through the door before you do this?"

THEY SPENT THE EVENING on the porch, catching up and gorging themselves on some of Avery's cupcakes before sundown, when Passover officially started. Ezra and Danielle, the twins, chased fireflies through the yard. No one stopped teasing Emma about Jo.

"You know the internet said she looked sad because you weren't at those awards with her," her mom said.

Emma remembered her drunken conversation with Jo and tried not to blush. "The internet says a lot of things, Mom."

Really, she and Jo had expected the GLAADs would calm the rumors down. Jo went by herself. People were supposed to realize Emma joining her was a fluke. Instead, everyone decided Jo was depressed either that Emma didn't join her or because they'd broken up.

Jo did look sad, though; no one had been wrong about that. Emma didn't like it. Jo's smile was strained and made Emma think about why Jo had taken her to the SAGs, as a buffer of sorts. It would've been worth the rumors, Emma thought, to go to the GLAADs with Jo for the same purpose. The rumors felt like a part of life now, neither bad nor good, just there. Even the photographers who had found her apartment weren't terrible. She hadn't told Jo about them, didn't think Jo needed to be bothered. They weren't usually there, but they were the morning after the GLAADs. Emma had held her head high and pretended she didn't see them.

"I like seeing my daughter in the news for dating a woman," her mom continued. "There are much worse reasons to be famous."

"I'm not *famous,*" Emma said.

"It was my turn to host book club last month," her dad said. "They all wanted to talk about you instead of about *Station Eleven.*"

Her dad's book club was all men over sixty. Emma didn't realize that so many people cared about the rumors.

"Did you tell them we aren't really dating?"

"Well," her father started, and already she rolled her eyes. "I told them you claim not to be interested in her?"

"Dad!"

"She's beautiful and famous, honey," he said. "All the guys agreed you should go for it."

"There's nothing to *go for!*"

Emma looked to Avery and Dylan for backup here, but they smirked at her.

"No one in this family loves me at all," Emma whined and the others laughed.

THE REST OF HER time at home went much the same. They had a seder with two other couples from their hometown temple, and even then, there was too much talk about Emma and Jo.

After the meal, alone in her childhood bedroom, Emma unlocked her phone. She opened her text thread with Jo. She wanted to tell her how ridiculous this all had been. She wanted to tell her about a group of sixtysomething guys deciding she and Jo were a cute couple. Jo would laugh, Emma thought.

But she'd never texted her boss about anything not work related. Not as the start of a conversation. Sometimes their texts ended up about something other than work, but they always began about it. Even though the rumors seemed work related, a little, Emma didn't type a message. She wasn't about to change the way their relationship worked after they had accidentally kissed. She couldn't do anything that would make Jo think she'd meant to do it. Plus, Jo was her boss, not her friend. And she wasn't even going to be her boss for long. Jo was pushing her out of the nest. Emma locked her phone and stared up at the glow-in-the-dark stars on her ceiling.

6

EMMA

UPFRONTS WERE WHEN NETWORKS TRIED TO WOO ADVER-
tisers. They were basically a dog and pony show—networks
did anything they could to promote their shows for a week in New
York. Last year, upfronts had been terrifying. Emma had just started
as Jo's assistant and had no idea what she was doing. But now,
rather than bumbling around trying to stay afloat, she'd be able to
learn about the production side of things from Jo, learn what it
took to win advertisers over. Outside of work, Emma planned to
sneak away when she could, walk the city, eat delicious food, go to
a museum or two. It would be an exhausting trip, but she couldn't
wait.

This year, their network was parading Jo and the stars—Tate,
Gina, and Holly—around. The main event for *Innocents* was a
panel with Jo and the other three where they would discuss what
they could of the next season without giving away spoilers. Emma
knew Jo hadn't written much of the next season yet. She'd been
focusing on Agent Silver instead, taking a break from *Innocents*
after the finale.

Emma and Jo worked seamlessly together, prepping for the panel. It was quiet, calmer with everyone else on break for summer hiatus. Emma quizzed Jo on the prepared answers to panel questions that the network sent. Jo peppered her answers with sarcasm and curse words the network definitely wasn't going to approve. Emma tried to be stern but always ended up laughing.

Jo dressed more casually, flowing maxi skirts and sometimes even a graphic tee. The atmosphere between them felt more casual, too. More than once when other people were still around, Emma had noticed Jo go to do something—put a hand on her shoulder or lead her by an elbow or something—before freezing. Jo always followed through with the motion, but it was obvious— at least to Emma—that Jo was considering how other people might see their interactions. It was nice to be away from that, to just be the two of them, grinning in Jo's office.

EMMA'S ASTHMA STARTED ACTING up on the flight. It was nothing severe, but she could tell. She couldn't breathe as deeply as usual. She'd keep an eye on it, up her meds if she needed to. She wasn't worried—her asthma was mild, and she'd dealt with it long enough to figure out how to work with it. Her lungs would be more sensitive than usual, but it shouldn't be a problem. She didn't mention it to Jo.

"Don't hesitate to ask me anything throughout the week," Jo said on the plane. "What questions do you have?"

"I'm sure they'll come up," Emma said. "I'll ask them when they do."

"But you have none right now?" Jo looked desperate for Emma to ask her something.

"Do you want to go over the schedule again, Jo?" Emma asked gently. "If you need to distract yourself?"

"I'm not distracting myself," Jo muttered.

She was, though. Which was why Emma didn't say anything about her asthma. The rumors were making Jo more nervous than usual—Emma assumed that was what it was, anyway. She'd listened in on that call with the network; any drop in advertising, and they'd blame it on Jo's refusal to deny that she was sleeping with her assistant. Advertisers were probably already wary about Jo leaving for Agent Silver and what effect that would have on *Innocents*.

It was Emma's job to keep Jo at the top of her game for the next few days, and she did it. She did it while trying to take in everything she could about upfronts, every lesson Jo imparted. She did it well. By the last day of the week, everything had gone smoothly. A few people had glanced knowingly between Jo and Emma, but Jo was charming, and the advertisers had been thoroughly wooed thus far.

Things were going well today, too, except they were running late. Jo needed to be at her panel in ten minutes, and she'd make it, but barely. Emma's chest felt tight. In any other situation she'd stop and rest, get her breathing under control. But she had to get Jo to the panel. Then she could sit down, catch her breath. And she'd be fine.

On their way, weaving through the crowds of the hallway, they passed a woman wearing too much perfume.

That was all it took.

Emma paused, trying to catch her breath. It—there wasn't— she was trying to breathe but the air wasn't moving. Her lungs refused to inflate. She tried to swallow. Bit at the air.

"Emma?"

Jo had continued walking before realizing Emma wasn't at her side. She was ten steps away.

"Emma?" she said again, looping back to Emma's side. "What's wrong?"

Emma's chest hurt. She wheezed in a breath, and it looked like Jo figured it out. Jo knew she had asthma, knew where her inhaler was in her desk, though Emma had never had to use it at work.

"Where is it?" Jo's hands frantically patted at Emma's pockets, front and back both, and the part of Emma's brain that wasn't solely focused on trying to breathe thought maybe her boss shouldn't grope her ass in public. When Jo couldn't find what she was looking for, she grabbed Emma by the shoulders instead. "Where's your inhaler?"

Her eyes were wide and her grip was strong.

"My bag," Emma got out. "In the—greenroom."

Jo yelled at someone over her shoulder. Emma coughed hard. The room was down the hallway. Her inhaler was not far away. It was going to be fine.

"I'm calling 911," Jo said, still holding Emma with one hand while pulling out her phone with the other. "You're going to be okay."

"No, Jo—" But Emma didn't have enough breath to tell her to calm down. Didn't have the breath to tell her she didn't have to call an ambulance unless Emma's rescue inhaler didn't work.

Jo spit rapid-fire words into the phone, pausing only to yell, "Hurry up with that bag!"

Emma's bag arrived, and Jo finally released Emma to fumble through it. Her fingers shook. There was a crowd of frightened onlookers around them. Emma leaned against the wall, closed her eyes. Opened them only when Jo shoved the inhaler into her hands. Emma took a hit off it. She wanted to vomit. Took another puff.

She still felt like something was caught in her throat, like she could only half fill her lungs. She closed her eyes again and slid down the wall so she was sitting on the floor.

"Emma?" Jo said. Her voice came closer. "Emma, breathe. Paramedics are on their way. You're going to be fine."

It sounded more like a directive than reassurance. Emma kept her eyes closed. She swallowed, coughed again, kept sucking in air. She didn't register someone right beside her until she leaned forward and a hand came to rest between her shoulder blades. Emma opened her eyes.

Jo was sitting on her knees next to Emma on the carpet, her feet tucked to one side. She rubbed soft circles on Emma's back. Emma stared at her.

"You're okay," Jo said. "Do you need anything?"

Emma didn't answer right away, her wheezing beginning to die down. As soon as she had the breath, she said, "You need to get to the panel."

"Fuck the panel," Jo growled. "Less talking, more breathing."

Emma rolled her eyes. "We didn't fly across the country so you could miss the panel."

"I'm staying here until the paramedics arrive."

"You shouldn't have called them!" Emma's chest was already feeling better. "I hadn't even taken my rescue inhaler yet. You panicked."

Jo's eyes flashed. "You *couldn't breathe,*" she said, like that was explanation enough.

Emma supposed maybe it should have been. Jo hadn't dealt with Emma's asthma. Emma hadn't had an attack at work before. It made sense that Jo wouldn't know what to do. It was sweet, really, that she was so worried. But she also had a panel to get to.

"Boss," Emma said quietly. The crowd around them had dissipated to just concerned looks from passersby, but Emma made sure not to be overheard. "Go to the panel. I'm fine, and we don't need to give anyone more ammunition."

Jo looked at her blankly.

"You can't miss a panel with potential advertisers because you're worried about your assistant who everyone thinks you're sleeping with." Emma managed to get it all out without blushing. Jo removed her hand from Emma's back. "I'm fine. Go."

"Text me if you need anything," Jo said. "I'll check in as soon as I'm done."

"*Go*," Emma said.

Jo's eyebrows were furrowed and her mouth was a gash of a frown, but she went. She somehow got off the ground gracefully, even in her heels. After a moment of smoothing down her dress and tucking her hair behind her ears, she went into business mode, striding off with purpose.

EMMA WAS SO EMBARRASSED when the paramedics arrived. Her breathing was almost back to normal by then, and she knew she was wasting their time. They'd given her an oxygen mask to breathe through, but she pulled it away to apologize again.

"I'm sorry," she said for the third time. "My boss didn't know what to do and she called you and I'm really sorry."

"It's no problem, ma'am," one of them said, also for the third time. "You're sure you're feeling all right?"

"I'm fine," Emma said. They had a thing to measure her lung capacity earlier, and it wasn't *high*, but it was good enough, she knew.

"It'd be best if you spent the rest of the evening avoiding any stressors that might cause your asthma to act up," the female paramedic said. She directed Emma's hand with the oxygen mask back to her face. "Pollution, smoke, that sort of thing."

"Crowds, too," the other paramedic said. "Since that seems to be what caused this attack."

"Right," Emma said. "Sure."

She wanted to go to the panel, was the thing. And then out to dinner, their last night here. She planned to venture out for bagels in the morning before their flight back. She wanted to be out and about, not avoiding stressors.

She considered ignoring the paramedics' advice, but she knew better. Plus, Jo would probably kill her if she ended up having another asthma attack. So when the paramedics packed up and left, Emma went back to her room instead of to the panel.

THE PANEL ENDED AT five. Emma's phone rang at 5:03.

She answered the call. "Hey, boss."

"Are you doing okay?"

"I'm fine," Emma said. She was, mostly. It had been almost two hours, and with the oxygen from the paramedics, she was better than she usually was at this point after an attack. "How was the panel?"

"They asked us questions and we gave prepared answers," Jo said, and Emma was almost certain she rolled her eyes. "Tate and Holly and G were worried about you, by the way."

"That's sweet of them, but like I said, I'm fine."

The line was silent for a few moments.

"Do you need anything?" Jo asked.

"What?"

"Do you need anything? Is there anything I could do that would help you?"

Emma needed a nap and some food, in that order. Asthma attacks always left her exhausted.

"No, boss, I'm good," she said. "I kind of can't leave my room, on paramedics' orders, but I can get room service later. Don't you have plans tonight anyway?"

Emma hadn't made the plans, which was rare, but the evening was blocked off on Jo's schedule. It was a personal thing, not a work thing, or Emma would've known what it was.

"Yes, well . . ." Jo didn't say anything more.

"I appreciate you checking in," Emma said when Jo stayed silent. "I have your six o'clock wake-up call already scheduled for the morning. Let me know if I can do anything else, yeah? Other than that, I'll just spend the night watching bad television or something."

"Right," Jo said. "I'd better go."

"Have a good night."

"You, too, Emma."

EMMA TOOK A NAP, and when she woke up, she felt almost normal. Almost like her lungs never had any issue. She was starving, though. She thought about the ramen place she went to last year at upfronts and again earlier this week. She thought about the best slice of pizza she'd ever eaten, from this walk-up window in Brooklyn. Maybe she could get away with sneaking out for dinner. Except there was still just the slightest twinge in her chest, and really, she knew better.

It didn't mean she couldn't get dinner brought to her, though. Thank God for technology. Emma scrolled through one of the three food delivery apps on her phone. The number of choices overwhelmed her. She had researched restaurants, as she did before any trip, but she hadn't fully narrowed them down. And for some, the ambiance of the place was important—ambiance she wouldn't be getting with delivery.

There was a knock on her door. She thought, wildly, that food was arriving before she'd even ordered it. But it wasn't delivery— obviously.

It was Jo.

"Hungry?" she asked when Emma opened the door. She waved the pizza box she'd brought in Emma's direction.

Emma was barefoot and not wearing a bra under her tank top. She crossed her arms over her chest. "What?"

"You haven't eaten, have you?" Jo asked. Emma shook her head. "Good. I'm starving."

Jo stayed in the hallway until Emma pushed the door farther open. Then Jo strolled in like she owned the place, set the pizza box and a plastic bag on the desk, and pulled paper plates and napkins from the bag.

"Ms. Jones," Emma said. She finally managed to close the door to the room. "You had plans."

Jo fluttered her hand. "Evelyn was being obnoxious," she said. "And you can't miss out on New York pizza."

Emma was not going to ask who Evelyn was.

Emma wished she'd closed her suitcase. The bra she was wearing earlier was strewn over the top. There was no way to surreptitiously close it. Jo didn't seem to mind. She took a seat in the chair at the desk and opened the pizza box.

"Extra-large cheese," she said. "We'll have to get drinks from the vending machine."

"Let me get it," Emma said, eager to contribute something to the meal.

"Paramedics said you had to stay in your room, I thought," Jo said. "Be right back."

As soon as the door closed behind Jo, propped open by the latch so that she wasn't locked out, Emma was in motion. She stuffed all the clothes on the floor into her suitcase, grabbing the bra before flipping the top closed. She hid in the bathroom to pull her shirt off, get the bra on, then put her shirt back on.

By the time Jo got back, Emma was serving herself a slice of pizza, fully clothed.

"Sprite or root beer?" Jo asked.

"Either is fine," Emma said. "Can I pay you back for some of this?"

Jo rolled her eyes and didn't even respond. She handed Emma the root beer.

"I'm serious," Emma said.

"Emma." Jo looked at her. "I was a millionaire as a teenager. I can afford dinner."

Right.

Emma ducked her head. If she didn't pay for anything, it felt too much like Jo was taking care of her, which was—it was weird, was all. Felt like when Jo bought her a dress, even though this time it was just pizza and a vending machine soda.

Emma climbed onto her bed, sat with her back against the headboard.

"You didn't have to do this, boss."

"It's pizza, Emma. It's nothing special."

"Well, I appreciate it anyway," Emma said. "And it's *New York* pizza. It's definitely special."

She took a bite.

The noise she made was probably inappropriate. If anyone knew

she was in the room with Jo and making that noise, they'd definitely think they were sleeping together. But what was Emma supposed to do? The pizza was *amazing*.

Jo smirked and didn't look at Emma. Emma couldn't bother to
be embarrassed.

"You've basically saved this night for me, boss," Emma said.
"This is—I cannot thank you enough."

Jo waved a dismissive hand.

They ate in silence for a moment.

"Emma?" Jo said, her voice quiet.

"Yeah?"

Jo was focused on her pizza, like whatever she was about to say
wasn't important. It made Emma think it *would* be important,
made her pay attention.

"Your shirt's inside out."

7

JO

THE NEXT MORNING, JO WAS READY TO HEAD OUT WHEN Emma knocked on her room door with a cup of coffee.

"I figured hotel coffee might not do the trick," Emma said. "This is from that cute café down the block."

Jo took a sip, and it was so good her mouth made words before she could think about them.

"I love you."

Emma's eyes went wide and Jo closed hers, took another sip of the coffee. It was just an expression, one she'd used before at work—on Chantal, certainly, and maybe even on Emma, too. Jo couldn't remember. Before the rumors, she hadn't paid nearly as much attention to every interaction between the two of them.

By the time Jo looked at Emma again, her assistant seemed to have decided to take the comment in stride. It was only fair—Jo had ignored Emma accidentally kissing her at the wrap party; Emma could ignore an innocuous phrase.

"The café also has good-looking breakfast options," Emma said.

"I have breakfast plans," Jo said. "I've already arranged for the car service to take you wherever you would like this morning, then pick me up on the way to the airport."

Emma swallowed. Jo wondered if she imagined the disappointment on her assistant's face.

"Sounds good," Emma said with a tight smile. "Enjoy your breakfast."

Evelyn texted then, letting Jo know she was waiting outside, and Jo started toward the elevators. She paused and looked back at Emma.

"Make sure you have your inhaler in your carry-on," she said.

Emma's smile went genuine. "Yes, boss."

JO WAS SUPPOSED TO have dinner with Evelyn the previous night, but at drinks Ev wouldn't stop giving her trouble about Emma. Apparently her asthma attack and Jo's reaction to it had made the internet. Evelyn had taken great pleasure in teasing Jo about it. It was the first time Jo had seen her best friend in six months, but it was *annoying*, made worse by the fact that Jo was still worried about Emma, wondering if she was recovering okay.

So Jo had bailed on dinner with an offer to buy Evelyn breakfast the next morning, provided she weren't as obnoxious then. Evelyn smirked and promised nothing.

But at breakfast, Ev did mostly behave. They talked about the GLAADs, how the panel went, and how Evelyn's work was going.

It wasn't until breakfast was almost over that Evelyn said, "So when do I get to meet her?"

Jo rolled her eyes. "She'll be in the car coming to pick me up in a few minutes if you want to come out and say hi."

Evelyn grinned so wide Jo recanted. "No, *no*, I was *joking*." She could tell Evelyn was still considering it, so she changed tactics. "Come out and visit me sometime. You can meet her then."

"I really do have to visit," Evelyn said. "It's been too long."

Evelyn had been in New York since she graduated from law school. When her parents moved cross-country to be closer to her, she stopped visiting the West Coast so often. Jo was glad to have heard from her so much this year, a strange windfall of the rumors. Even though Evelyn primarily called to tease, Jo didn't mind, happy to hear her best friend's voice.

Breakfast ended with Evelyn promising to visit no later than Thanksgiving. Jo was surprised she didn't follow her to the car to meet Emma.

"Have a good breakfast, boss?" Emma asked as Jo settled beside her in the back seat.

"I did," Jo said.

She spent the drive to the airport staring out the window, relaxed. With upfronts behind them, it was officially the least stressful time of year. Her half-finished Agent Silver document beckoned, reminding her there was still a large source of stress, but she pushed it aside for the time being.

JO'S NEPHEW'S FIRST BASEBALL game was the next week. She got there early and climbed to the top corner of the bleachers. Her sunglasses went all the way to where her baseball cap sat, hiding as much of her face as she could.

She didn't get recognized that often, but today was a day she absolutely did not want to be. It wasn't something that usually bothered her, but family days were off-limits, in her mind.

She used to not be able to go out for dinner without giving

autographs and posing for pictures. When Jo was thirteen, she was cast as Amanda Johnson, the adopted Chinese daughter of a typical white family in the suburbs. *The Johnson Dynasty* ran for seven seasons. Jo grew up in living rooms across the nation. She was a household name—world famous, even.

Every other series regular was white.

Jo never mentioned it. No one ever mentioned it. Jo had never known if people were ignoring it or simply didn't notice. She said nothing, and had her pick of scripts when the show ended. Her transition to film went smoothly; she did four movies, all blockbuster hits.

On the ten-year anniversary of *The Johnson Dynasty*'s premiere, Jo published a column.

She wrote about what it was like being a Chinese American in Hollywood. What it was like to be the butt of racist jokes on her own television show. About casting notices asking for white actresses only.

She stopped being offered scripts.

It was five years later that she wrote her own. The network billed it as a Cinderella story, made themselves seem like they were doing a good deed, giving a disgraced actress a chance at writing. Jo won four Emmys in a row.

She'd stuck to writing and producing ever since, so she wasn't usually recognized in public, or at least not bothered.

But of course today, the day she wanted to just sit in the bleachers and cheer for her nephew, a set of parents climbed toward her, and even though she was looking at her phone and hoping they weren't talkative, the wife said, "Oh my God, *Amanda*?"

Jo cringed. Being called by a character's name was *awful*. She thought she'd be done with it now that it had been twenty years. She tried to plaster a smile on her face.

When she turned to look at the woman, though, she recognized her.

Avery Kaplan, smirking.

"The sister," Jo said.

"The fake girlfriend," Avery said.

Jo rolled her eyes.

Avery set her bag down, not right beside Jo, but closer than Jo would have liked. "Who do you know out there?" she asked, elbow gesturing toward the field as she set up her bleacher cushion.

"Ethan Cheung," Jo said. "Nephew."

"Ah, the new kid on the team," Avery said. "You get to come to your nephew's game but Emma's not allowed to?"

"Emma didn't ask."

Jo would've let Emma out early if she had, since it was summer. When they were shooting, though, she'd rather Emma be at work if she wasn't. Jo surrounded herself with people she trusted because it was the only way she wouldn't micromanage. She could leave Chantal in charge, or leave Emma to report back on anything that Jo needed to know; that was how Jo could be away from work and not be anxious. Her production company, the Jones Dynasty—yes, she threw shade in naming it and it made her laugh every time—was her baby, had her name in big bold letters. She needed to be sure its output was up to standards. Emma helped.

"I'm Dylan," said the man who Jo assumed was Avery's husband, offering his hand. "We've got Ezra and Dani out there."

Jo shook his hand. "Jo."

He grinned but didn't mention he already knew who she was. She gave him points for that.

"How's the bakery?" Jo asked, because this was one of the rare situations where small talk might be preferable to silence. Avery would probably report this whole game back to Emma, and Jo did not want to come off looking like a bitch.

"*Busy*," Avery said.

"You should hire someone," her husband singsonged at her.

"If I could pay them a decent wage, I would," she said, mimicking his pitch back at him. She turned to Jo. "Business is good, really. How's the hiatus treating you?"

"Gently," Jo said, "now that upfronts are over."

"I heard you had to deal with an asthma attack," Avery said.

Jo stiffened, frozen by the memory of Emma gasping.

"Thanks for keeping her breathing."

Jo let out her own breath. She tried for a smile. "Yes, well, an employee dying on a business trip would have been terrible press."

Jo's stomach twisted at joking about it, but Avery chuckled and let the subject drop.

"How old is your nephew?" she said.

"Just nine," Jo said. Her heart was still racing thinking about Emma's asthma attack. It had shaken her, and even though she knew Emma was fine, she was terrified of the idea that it could happen at any time. "His first year past the pitching machine. What about your boys?"

"Boy and a girl, actually; Dani is Danielle," Avery said. "They're ten."

"Oh, I didn't realize—"

"Their goal for the season is to trick people," Avery said.

"Dani's the one girl in the league," Dylan explained. "She got a lot of crap for it last year, so this year she cut her hair short and Ezra grew his into a ponytail."

"Clever kids," Jo said. "They must get that from their father."

Jo's brother arrived then, right as Jo was chatting with a set of parents and making them laugh. He gave her a look.

"What do we have here?" he said.

"Making friends, don't I always?" Jo said.

"Not usually?"

Avery offered her hand. "Avery Kaplan."

Realization dawned in Vincent's eyes. "Ah. The girlfriend's sister."

Avery immediately grinned, delighted.

"Do you have any tips?" Vincent asked as he shook her hand. "On how to handle the burden of being the cooler sibling?"

Avery laughed, and Jo rolled her eyes.

It wasn't bad, though, sitting with Avery and Dylan as well as Vincent and his wife, Sally. Thomas, Jo's younger nephew, said hi and then immediately joined the other younger siblings playing under the bleachers. Once the game started, the adults didn't keep up inane small talk, and when they did talk, Avery was sharp and witty. She reminded Jo a lot of Evelyn, actually.

The kids won, and Jo got dragged to ice cream with the team after, because Ethan asked her with too big a grin for her to say no. Avery chuckled as she walked beside Jo toward the parking lot.

"Who knew Jo Jones was such a softie?" she said.

"Only for my nephews," Jo said. "And if you tell anyone, I'll have to have you killed."

Avery chuffed out a laugh, and Jo almost wished she weren't Emma's sister. She wouldn't mind having a friend, but that seemed complicated here.

"GOOD MORNING, BOSS," EMMA said the next day, handing Jo her coffee.

"Morning," Jo said. "Thanks."

She was a little wary, but there didn't seem to be anything behind Emma's smile. Perhaps Avery hadn't discussed last night with her yet. In that case, Jo wouldn't bring it up, didn't know exactly what to say anyway. *I watched your niece and nephew play baseball last night* sounded a bit strange. She took her coffee and went to work instead.

Jo wouldn't have admitted it to anyone, but she'd expected that writing Agent Silver would be easier. She was used to being television Jo Jones—a powerhouse who got what she wanted because she'd already proven herself. And while the whole point of branching out and doing Agent Silver was to push herself to do something she didn't have experience with, it felt unsteady, not having a reputation and history of work to rely on. Film was brand new. Action was brand new. There wasn't room for mistakes.

So she worked hard during the beginning of hiatus. She'd dive back into *Innocents* as summer went on, but she wanted a good first draft of Agent Silver before then. It meant she was a little busier than usual. Still, she made an effort to go to every one of Ethan's games.

She waited for Emma to say something about it or to ask for the afternoon off, too, but Emma never did.

Things were good with Emma, though, and better with no one around. The asthma attack at upfronts had caused the rumors to flare up, but they had quieted down since then. Jo no longer felt like she had to analyze every interaction they had. She gave Emma directing "homework"—books to read, movies to watch. While it would likely be some time before Emma had the chance to direct, it was never too early to learn.

One day Jo was having trouble with a scene in Agent Silver, so she called Emma in to work in her office. Emma, as always, got to work silently, no questions asked. It wasn't until Jo sighed for perhaps the forty-fifth time that Emma cleared her throat.

"Boss?" she said.

Jo *mmm*ed at her but didn't look up, her head buried in her hands.

"Is there anything I could help you with?"

Jo stretched, cracked her neck. "I cannot get this scene right."

"Let me read it," Emma said.

Jo stared at her. Few people had ever read a Jo Jones work in progress, and no one should've seen this particular one—the studio kept everything for Agent Silver on lockdown.

"I mean," Emma said, shrugging slightly, "if you want. I could be a new set of eyes."

Jo wasn't supposed to show the script to anyone.

"Look, it's not like I'm a writer or anything," Emma said. "If you don't want me to read it, will you at least take a walk or something? You need a break."

Jo thought of that day back in February, when Emma swore to always remind her that she could do this.

"I can't share the file with anyone," Jo said, "but you could read it on my computer?"

Emma beamed. "Works for me."

Jo scrolled to the beginning of the scene in her script. She brought her laptop to Emma on the couch and practically dropped it in her lap. She knew she was tipping her hand in terms of nerves, but she couldn't help it.

"I need a refill," she said, grabbing her tumbler and heading toward the door.

"I can get it—" Emma started.

"No, you read. It's fine. I'll just—"

Jo did a loop of the hallways, did another for good measure, before heading to the kitchen for more cold brew. This was why she didn't share her writing before she was done with it—her skin felt like there were bugs crawling all over it. She was a good writer, she knew she was a good writer, obviously, had Emmys to prove it, but it still felt as if she'd cracked her chest open and Emma was rooting around inside right now.

It was almost fifteen minutes later by the time Jo finally returned to her office. Emma was still on the couch, refocused on her own tablet, Jo's computer on the table in front of her rather than her lap. She looked up when Jo entered and gave her a small smile.

She hated it. She thought it was awful. This was fine. Jo would just go fling herself off the nearest building. This one, she realized, was the nearest. She should turn and head to the elevators.

"Boss," Emma said gently.

It was all Jo could do not to tell her it was okay, she didn't have to say anything, they could pretend this had never happened. She grabbed her laptop and took it to her desk.

"I'm really excited you're writing Agent Silver," Emma said.

Jo's eyes snapped to Emma's. That wasn't what she expected.

"You're an amazing writer," Emma said. "Your stories are great."

"But?" Jo offered.

"But this isn't your story."

Jo scoffed. Emma put both hands out in a "give me a minute" gesture.

"Hear me out," she said. "In a lot of the Silver movies—too many, really—the women are background characters even when they're main characters, you know what I mean?"

Jo inclined her head in agreement.

"In a lot of the movies, Silver's kind of an asshole. But, like, an asshole who is written by a dude who doesn't think he's writing an asshole character."

Normally that would garner at least a chuckle, but Jo still felt like she was sitting on a bed of nails. Any wrong move and she'd be impaled.

"You're not an asshole, and your Silver isn't going to be, either," Emma said. "You shouldn't make him a dick just because other people are afraid you're going to make him too nice."

It was a nice sentiment, but—"A writer changing doesn't mean a character changes," Jo said. "Especially when the actor is the same."

"You're a writer, Jo," Emma laughed, not meanly. "Use your imagination. You really don't think Silver has any hidden depths?"

A light bulb went on in Jo's head. She let out her breath.

Hollywood decided people's reputations for them. It was the same for Jo as it was for Agent Silver. Just because people thought they knew everything about her didn't mean they did. Emma was right—of course there was more to the character than had been shown in previous movies.

"Okay," Jo said. "I think I can do this."

"I know you can, boss."

Emma beamed at her, and Jo couldn't help but grin. She selected three full pages of text. Pressed delete. Before she could be overwhelmed by the blinking cursor, Jo's fingers flew across the keyboard, a new idea coalescing. She could've kissed Emma for making it so easy on her.

The next day, Emma knocked on Jo's doorjamb in the afternoon. She held a stack of papers.

"I need more room than my desk to spread these out on," Emma said. "Can I work in here?"

"Of course."

Later in the week, they ate lunch together in Jo's office. Jo wasn't always committed to feeding herself; she got too involved in her work and forgot. Without Emma, Jo might have starved by now. Emma brought her sushi, and Jo made Emma join her to eat. When they finished, Emma started working on her tablet. Neither of them ever addressed the fact that she stayed working on Jo's couch until five.

It became habit. Jo invited Emma in or Emma invited herself in or neither of them said anything, Emma just brought her work into Jo's office. It was easy, and less distracting than it should've been. They both got work done, and Emma made sure Jo never skipped lunch. Jo did catch herself looking at Emma occasionally. She was always impressed by the other woman's focus, her work ethic. It was rare that Emma even noticed Jo's eyes on her, but if she did, she'd give her that soft smile. Then she'd raise her eyebrows and make Jo get back to work.

Even while they worked so closely, Jo didn't do much supervising. Emma knew what she was doing, and Jo trusted her. Jo was vaguely aware of what Emma was working on day to day— planning things for when the cast and crew came back, beginning the search for her replacement, learning more about directing— but Emma was independent. So when Jo heard a disgruntled huff from her couch one day, she didn't know what it was about.

"Problems, Ms. Kaplan?" she asked, not looking away from where she was editing the Agent Silver script.

"This doesn't have half the stuff I do on it!"

Jo hit save, then looked to Emma.

Normally, Emma's feet were tucked under her, or sometimes at the other end of the couch, legs stretched long. She almost never sat on the sofa in a normal fashion. Today, though, both her feet were on the floor, her elbows on her knees, brows furrowed at the tablet propped up on the table in front of her. Jo watched until Emma stopped glaring at whatever was on her screen, and made eye contact.

"I got the job description for my position from HR," Emma said. "I figured I'd tweak it a little and then post it to find my replacement. But this is missing a ton of stuff I do."

Jo chuckled. "Why do you think you're being promoted?"

Emma went back to squinting at her tablet.

"This makes it sound like I'm just a secretary." Emma, being Emma, quickly amended, "Not that there's anything wrong with being a secretary, but I do more than this."

Jo was well aware of that.

"Of course you do," she said. "You could've had the associate producer title from day one with the amount of work you took on."

Emma's work ethic was why Jo stole her away from Aly in props at the end of the previous season.

"You're hiring my next assistant," Jo said, "not my next Emma."

"Oh."

Emma's voice was quiet, underpinned with wonder. Perhaps she hadn't realized how valuable she was.

Honestly, it was something Jo had been worrying about. As though the move from *Innocents* to Agent Silver full-time wouldn't be stressful enough, Jo would be doing it without Emma. She'd have an assistant, of course, but not one who had figured out how she ticked, knew when to interrupt with food, wasn't afraid to throw sass at her when she got snippy. There was no one else she'd trust to read scenes from her scripts, the way Emma occasionally did, ever since that first day she offered.

Emma was Jo's cheerleader, but she was never afraid to give Jo a kick in the pants if she needed it. She made Jo better.

"The job description likely only needs to be edited regarding Agent Silver instead of *Innocents*," Jo said. "Other than that I'm sure it's fine."

Emma's brow hadn't unfurrowed.

"Is there some other issue with it?"

"No," Emma said. She took a breath. "I guess it's just weird—hiring my replacement."

Jo had no doubt Emma would hire a capable new assistant. But she wouldn't be able to replace herself.

"Want to take a break to look at the new opening?" Jo asked.

Emma blinked the concern off her face. She set aside her tablet and reached toward Jo's computer, opening and closing her hands. "Gimme."

Jo handed over the laptop. She still had to leave the room when Emma read her writing. She'd grown more comfortable with it, but she wasn't *that* comfortable.

She did a lap, refilled her tumbler with cold brew from the fridge in the break room, then returned to her office.

Emma grinned at her.

"I think you've got it this time."

Jo's jaw dropped. "You do?"

"I do."

If Jo weren't more than half a foot shorter than Emma, she'd tug her off the couch, lift her off her feet, and spin her around in a hug. This was the fourth iteration of the opening scene. Emma had altogether dismissed the first—and for good reason. The second hadn't fared quite so poorly, but Emma pointed out its every weakness as well. The third revision earned a smile, at least. The fourth, apparently, was the charm.

"We've got to celebrate somehow," Jo said. "Champagne in the workplace is frowned upon, right? Perhaps we should get some cake delivered."

Emma suddenly sat up straighter, mischief behind her smile. "Or"—she dragged out the word—"we could go on a field trip?"

"A field trip?" Jo raised her eyebrows. Was this elementary school?

"To Floured Up?"

Emma's lips turned up, her head tilted, and she employed what could only be described as puppy-dog eyes. Jo knew she was being manipulated. She said yes anyway.

"THERE IT IS," EMMA announced, beaming as they approached the bakery.

There was a rainbow flag hanging out front of a two-story brick storefront. It fit right in in West Hollywood. Chloe dropped them at the curb, and Emma clambered out of the car. She flounced to the door and pulled it open with a flourish, a bell ringing from inside the store. Jo thanked Emma for holding the door for her.

The inside was as bright as the flag outside, yellow walls with thick lime-green chevrons, tables and chairs of all different colors. There was no one at the register. Emma marched right into the employees-only section, behind a long display case filled with pastries, loaves of bread in baskets on the wall on her other side.

"Hi, welcome to—oh, it's you." Avery appeared from the back. "This is the first time all day I've had a minute to actually get work done and not deal with customers. Why are you bugging me at work? Why aren't you at work?" Regardless of the annoyance in her voice, she hugged Emma tight. Then she spotted Jo. "Oh. It's both of you."

"Hello," Jo said.

"Avery, Jo. Jo, Avery," Emma said. "I know you met at the wrap party, but always better to reintroduce people than not."

Right.

That answered that question, then. Apparently Avery had never said anything to Emma about baseball. Jo shifted on her feet.

"Nice to, uh, see you again," Avery said.

"Likewise."

Emma slid open the back of the display case, reached in, and grabbed herself a cookie. She closed her eyes and hummed at her first bite.

"You're the best baker in the world."

Avery flushed at the hyperbolic comment. "Whatever," she said. "I'm going back to the kitchen. Stop being a glutton and get your boss whatever she wants."

She disappeared to where Jo assumed the kitchen was. When Jo looked back to Emma, her assistant grinned at her. Jo couldn't help but smile back.

Emma held up the cookie she'd chosen. "This is the best snicker-doodle you'll ever eat." She gestured to the display case. "But you can see the great variety to choose from."

There were cookies of various kinds, cupcakes, coconut maca-roons, pastries—some of which Jo recognized, some she didn't. Jo pointed to a sliced loaf of bread, a complicated, intricate swirl of something dark inside it.

"This looks good. What is it?"

"Chocolate babka!" Emma crowed. "A Floured Up specialty and an excellent choice."

She used a sheet of wax paper to retrieve a slice for Jo and pre-sented it to her on a bright red plate with a fork.

"C'mon," Emma said. She leaned into the display case one more time to grab herself a second cookie, the first still half-eaten in her hand. "Let's go bother the baker."

Jo followed her into the back. The kitchen was smaller than Jo expected, but it was nice. Organized, clean. Avery was measuring flour on an electric scale, a commercial-sized KitchenAid mixer beating away on the counter beside her.

"What are you two even doing here?" Avery asked. "Don't you have your own work to do?"

"That's no way to greet guests," Emma said. She took a bite of her cookie and talked while she chewed. "We're here because we're celebrating Jo getting the opening of Agent Silver figured out."

"Oh yeah?" Avery glanced over her shoulder toward Jo. "Congrats."

"Thank you," Jo said.

She set her plate of babka on the stainless-steel-topped table in the middle of the kitchen. She barely suppressed a groan of pleasure at her first bite.

"This is delicious," she said. "My compliments to the chef."

Avery poured some of the flour into the mixer. "Thanks," she said, grinning at Jo.

Emma hopped up to sit on the table, a few feet from Jo's plate.

"You know," Avery said, "for a girl who always liked to follow the rules in school, you're sitting on my tabletop. If the health department came in here, they'd shut me down."

"Oh, shut up, they would not." Emma rolled her eyes. "Plus, I'd jump down. I'm very quick."

Jo pressed her lips together to keep from chuckling.

Emma and Avery continued to banter as Avery combined ingredients. Jo almost joined their conversation to ask after the twins, before worrying that that was too friendly. The sisters were a study in contrasts: Avery short, soft, and focused, where Emma was all long legs and ease. Emma's hair cascaded everywhere, while Avery's bob was hidden beneath a bandana. Emma seemed loose, her smile effortless. It was nice, as long as Jo didn't think about how she and Avery were lying to Emma. By omission, at least.

The bell above the door rang from the other room. Emma leapt off the table.

"See? If it's the health department, you're fine."

Avery swatted her with the kitchen towel she had over her shoulder. "Please do not mention the health department where customers can hear."

"No promises."

Avery's laughter carried as she left the kitchen. Jo and Emma stayed put. Jo finished her babka. Emma climbed right back up onto the table and ate her second cookie. She swung her feet back and forth beneath her.

When Avery returned, Emma kicked out at her. Avery avoided it and gave her sister a fake glare.

"Why are you here, again?" she said.

"Field trip!" Emma grinned. "We should take them more often. I get to eat cookies and hang out with two of my favorite people."

Jo caught Avery's raised eyebrows, and Emma's eyes cut from Avery to her.

"I mean, whatever," Emma said. "It's not weird. You know I love working for you."

Jo didn't admit it, but she was hanging out with two of her favorite people, too.

ONE AFTERNOON THE NEXT week, Emma was working in Jo's office when it was time for Jo to leave for Ethan's game. Jo was fully packed up before Emma realized she'd stopped working.

"Oh," Emma said. "I can—"

"Lock up when you're done," Jo said. She considered it. "You're welcome to leave early if you'd like."

Emma smiled gently. "Thanks, boss. Have a good night."

"You too, Emma."

Maybe this would be the day Emma came to a game.

Jo had been sitting next to Avery throughout the season. Avery told Jo stories about obnoxious customers at the bakery, and Jo told Avery stories about obnoxious suits at the network, and neither of them mentioned Emma again, after that first game.

Today, Dylan arrived without Avery. He gave Jo a half roll of his eyes and said, "Bakery crisis."

Avery showed up in the third inning, flour smeared in her hair. She and Dylan spent much of the game bickering. Jo tried not to eavesdrop, but they were too close not to overhear Dylan insisting she hire more help and Avery claiming she didn't have the money to pay them enough yet.

An idea formed in Jo's mind.

Emma didn't show up, and Jo was glad. There was enough tension between Avery and Dylan; she didn't need to add to it with whatever would happen if Emma arrived. After the game, Jo caught Avery while Dylan was distracted with the kids.

"If I swing by the bakery in the morning, will you have time for a conversation?"

Avery looked skeptical. "Why?"

"I think I may have a proposition for you," Jo said.

"What are you talking about?"

"I'll tell you in the morning if you have time for me."

Avery rolled her eyes. "Fine," she said. "But you might have to tell me while I make babka."

———————

JO WAS RIDICULOUSLY WEALTHY. She was absurdly rich. There was no polite way to put it. Her first paycheck, when she was thirteen, had gone in part to an accountant. Her parents wanted to teach her to be responsible, not wasteful. Jo's money made money for itself. She had more than she could ever use.

So she gave it away.

Of course she bought things for herself. She probably owned too much property and definitely owned too many shoes. But the majority of her money went elsewhere, always to causes she cared about. She didn't like to be ostentatious about it, didn't do it on a grand scale. Or, well, not grand to her. She liked to spread it out. Instead of millions of dollars to get a hospital wing named after her, she paid off student loans or bought medical debt and immediately forgave it. She found fund-raisers looking to make ten thousand dollars and gave them twenty-five thousand instead. She bought out every Girl Scout she saw come cookie-sale time. The crew loved her most then, she was pretty sure, with cookies on every flat surface at the studio.

Restaurants weren't new to her. She'd sent kids to culinary school and bought a food truck for a guy who to this day was willing to bring it anywhere she'd like and serve people for free. Floured Up seemed like a perfect investment.

Jo scrolled through her contacts that evening, sure to select Emma, not Evelyn.

She chewed on her bottom lip. She didn't have to tell Emma why she'd be late tomorrow. She did plenty of things, business and otherwise, Emma didn't know about. Just because this involved her sister didn't mean it was any different. Avery hadn't even told her.

Jo was aware that that reasoning was flimsy, but it was all she had.

Will be late in the morning, take your time getting in

Emma replied almost immediately, as she usually did.

Sounds good, boss

She included a smiling emoji, because Emma always had a smile for Jo, even when Jo was lying to her.

Jo wondered if Emma realized she only called her *boss* when no one else was around to notice.

THE BELL ABOVE THE door rang as Jo entered Floured Up. Unlike the last visit, the bakery was filled with people, the tables all taken and a line of four at the counter. Jo sipped on the coffee in her travel mug and wondered if it would be rude to cut to the front. There were two workers waiting on customers, and neither of them Avery. Jo decided to wait.

"Good morning, what can I get for you?" The young man behind the counter was altogether too cheery given it was before eight a.m. His eyes went wide when he fully looked at her, and she offered him a still-not-caffeinated-enough smile.

"I believe your boss is expecting me," she said. "Could you check in with her?"

"Yes, of course, right away."

He disappeared into the back, and Jo stepped out of line to let the next person go. When the worker returned, he waved her to the back as well, smiling too wide. Jo was glad he wasn't asking for an autograph.

"Thanks, Scott," Avery said.

True to her word from last night, she was busy rolling out dough. She didn't pause when she greeted Jo.

"So what's your proposition for me?" Avery said.

She reached for a bowl of a chocolate mixture and started spreading it on the rolled-out dough in front of her. Jo knew exactly how delicious the bread would end up being.

"You need to hire another worker," she said, "but you can't afford to pay them what you'd like."

"I'm aware of my business situation, Jo," Avery said.

"If I were to cover their salary, you wouldn't have a situation," Jo said.

Avery stopped what she was doing. "What?"

"I could pay the salary for another worker, or a couple workers even."

Avery stared blankly at her.

"It's simple," Jo said. "I pay a salary or two—what? Fifty thousand each?—until you get to the point where you can cover them."

Avery sputtered. "Fifty thousand? You're just offering me a hundred thousand dollars a year? In exchange for what?"

"For you hiring two more workers so you're less stressed."

"In exchange for what *for you*?"

Jo shrugged. This wasn't how she expected the conversation to go. People tended to be disbelieving but rather excited to get money, not hostile.

"I'm not interested in charity," Avery said.

Jo rolled her eyes. "It's *investment*, not charity."

"Investment generally means you get something in return."

"I do," Jo said. "It's easier for me to hire you to cater, which means my cast and crew love me more."

Avery leveled her with a look. "God, you really have no idea how money works, do you?"

Jo rolled her eyes again. "I have a lot of it—"

"Which is why you don't—"

Jo held up a hand and Avery stopped talking. "I have a lot of it, more than I need. And I know I can use it to make my friend's life better. So I'm fairly certain I know exactly how money works."

Avery's eyebrows went up. Perhaps Jo shouldn't have admitted to thinking of her as a friend.

Avery went back to her work. She finished with the spread and started rolling up the dough in front of her. "One worker," she said. "And you don't have to cover their whole salary, just the difference between what I can pay them and I'd like to pay them."

"You can work out the specifics with my accountant," Jo said.

"I was right at that first game," Avery said. "You're totally a softie."

Jo let out a chuckle. "Look, I don't like that many people, but your family seems to be the exception. So shut up and take my money."

Avery smirked at her. "You basically offered me a hundred thousand dollars a year, just because you're nice."

"I'm no such thing and I won't stand for this slander."

Avery laughed outright, and Jo grinned. She didn't think about how it helped, the ice queen persona. That people tried to hurt you less if they didn't think you had feelings. That the only way to get anything done as a woman in Hollywood was to have everyone assume you took no shit. And even with that reputation, people still thought she was too soft to write Agent Silver.

"I'll leave you to your work," Jo said. "My accountant will call later to set up a time you can sit down and figure things out while you're not simultaneously making food."

8

EMMA

EMMA LOVED IT WHEN AVERY INVITED HERSELF OVER FOR dinner, because Avery inviting herself over for dinner meant Avery making or buying dinner, and cleaning up, too. She did it when she needed a break from her family or she had to girl-talk something out or she just hadn't seen her sister recently. Whatever the reason, Emma was always happy to oblige.

When Avery said she was coming over with homemade lasagna to throw in the oven, Emma didn't think anything of it. It was a little unusual for Avery to come over on a Friday night, but nothing seemed suspicious. Emma spun on one of her kitchen stools and told her sister about her day.

"Jo says I should consider being a script doctor," Emma said, rolling her eyes. "But I don't even actually do any of the writing, I'm just good at helping her figure out what she needs to do."

"Cool," Avery said. Her voice was flat.

Emma stopped spinning on her stool. "What?"

"Nothing," Avery said. "What?"

"Why are you being weird?"

"I'm not being weird!" Avery sounded way too panicked for someone who supposedly wasn't being weird.

Emma narrowed her eyes. "What's going on?"

Avery sighed heavily. She leaned on her elbows on the kitchen island across from Emma's stool.

"I don't know how to explain this to you," she said.

"Okay, you know you're going to have to explain it immediately now because otherwise I'm going to freak out about all the bad things it could be," Emma said. "Do you have cancer? Did Dani and Ezra read Harry Potter and decide Hufflepuff was a bad house? Are the dogs okay?"

"I'm going to pretend I'm not offended that you made me having cancer sound like the least bad of those situations," Avery said. "But no. None of that. It's . . . what it is, is . . ."

Emma's chest tightened with worry. *"Ave."*

"Jo's nephew is on Ezra and Dani's baseball team."

Emma blinked. That didn't seem that bad. "Okay?"

Avery flailed her hands a little like Emma wasn't understanding. Emma flailed back at her.

"Jo's nephew is on Ezra and Dani's baseball team and I've been sitting next to her at every game."

"Wait, what?"

Avery moved from leaning on her elbows to a more upright position, leaning on her hands instead.

"I haven't told you because I was trying to get you to come to a game," she said. "I thought it'd be funny to see your face when you saw Jo. I know I let it go on for too long."

Emma pointed her toes toward the ground, then switched and flexed them toward the ceiling. It didn't help the squirmy feeling in her body.

"Okay?" she said. "So you're, like . . . friends?"

"No," Avery said, immediately amending, "well, maybe. Sort of. She also—you know how Molly called in sick Monday and it was a bit of a disaster?" She went on without waiting for Emma to respond. "I was late to the game, and I guess Jo asked Dylan why and he said bakery emergency and—I don't know. I'm sure she heard us bickering about it all game. So she came to Floured Up in the morning and made me an offer."

Jo came in late Tuesday. She hadn't explained why.

"An offer?" Emma asked.

"She wanted to cover the salary of a worker or two," Avery said. "To help. We worked it out so she's just covering the difference between what I *can* pay a new pastry chef and what I *should* be paying them."

Avery was watching Emma, like maybe she thought Emma was going to bolt. Emma pointed her toes again, shrugged at her sister.

"Okay."

Avery furrowed her eyebrows. "Okay?"

"Yeah."

"Just okay?"

"I don't know, Avery, what else do you want me to say?"

"I don't know. How you feel about it? Is it okay? Do you forgive me for not telling you?"

"I mean, of course it's fine you're friends with Jo," Emma said. "Or business partners or whatever. I don't know why that wouldn't be fine. It's none of my business."

"Emma."

Emma didn't say anything.

"Of course it's your business," Avery said. "I'm your sister and you're her—she's your—" Emma didn't like the way Avery paused. "She's your boss. It's weird. I mean I feel weird about it."

"About which part? The being friends with her without ever telling me, or her supporting your business?" It came out snappier than Emma intended.

"All of it," Avery said. "I'm sorry I didn't tell you sooner."

"It's fine," Emma said dismissively.

It was. Avery didn't have to tell her everything. And if she had gone to a game, she would've found out. Maybe Avery was right and it would have been funny. It was good that Jo was helping with the bakery. Avery was successful enough to need to hire another person, and Jo's help allowed that to happen. That was better than fine.

Except Emma also inexplicably felt like she was going to cry.

"Em."

"Seriously, Avery." Emma laughed. It came out fake. "I'm really excited you're hiring a new person. I'm so glad the bakery is doing that well."

Avery's smile came slowly, but it was sincere. "Yeah. It's kind of great."

Emma hopped off her stool and went around the island to hug her sister from behind. Avery let her, for a moment, before turning around in Emma's arms to squeeze her back. Emma sank into it.

"I'm sorry I didn't tell you sooner," Avery murmured. "I thought I'd convince you to come to a game and it'd be a funny surprise, but it got out of hand. I didn't mean to hurt you and I won't do it again."

Emma had never been good at holding grudges against her sister.

"Thank you," she said.

"I'm sure it got out of hand for Jo, too," Avery said. "She probably didn't know how to tell you."

That Emma didn't believe as easily. She closed her eyes and

pretended water wasn't welling in them. Took a deep breath, then she pulled away from Avery's embrace.

"You know, I'm really tired." She ignored the way Avery's face fell. "I think I'm just going to eat and shower and hop in bed. I don't think I'll be very good company."

"Emma," Avery said quietly. When Emma didn't reply, Avery nodded. "Okay. Yeah. I'm gonna leave you everything, okay? I can eat with Dylan and the twins. Don't forget to put leftovers in the fridge before you go to sleep. Then you can feed yourself for a couple days."

"Great," Emma said. "Thanks."

Avery didn't push her. She hugged her one more time instead, then came up on her tiptoes to press a kiss against Emma's forehead.

"Love you."

"Love you, too," Emma said.

She collapsed onto her couch as soon as the door closed behind Avery. Stared blankly at the ceiling.

It didn't seem fair.

Emma was happy that her sister's bakery was doing well. Of course she was. She loved Avery, wanted her to be successful in everything she did. And Avery *was* successful in everything she did. Since high school, or really their whole lives, Avery had always been successful. Not that Emma wasn't—she got an all-state honorable mention in cross-country and stage-managed the school play every year. She did well. But Avery was always the best.

Emma had adored her back then. Still did. Rationally, she knew it was a little bit of a case of sibling worship, but it never stopped her. Avery had always been great, and Emma had always wanted to be like her. When they were younger, Avery had known what she wanted to do and so had Emma. But Avery flew through training as a pastry chef, while Emma dropped out of film school. Their paths diverged.

Emma was back on track, though. She was finally figuring out who she wanted to be, was taking steps toward a career she yearned for. Jo was a part of that. Jo was helping her.

It wasn't that Emma didn't want Jo to help Avery. But it didn't seem fair. Emma had finally found something for herself—not that Jo was a something, but—

Emma didn't want to share her.

She didn't think Avery should get her. Avery didn't really need help with accomplishing her dreams, did she? She already had the bakery. She was already living her dream. Emma was just figuring hers out. She wanted to carve out her own space for once, not to follow in Avery's footsteps or her shadow.

Jo wasn't Emma's to share, though. Clearly. She'd lied to her. Emma wasn't important enough for Jo to tell her anything. Jo breezed out of work early so many afternoons, came in the next morning and never mentioned anything. Emma thought—she thought they were closer than that by this point. Thought she would have warranted some kind of acknowledgment.

But Jo was her boss, not her friend. She was Avery's friend, apparently, but not Emma's. Emma *liked* being Jo's assistant, but—it had felt like a job that mattered, and if she could've been rational about it, maybe it would still feel like that. She used to love how she knew every part of the show, like it was a machine she could tinker with. Now she felt like a cog in that machine. Necessary but replaceable. Jo had said she was hiring a new assistant, not a new Emma, but clearly Emma was just a slightly more complex cog.

It didn't matter. Six months from now Jo would move to Agent Silver, and Emma would be an associate producer. It didn't matter if they weren't friends.

When the lasagna was ready, Emma took it from the oven and left it on the counter. She showered, the water cold enough to leave goose bumps in its wake. Then she put the entire dish of lasagna into the refrigerator and went to bed at eight p.m.

EMMA DIDN'T GO TO temple on a regular basis. She went—when she had time, when she was thinking about it, when she needed to surround herself with community. She went Saturday morning.

Emma liked the routine of services, liked the tradition. She liked losing herself in recitation and song. She liked sitting next to Ruth, whom she sat by at every service she attended. Ruth was fifty-something with wild brown curls and a vibe of someone who took no shit. She grinned wide when she saw Emma that morning.

Everyone at temple was so nice, and it was wonderful, really, but it made Emma sadder. These people weren't strangers, but she saw them once a month at most. The fact that they could seem to care so much for her highlighted how little Jo cared.

It shouldn't matter. Jo had always just been her boss. This was no different, really. Except this was the first time Jo made Emma feel unimportant. That part was new. Emma hated it.

Ruth gave Emma a look when she skipped kiddush, the meal after service, and left right away. Emma waved her off. She wanted to be alone, maybe wanted to wallow a little.

EMMA TALKED TO HER mom every Saturday. Sometimes they talked during the week, too, but her mom got mad if she didn't call on Saturdays, even if they talked on Friday.

She didn't want to talk to her today, would rather get a lecture on not calling than a discussion of her week. But her mom called her, and she couldn't not pick up.

There were the standard pleasantries, and then:

"Honey," her mom said, and Emma already sighed, knowing what was coming. "I talked to your sister. Are you okay?"

"I'm *fine*, Mom," Emma said. "I told Avery I'm fine. I'm not mad at her."

"I know, sweetie," her mom said. "We're just worried about you."

Emma rolled her eyes and collapsed onto her couch. She stared up at the ceiling just like she had after Avery left last night.

She wasn't mad at Avery anymore, truly. Avery had apologized. They were fine. But her stomach still felt queasy when she thought about Jo. Over and over again she told herself: Jo was her boss, not her friend. Her boss, not her friend.

"Do you think . . . ," her mom started. "Do you think maybe just because you're not mad at Avery anymore doesn't mean you're not mad anymore?"

"It's fine," Emma said. "It doesn't matter that they're friends. Or business partners. I honestly don't care."

Her mom was quiet.

"I just think—" Emma half scoffed. "I'm just surprised, is all. That Jo didn't care enough to mention it to me? I've been reading scenes for Agent Silver, you know? Don't tell anyone, because I'm not supposed to, I don't think. But I am. So I guess I thought she—we—I'm just pretty involved in her business dealings, usually. But apparently I'm not important enough to know anything about her sponsoring a pastry chef for Avery."

"I'm sure that's not it," her mom said. "She probably just didn't know how to tell you."

"Didn't know how to tell me, 'Hey, I saw your sister' after the first game. It'd be that easy. If she had cared enough to tell me, it would be that easy."

Emma rolled over, pressed her face into the couch cushions. She felt stupid for pouting. It shouldn't even matter. Jo didn't have to tell her anything. And just because she was helping Emma figure out her career didn't mean she couldn't sponsor a pastry chef for Avery. There was no reason for Emma to feel like this.

"I don't think she doesn't care about you, honey," Emma's mom said gently. "You told me how worried she was when you had that asthma attack in New York."

Emma shrugged even though her mom couldn't see her.

"Sweetheart," her mom said. "I'm not saying this to tease and I don't want you to get mad."

"That's always a good start to a sentence," Emma grumbled.

"Sweetheart," her mom said again, and Emma felt mildly bad for being rude. "Do you think maybe the rumors about you two might have a point? One that maybe you didn't realize before?"

Her mom was asking if she had feelings for Jo, had a crush on her. Emma's instinctual reaction was to roll her eyes and brush it off like she'd been doing since the SAGs, but today her chest ached. Today she was lying facedown on her couch complaining to her mom about her boss not caring about her enough. Today she blinked, and her eyes were wet.

When she finally responded, her voice was barely above a whisper. "Maybe."

JO THANKED EMMA FOR her coffee Monday morning like nothing was different. Nothing was for Jo, Emma supposed. She was still lying to her assistant like she had been last week. Or—not lying, exactly. But not telling the truth. The whole summer of them working so well together. Emma in Jo's office and Jo asking for her help with the Agent Silver script. But she wasn't important enough to know that Jo had befriended her sister.

Though Emma had told her mom she might have feelings for Jo, she wasn't sure. That was still a solid maybe. Maybe this hurt so much because she had feelings for Jo and it was obvious now that Jo didn't feel the same way. But Emma didn't have to have some stupid crush for this to hurt. This sucked, the way Jo lied to her, the way Jo treated her like a cog in a machine. Even if she didn't have a crush on Jo—and she might not!—this would feel bad.

It felt like a breakup whether romantic feelings were involved or not. Emma thought she and Jo had a certain type of relationship. Thought they were friends. But Jo was only helping Emma advance her career because of business. She needed Emma to do well because Emma was her assistant and Jo couldn't have a reputation of assistants who went nowhere. Especially not Emma, because then it would prove what everybody thought—she was only there because Jo was sleeping with her. Emma was basically a business expense to Jo. Meanwhile, barely two weeks ago, Emma had called Jo one of her favorite people. How *mortifying*.

Jo didn't ask Emma to work in her office all day. Emma didn't know how she would've replied if Jo had. At five, Jo gave her a smile and told her to have a good night. Emma nodded and left.

The next day, Jo called Emma into her office within an hour of Emma handing over Jo's coffee. Emma assumed Jo wanted her to bring her work in. She didn't expect Jo to scrutinize her.

"Are you okay?" Jo asked.

"Uh," Emma said. "Yeah. Of course. I'm fine. Why?"

Jo shrugged. "You've been quiet. I thought maybe something was bothering you."

You're bothering me, Emma thought.

"I'm fine, Ms. Jones," she said instead.

Jo's smile looked brittle. Emma told herself she didn't care.

EMMA WAS GOING TO ask for Wednesday afternoon off to see the twins play. She didn't know how she'd say it, didn't know whether she'd admit to Jo that she knew or if she'd just surprise her by being at the game. But she woke up Wednesday to rain. The one day it rained in Southern California.

When the rain hadn't stopped by noon, it was clear the game would be canceled. At least Emma didn't have to figure out how to talk to Jo about it.

She was trying to be less awkward with Jo, to not show her feelings—frustration and hurt and maybe, *maybe* a crush or whatever—quite so obviously. Jo had noticed, had asked her about it, and Emma didn't want her to push. Not that Jo would, of course. She probably didn't even care that much. Emma only had to make it until Monday for the cast and crew to come back. Then she could distract herself with work and other people.

Jo invited Emma into her office for lunch. Emma went, but as soon as she finished, she started packing up to go back to her own desk.

"I have a bit of a surprise for you," Jo said.

Emma stopped crinkling up the wrapper to her sandwich. "What?"

Jo was focused on her own lunch, a sly smile on her face. "Barry Davis is coming to set."

Emma's jaw dropped.

"And you're going to be shadowing him."

She almost fell off the couch.

Barry Davis was her favorite director. Her absolute favorite. And she was going to shadow him? An Oscar-nominated director?

Jo was looking at Emma now, that smile turned into a rare beam.

"I called in a couple of favors," Jo said. "He could direct an episode, maybe, but mostly he'll be here for you. To learn from. To impress, in all likelihood. He'd be a great connection for you."

This couldn't just be business, could it? Jo didn't call in favors to bring Emma's favorite director to set for a *business expense*. It had to be more than that.

Jo's smile slowly faded as Emma took too long to respond.

"You like Barry Davis, right?"

"No, yes, of course," Emma said. "Yeah. I'm—that's great. I'm really excited. I'm speechless."

It was true, at least, that she didn't have words. She couldn't even understand how she was feeling, much less explain it. She was still confused, still hurt at Jo keeping everything with Avery from her. But she couldn't not be excited for Barry freakin' Davis.

"When is he coming?"

"Tuesday. Not next week but the week after," Jo said.

Whatever was going on between her and Jo, the cast and crew were coming back from hiatus on Monday, and Barry Davis was coming to set the next week. That much, at least, was great.

9

JO

J O ALWAYS ENJOYED THE FIRST DAY BACK FROM HIATUS. IT was more of a reunion than a day of work. The schedule was never tight, plenty of room for people to reconnect and reminisce. It was like a wrap party with less alcohol and more responsibilities. Lunch was a big catered event, and this year Jo got breakfast, too, croissants and honey cakes and a variety of pastries she didn't know the names of. Emma squealed when they arrived in bags with the Floured Up logo on the side.

Emma spent much of the day squealing, really. She seemed back to her usual self, filled with enthusiasm for her coworkers. Tate hugged her hard enough to lift her off the ground even though she had an inch on him. She grinned widely at Chantal, who was categorically not a hugger. Aly, Gina, and Holly all clamored around Emma, voices overlapping with updates and *it's so good to see you*s. Emma bumped one of the props assistants—Phil, Jo thought his name was—out of line around the pastries, laughter booming over his outrage.

Jo stayed to the side of the room, sipping her coffee and considering getting a croissant. Chantal joined her, and Jo felt a bit like the adults at a kids' party—everyone else thrilled and boisterous. She hadn't had enough coffee to be too excited about anything.

Before Jo gathered the energy to even say good morning to Chantal, Emma swooped in, pressing a napkin holding a filled, crescent-shaped pastry into her hand. Their fingers brushed as Jo took it from her. It was as close as they'd been to each other in a week.

"Okay, I know you don't like sugar in the morning but you need to try this," Emma said. "My sister makes the *best* rugelach. Eat it, you won't regret it."

And she was off again, not giving Jo the chance to protest.

Jo watched her go, then looked at Chantal in hopes of commiserating—*Can you believe this girl?*—but Chantal just had one eyebrow raised at her.

"And how was your hiatus?" Chantal said, not as pointed as it might have been but pointed enough.

Jo waved the rugelach dismissively. "You know how it was," she said, because Chantal did. She would be the one fully taking over the production side of *Innocents* when Jo officially moved on, so she had been plenty involved over the summer. "Good luck wrangling this crew when I'm gone."

Chantal chuckled. Jo took a bite of the pastry and let out a hum of pleasure. It was *fantastic*. Jo decided to save another one for later before she'd even finished the first. Investing in Floured Up was definitely the right choice.

THAT AFTERNOON, JO ANSWERED emails while Emma sat on her couch working on something; Jo wasn't sure what. Emma had been there since lunch, one foot tucked under her. It was louder than it had been in months—the door open and the building again filled with other people—but Emma was quiet. She'd been quiet for a week now. Subdued. Jo had asked and been brushed off. She didn't want to intrude. She was Emma's boss, not her friend. Emma didn't have to tell her if something was wrong, though it didn't mean Jo didn't worry.

Jo never tried to write the first day back—too many interruptions and distractions. Aly and Phil came in first with props questions. Emma scrunched her nose in greeting to them but stayed focused on her work. Jo solved some of their issues and gave Aly leeway with the rest. Tate interrupted next—not directly, but via a new intern, shaking with nerves, asking for the scripts for the entire season. Jo didn't roll her eyes, because Tate sent a new kid on a fool's errand every year, and it wasn't the intern's fault.

"You'll learn not to believe half of the things out of Tate's mouth," Jo said gently. "Feel free to tell him I'm killing his character off this season. See if it'll make him behave."

After the intern left, looking exactly as nervous as he had when he came in, Emma smiled at Jo. It had been too long since Emma had done that.

"Maybe he'll also learn you're not nearly as intimidating as he seems to think," she said.

Jo shrugged. "It helps to have them terrified the first few weeks. Keeps them in line."

She tried not to think about the other Kaplan sister—how she, too, knew Jo wasn't as tough as her reputation made her seem. Jo expected Avery to have told Emma about the baseball games by this point, especially after Jo invested in the bakery. Every time Jo thought about it, she got an unfamiliar anxious feeling in her stomach. She didn't know what to say to Emma, so she didn't say anything.

Chantal came by soon thereafter. Emma said hello and went

back to her work. When Jo looked up to see what Chantal needed, she was met with more raised eyebrows. Chantal didn't say anything about Emma being there, but Jo could tell she had thoughts on it. It was unnecessary—no one else seemed to think it was strange. Emma had always worked in Jo's office on occasion. There was nothing different about it just because the world had decided they were dating.

Jo had almost forgotten about the rumors over the summer. There had been a few photos of their lunch when they discussed Emma's promotion—including a shot of her squeezing Emma's hand on top of the table. She should've been smarter than that. Other than that one outing and upfronts, though, they hadn't made the tabloids. It didn't mean the tabloids had forgotten about the rumors; nor had Chantal, apparently. The thought chafed Jo for two days. She'd worked with Chantal for more than half a decade. The woman should've known her better than to put any stock in gossip.

Wednesday afternoon, Jo was stuck on a scene and annoyed as hell. She was annoyed that Emma wasn't already in her office, as she'd been so many other days. She was annoyed that she hadn't already asked her in—Chantal's raised eyebrows influencing Jo's actions. The summer had been such a nice respite from worrying about how her interactions with Emma might have looked to outside observers. Jo would have really liked to not care about appearances, but this was Hollywood, and she wasn't naive.

That was why she waited so long, struggled for so long, before finally calling Emma to work in her office.

Emma came, as she always did, but instead of sitting down and getting to work, she stood next to the couch, clutching her tablet to her chest.

"Are you sure I should be working in here?" she asked.

Jo looked up distractedly, her brow furrowed. "Why shouldn't you?"

"I just don't want anyone to think . . . anything."

It was the reason Jo had taken so long to ask her to, but she bristled anyway.

"Think anything like that you're my assistant and sometimes I have work that requires you to be in my office?" she snapped. She was peevish about the dialogue she was working on and about caring what others thought. That frustration was worsened now that her dynamic with Emma had changed enough with people around that her assistant was making a big deal of this.

"I just meant—" Emma started.

"If you're going to talk, get out. I can't work with you talking at me."

Jo could feel the weight of Emma's stare on her even though she wasn't looking back.

"You're the one who asked me to come in here," Emma said. Her voice was quiet, hurt.

"And now I'm asking you to leave," Jo said.

There was a beat, but still Jo refused to look up. Emma closed the door on her way out.

Jo didn't finish the scene.

JO ALMOST DIDN'T PICK up her phone when Evelyn called that evening. She was alone with a glass of red wine and considered staying that way, not letting anyone interrupt her over-the-top moping, but she ended up answering right before it went to voicemail.

"I hear your girlfriend is quite comfortable working in your office," Evelyn said.

"What?"

Evelyn paused at the vitriol in Jo's voice. Jo sighed, and took a sip of her wine.

"I'm sorry," she said, gentler. "What are you talking about?"

"On *Star*'s website," Evelyn said. "They have an article about how you and Emma must have gotten cozy over the summer, given how comfortable she was working in your office, even with other people around."

Jo rubbed at her eyes. They were dry, tired. She should take her contacts out.

"When did this article go up?" she asked.

"Ā-Jo, what's going on?" Evelyn said. "Why do you sound . . . exhausted?"

"You sound great, too," Jo said, no bite to it. Evelyn didn't respond, and Jo knew she might as well tell her what was happening, because otherwise Ev would simply wait her out. "Emma was concerned about working in my office today, and I didn't know why and I snapped at her. I didn't know someone—God, someone had to have leaked that. People are back for two days and we're in the fucking tabloids again. If I find out who it is, I'm going to kill them."

"I'd bet Emma saw the article," Evelyn said, "because it was published this morning and she probably has a Google alert set for your names together."

"Don't accuse her of things I know *you* do," Jo said, smiling slightly. "Anyway, now I'm going to have to apologize to her in the morning."

"They always say makeup sex is the best sex."

"I'm hanging up now."

"No, no, come on, I'm teasing," Evelyn laughed. "How is it with everyone back, other than your spat with Emma?"

"Louder than usual," Jo said. "More distractions. It always takes me a while to get used to it."

"Tate do anything stupid yet?"

"When does he not?"

"I'm going to meet him when I come visit, okay?" Evelyn said. "I'm coming to set this time, meeting everyone."

"Have you decided when you're coming yet?" Jo needled, setting her wineglass down and settling deeper into the cushions of her couch.

"Your birthday, maybe? Or I'll just show up and surprise you one day."

Jo would've been happy with either.

"I'll have to see if Sammy's free, too," Evelyn said.

Jo knew she was mostly joking—Sam had played Jo's older brother on *The Johnson Dynasty*, and Evelyn had fawned over him ever since. Jo was fairly certain that Evelyn started her infatuation as a way to bother Jo, decades ago, but she had kept it up so long by this point that there must've been some truth to it.

"You'll have to fight me for him," Jo teased. "We're actually going to dinner on Saturday."

"Tell him I'm single."

Jo rolled her eyes and couldn't help her grin. More of her tension bled away the longer she talked to Evelyn. She felt bad about snapping at Emma, but with context, it all made sense, and it would be an easy fix, apologizing in the morning.

10

JO

"CAN I TAKE THE AFTERNOON OFF?" EMMA ASKED THE NEXT morning before Jo even had a chance to thank her for the coffee.

Jo blinked. Emma took time off only for dentist appointments, holidays, and the one time a year she got sick.

"Of course," Jo said.

"Thank you." Emma turned back to her computer before Jo could say anything else.

Jo stood beside Emma's desk for a moment, but when Emma continued to not look at her, Jo headed into her office and closed the door behind her.

So much for an easy fix.

On a normal day, Emma would tell Jo why she needed the afternoon off. Today, Jo could only assume she'd be at the twins' baseball game. Jo had to apologize to her before she left for the day. She'd snapped at Emma when Emma was trying to do her job—or, not her job, not exactly. Emma was trying to rein in the rumors, and Jo didn't bother listening before dismissing her. Emma was doing more than her job, was doing what she could to make Jo's life easier. Jo hadn't understood that yesterday, but she did today. She needed to tell Emma.

But all morning, Emma avoided letting any pauses linger in their interactions. Jo would open her mouth and Emma would interrupt with something, and so Jo never apologized.

When Emma dropped off Jo's lunch, she didn't stay to eat with her.

"I'm going to head out," she said instead.

Jo looked up at her and smiled gently. "Have a good afternoon, Emma."

"You, too, Ms. Jones."

Jo could feel her smile go strained. Emma turned and left without another word.

JO CONSIDERED NOT GOING to the game. But Ethan didn't deserve her not showing up because of personal issues. And it provided another opportunity to apologize to Emma.

Like she did every game, Jo wore her standard baseball cap and big sunglasses and sat in the top row of the bleachers. She scrolled through various apps on her phone instead of anxiously watching the parking lot to see when Emma would arrive.

She saw her immediately anyway. Dani and Ezra raced to the field like they always did, Dylan and Avery moving more slowly, three rottweilers and Jo's assistant with them today. Emma was in a tank top and shorts, waves of hair past her shoulders and sunglasses on top of her head. It was the most casual Jo had ever seen her. Jo's breath caught.

She prepared herself for Emma noticing her, realizing where she sneaked off to all these summer afternoons. She expected Emma to freeze, to look confused, maybe even hurt. She did not expect Emma to smile up at her and wave as she climbed the bleachers. Jo attempted her typical nonchalant wave, but her fingers were rigid.

Avery was quiet as she and Emma joined Jo in the top row. She sat next to Jo, Emma on the other side of Avery. Jo and Avery's eyes met, then Avery's darted away, back toward her sister.

"Nice day for a ball game, isn't it?" Emma asked, flicking her sunglasses down over her eyes.

"It is," Jo said.

She had no idea what was going on.

Emma knew she'd be here. Did Avery tell her today, or had Emma known for some time? Had Jo been confused about how to tell her for no reason? Emma knew but didn't think it was important enough to discuss? Jo needed to ask Avery, or even Dylan, who was still in the grass with the dogs.

Jo had been in plenty of awkward situations at work. She could be charming and disarming and win the day. Here, though, she couldn't figure out how to keep conversation going. She sat silently until Vincent arrived. She saw his smirk when he noticed Emma and prayed he wouldn't say anything stupid.

"Emma," Jo said, "this is my brother, Vincent."

Emma smiled and shook his hand. Was Jo imagining how her movement seemed stiff?

"It's nice to meet you," Emma said.

"Likewise," Vincent said, his smirk fading into a smile. "Surprised my sister let you take the afternoon off. The way she talks about you, you'd think the show would fall apart without you there."

Jo could have hugged him.

"I'm quite sure that's not true," Emma said.

Jo shifted on the bleacher. Emma glanced down the first baseline.

"Anyway," she said, "now that Dylan has been the one who had to pick up the dog poop, I'll go take those pups off his hands."

Emma was gone before Vincent even sat down. Jo should've stopped her. Should have gone after her. Should have told her it was true, not only that she talked Emma up to her brother, but that the show wouldn't be half as good without her. Jo had told her once, back at the wrap party that seemed so long ago now. They'd had that ridiculous drunken kiss and upfronts and asthma and a summer of getting closer since then, and still Jo felt like she'd never been further away from her assistant.

"How did it take you this long to let her come to a game, Jo?" Vincent said. "Honestly."

Jo shrugged, looking at Avery. Her brother let the topic drop, thankfully.

"I told her when you invested," Avery said out of the corner of her mouth. "It felt like too much not to."

"Right," Jo said.

The timing of Emma's melancholy made sense now. Or—it didn't make sense, really, but Jo had context. It didn't *make sense*, because why would Emma be sad that Jo invested in Floured Up? Jo's investment was because Avery's bakery was doing well, and her money allowed it to do even better. Emma should be happy about that.

"She won't talk to me about it," Avery said, an undercurrent of pain in her voice.

Jo still needed to apologize to Emma for snapping at her the previous day. Perhaps it would be a good opening to a larger conversation. Not that Jo felt the need to apologize for not telling Emma about investing in the bakery, but if they could discuss it, Emma might be able to understand her perspective. They could move on.

Jo only lasted half an inning before excusing herself. Emma had taken the dogs toward the outfield along the first baseline. Jo climbed down the bleachers and headed toward her. It looked, for a moment, like Emma might flee, but two of the dogs were lying down, and they anchored her to the spot.

"Hi," Jo said, still a few yards away.

"Hi." Emma barely opened her mouth to say it. She didn't take her eyes off the field.

"I'm sorry for snapping at you yesterday," Jo said. "I know now you were just being conscious of the rumors. I didn't understand at the time, but I do now."

"Great," Emma said, and nothing more.

So much for opening up a conversation.

Emma couldn't be this mad at her. For what—not saying anything about the baseball games? Why was that Jo's responsibility? She was Emma's boss, not her friend, and certainly not her *sister*, who also had said nothing. And when it came to investing in the bakery, that was a business decision—Emma didn't need to know what Jo did with her money. Not to mention that Emma should be happy about that particular investment.

When Jo was in the wrong, she apologized. The practice had helped her throughout her career. Admit when you were wrong, apologize, do better. But Jo shouldn't need to apologize for supporting Emma's sister.

Jo had been the one who felt uncomfortable, though, texting Emma that she'd be late the morning she went to Floured Up. Even then, she'd felt like she should tell Emma. And now it was clear that she'd hurt her. She wished she hadn't.

But that didn't mean her behavior necessarily warranted an apology.

The argument sounded weak, even in her head.

In silence, they watched two batters ground out.

"I—" Jo started. She didn't know what to say. "Do you have your inhaler? It's fairly dusty."

"Yep," Emma said.

Jo felt so small, in sneakers instead of heels. Emma seemed towering, shoulders back, head high.

"You should come to the last game," Jo said. "If you'd like."

Emma scoffed. There, perhaps, her frustration was justified. Had Jo told her sooner, Emma could have come to support her niece and nephew the whole season long.

Jo wanted to stay, wanted to explain. But she didn't have an explanation, and she tried to convince herself she didn't need one anyway. Emma never looked at her again. Finally, Jo headed back toward the bleachers.

She stood beside them rather than climbing to the top again. She couldn't stomach sitting next to anyone, having to make small talk. In the fourth inning, Avery came down. She paused beside Jo.

"Gonna go make my sister put on sunscreen," she said.

Jo nodded. "Good. Take care of her."

THE KIDS' TEAM LOST, but their sadness evaporated when Avery announced they were going for ice cream. Then it was all smiles and cheers as the parents loaded things into cars. Jo stood near Vincent's car, not quite looking at Emma, who was on the side of the parking lot with the dogs.

"Vincent, are you and Ethan coming to ice cream?" Dylan asked.

"As long as Ethan doesn't tell his little brother he got ice cream before dinner," Vincent said.

"I won't, I promise!" Ethan said, his eyes wide.

"Jo?" Avery asked.

Jo was looking at Emma when Avery asked, and Emma's eyes snapped to hers. Jo turned to Avery instead.

"I don't think so tonight," she said.

"Come on," Emma said. "You should come."

Jo looked back at her. Emma blinked a few times, smiling like everything was fine. Why was she putting up this front?

"No, I'd better—I'd better get home," Jo said. She looked at her nephew. "Your brother wouldn't be happy if I took you to ice cream but not him. I'll take you both next time, okay?"

Ethan grinned. "Okay!"

Emma's shoulders were almost up by her ears, like she was trying to sink into herself. She didn't look at Jo again, didn't smile until Dani and Ezra said they wanted to ride with her. Jo got in her own car and drove away.

JO CALLED HER PREFERRED coffee shop the next morning, the one where Emma picked up her latte every day. She added an iced chai to her standing order. It was something she did sometimes, after late-night shoots or before a long day. A little pick-me-up for Emma.

Usually, when Jo got to work in the morning, Emma stood and handed Jo her coffee. Usually, Emma smiled at Jo. Usually, Emma made sure that Jo had everything she needed before going back to her own work.

That morning, Emma sat at her desk and pushed the coffee cup in Jo's direction without looking up. A second cup, with her chai, was nowhere to be seen.

"Thank you," Jo said as she took the coffee. "Good morning."

"Morning," Emma said.

Jo stood there for a moment.

"Emma."

Emma finally turned to her. "Did you need something, Ms. Jones?"

Jo bristled at the formality, the distance in Emma's tone.

"Don't forget you're shadowing Barry Davis on Tuesday, Ms. Kaplan," she said instead of any sort of apology.

Jo had arranged Barry Davis's visit because she knew he was Emma's favorite director. She pulled strings with various connections and adjusted the *Innocents* schedule. There was a chance he'd end up directing an episode this season, a chance he'd like Emma enough to help set her on the right path within the Directors Guild, maybe even hire her himself. Emma needed to be prepared.

"Do you have any questions beforehand?" Jo asked.

"Nope."

Emma turned back to her computer. Jo went into her office and closed the door.

AFTER LUNCH, JO HAD a meeting with Chantal. Emma sat in to take notes. It was general updates about the beginning of filming, including a bit about Barry Davis's visit. At the end of the meeting, Jo gave Emma specific instructions about following up on something. She almost stopped halfway through the directions, when she noticed Emma looking over her shoulder instead of making eye contact. The woman couldn't even look at her. This had snowballed much more quickly than Jo expected.

They didn't interact again until five o'clock.

"You can go home, Emma," Jo said. "Have a good weekend."

Emma normally made sure Jo was going home, too, before she

left. She normally didn't leave Jo at the office alone without a fight. Today, she nodded.

"Good night, Ms. Jones," she said, and left.

THERE WERE PLENTY OF assholes in Hollywood. The assholes walked all over their employees. You worked for them because you had to, not because they were good bosses. Their recommendation letters were written by assistants because they didn't know their employees well enough to write anything themselves.

Jo could've been one of those assholes if she wanted to. She had enough money, enough power. She got called a bitch simply because of her standards, but being an asshole wasn't a reputation she had. Her employees liked her—liked her enough to tell a reporter she'd be amazing writing Agent Silver. There was a leak now, yes, but there were also people like Chantal who had been with Jo since before *Innocents*. They were loyal, because Jo had never been an asshole.

She felt like one now, though. The longer Emma was mad at her, the worse a job Jo did at convincing herself that she didn't need to apologize. Yes, Avery should have told Emma about Jo coming to the baseball games, but that didn't absolve Jo of the responsibility. Yes, Jo was Emma's boss, but she didn't have to be an asshole. Emma had been helping her with Agent Silver—with her presence and support, sure, but also by actually reading the script. That wasn't in her job description, but she did it. Why, then, was Jo acting like their relationship was nothing more than professional? It wasn't intimate like the tabloids claimed, but being friends with Emma didn't give the rumors merit.

Jo had hurt Emma. She had been so focused on how telling her seemed hard and confusing that she gave no regard to how Emma might feel about the situation. That was worth apologizing for. She considered sending a text Friday evening, barely more than twenty-four hours after the baseball game, but decided Emma deserved the apology to be delivered in person.

Jo continued fretting right up until she met Sam for dinner Saturday night. He met her in front of the restaurant, wrapping her up in a hug that made her feel cherished. He towered over her—she remembered when he'd hit his growth spurt while they were filming *The Johnson Dynasty*, how awkward and gangly he was back then. Almost thirty years later, he had more than grown into it. His hair was still brassy blond, no sign of gray. Just seeing him made Jo feel better than she had for days.

He had chosen a restaurant that specialized in molecular gastronomy. It was supposed to be all the rage. Jo couldn't help but make fun of it.

"Cotton candy foie gras?" She snorted a laugh. "Sam, were you always this pretentious?"

"We're ordering that now," he said. "And you're going to like it."

She did end up liking it, though she absolutely refused to admit it.

At the coffee and chocolate bar they went to after dinner, Sam crowded into the same side of the booth she was in. He poked her in the side like he did when he wanted something from her when they were kids.

"So tell me about Agent Silver," he said. "How's the script thus far?"

"You know if I told you anything, the studio would have me shot on the spot," she said.

"C'mon," he whined. "Just one little thing."

She mimed locking her lips and throwing away the key. Spoilers were on lockdown for something as big as Agent Silver.

But that hadn't stopped her when Emma asked to help. Emma didn't just know some of what happened, she'd read it, right there in the script.

Sam hadn't mentioned Emma all evening. Jo didn't know whether he was being a gentleman or he simply didn't put any stock in the rumors and thus didn't feel a need to bring them up. The thought of Emma made Jo's chest clench. What would she do if Jo asked her to take a look at the script now? Was she so hurt that she'd refuse? Jo picked at her fingernails.

Sam poked her in the side again, pulling her out of her thoughts. "I'm looking forward to all the assholes who thought you couldn't do it eating their words when you blow this thing out of the water."

Jo laughed at the sudden compliment. She tried not to think about who else believed in her so strongly.

11

EMMA

WHEN EMMA'S ALARM WENT OFF ON SUNDAY, SHE snoozed it and lay staring at the ceiling until the alarm went off again. She shoved the covers down and dragged herself out of bed.

She shivered against the chill in her apartment as she put a protein waffle in her toaster. She'd blasted the AC the past few days, keeping it cold so she could sleep with heavy blankets and not sweat through her sheets. The highs were near ninety, but Emma wanted to burrow into her mattress. She'd cleaned her apartment twice, and she'd clean it again if it weren't already spotless by this point. She used a plate for her waffle and left it on her counter just so she'd have something to tidy when she got home. The boxers and tank top she wore to sleep ended up in a pile on her bedroom floor.

She was up early enough that when she headed to Griffith Park this time, it was neither too busy nor too hot. The tourists weren't out yet and the sun wasn't too high in the sky.

Jo had apologized for snapping at her. That was nice, Emma guessed. But it was like she didn't even realize she'd done anything else wrong. Who cared that she'd been lying to Emma for months? Emma had admitted that Jo was one of her favorite people, but Emma was just her assistant, didn't matter enough for Jo to consider her feelings.

Emma felt stupid, being stuck on this. But she'd loved her job for so long, loved going to work, loved working for Jo. All of that left a bad taste in her mouth now. Emma deserved better. She deserved to be treated better. Even if Jo was just her boss, she still should have been honest with Emma.

Emma doubled the length of her run this morning. She finished the observatory trail, up and back down, her calves burning, and then kept going. This section was flatter, letting her catch her breath even while she kept pace. The slap of her feet against the ground was steadier here. Consistent. Like a mantra.

She decided not to be sad anymore.

How she felt about Jo didn't matter. Neither did how Jo felt about her. Emma was smart and capable, and she knew what she wanted to do. Tuesday she'd be shadowing an accomplished director, taking steps toward her new career. Jo had set that up, yeah, but it didn't matter why. If Jo needed her to do well so Jo herself looked good, who cared? The means to success weren't as important as the ends.

And Barry Davis was a great means to Emma's success anyway. Emma tried not to fangirl, and she was usually pretty successful at it. She'd dealt with so many famous and powerful people as Jo's assistant that it was easy to remember that everyone was just a person. But Barry Davis was an Oscar nominee who had directed some of Emma's absolute favorite movies. The thought of getting to see him in action was *thrilling*, even if he was just a person. He was an incredibly talented person, and Emma couldn't wait to see him work. Better still, she got to shadow him.

She was actually looking forward to the workweek by the time she got back to her apartment. Her shower was refreshing, and she smiled as her phone buzzed with a text from Phil.

Is your girlfriend cheating on you?!

There was a shocked emoji and a link to a TMZ story. Emma tried to hold on to her good mood, but its tendrils slipped through her fingers. She clicked the link.

JO JONES AND SAM ALLEN:
REUNION OR ROMANCE?

There were pictures of Jo and a former costar. Emma of all people should have known better than to judge a relationship based on pictures, but they sure seemed cozy, first leaving a restaurant together and then sitting on the same side of a booth in a coffee shop. Jo's eyes sparkled. Her smile was wide. Whether she was dating the guy or not, she certainly hadn't spent her weekend worried about how Emma might be feeling.

Emma locked her phone and climbed back into bed. It wasn't worth crying over, but Emma cried anyway.

AS EMMA STEPPED OUT of her apartment building Monday morning, she heard shutters click. Paparazzi. The first time they'd been around since before hiatus. Of course it was the week after Jo had been seen out with someone else. Emma probably looked exhausted, and she hadn't expected the cameras, so she was grimacing. It was going to be an all-around terrible photo. It would look like she'd just been broken up with.

Just like there had been on Friday, there was an iced chai waiting for her when she picked up Jo's coffee. She hadn't taken it then, but she did today. She could be mad and enjoy a free drink at the same time.

Just like she had on Friday, she slid Jo's coffee across her desk when Jo got in without bothering to look up.

Just like she had on Friday, Jo stopped beside Emma's desk after picking up her coffee.

This time, she actually had something to say.

"I'm sorry, Emma," she said. Emma's pulse shot up. "I should have told you I was spending time with Avery."

Emma looked up at her. That was apparently the end of her apology.

"Okay," Emma said.

"Okay?"

Jo admitted she did something she shouldn't have. That had no effect on Emma.

"Just because you apologize doesn't mean I'm not still hurt," Emma said. Her voice wavered, but she held eye contact. "Just because you apologize doesn't mean you suddenly have my trust again."

Jo's face fell so much, Emma almost took her words back. Her boss looked *crushed*, and Emma hated it. But she was right. Hurt didn't go away with an apology. And trust was earned. Emma deserved to be treated better.

"I understand," Jo said quietly. "I hope you'll let me earn your trust back."

"That's really up to you," Emma said.

She wasn't quite sure where the steel in her blood had come from. Jo probably didn't know, either. She probably expected to be easily forgiven and they'd move on. She didn't look prepared for

Emma to actually stand up for herself. Jo opened her mouth, but Emma didn't want to give her a chance to try to further apologize.

"Everything is ready for Barry Davis's visit tomorrow," Emma said. "I appreciate you letting me go for the day so I can learn from him."

She did. She knew it was all business, and that was fine. She could be professional.

Jo nodded, head hanging like there was an albatross around her neck.

"I hope it goes well," she said, and disappeared into her office.

AFTER LUNCH, JO LEANED against her doorjamb and looked at Emma. Emma tried to stay focused on her email. She considered asking what Jo was doing, but she wanted to see where this was going to go.

Finally, Jo said, "You have your inhaler, right?"

Emma opened her desk drawer, picked up her inhaler, and waved it at Jo.

"Good," Jo said. "Good."

She went back into her office.

There was a part of Emma that wanted to make this easy on her, wanted to forgive and forget and make Jo smile again. But as Emma kept reminding herself, she deserved better. She appreciated the apology, but it didn't matter if Jo was sorry that she hadn't considered Emma's feelings unless she wasn't going to do it again. Sorry meant nothing without changed behavior. That was what Emma had told herself, months ago, her mouth accidentally landing on Jo's at the wrap party. She hadn't had to apologize out loud then, because her apology was changed behavior, never letting anything like that happen again. Jo needed to do the same. Emma had forgiven too many people in her life too easily. She was finally learning to stand up for herself.

TUESDAY MORNING, EMMA HANDED off Jo's coffee.

"Is your asthma worse in this heat wave?"

"It's fine, Ms. Jones," Emma said.

"Okay," Jo said. "Good."

Emma managed not to roll her eyes. She was sure Jo wasn't really that hung up on her asthma—it wasn't what she intended to keep talking about. But if she couldn't come up with the words of a better apology, couldn't figure out how to promise Emma she'd be better, Emma wasn't going to help her.

Especially not on the day of Barry Davis's visit. It was basically a simple set visit for now. He might end up directing an episode, but he might not. He might like Emma enough to help her get a job, which was something Emma tried not to think about too hard or her throat would close up with anxiety.

Barry was to arrive around ten, and Jo would be greeting him, rather than Emma, who would usually. He was important enough that they were pulling out all the stops.

Emma sat at her desk with nothing pressing to do while Jo went to greet Barry. She tried not to fidget too much. When she heard Jo returning, talking to someone who must have been Barry freakin' Davis, Emma made sure to look like she was hard at work.

She was typing a fake email when Jo and Barry rounded the corner. She looked up at them and smiled. Barry Davis, in the flesh. His shrewd eyes behind his distinctive rectangular glasses. He had a five-o'clock shadow even though it was morning.

"Barry, this is my assistant, Emma Kaplan," Jo said.

Emma stood and hoped her face wasn't too flushed. She offered her hand.

Barry shook it with a grin. "It's nice to meet you, Emma."

"You, too, Mr. Davis."

He laughed. "Please, call me Barry."

Emma nodded and could tell she was blushing. Jo gave her an inscrutable look.

"I just need to grab my water from my office," Jo said. "And we'll be on our way."

As soon as Jo disappeared into her office, Barry stepped closer to Emma. His cologne smelled like . . . lumber? Was that a thing expensive cologne smelled like? Emma smiled at him and tried to remind herself that he was just a person like anyone else.

"I'm excited to take a look at set. See what Jo Jones can do," he said.

"She's incredibly talented," Emma said. It was true, even if she was still mad at Jo.

"And you know those talents well, don't you?" Barry said.

Jo returned with her tumbler then, and Barry slid easily into step with her, somehow making it look like he hadn't been in Emma's personal space, like he hadn't made an inappropriate comment. Emma's feet stayed rooted to the ground.

Maybe he didn't mean it that way, she told herself. She was just being sensitive.

Jo and Barry were almost around the corner before Jo stopped and looked back at her.

"Emma, are you coming?"

Barry's smile was guileless.

"Of course," Emma said. "Sorry, one moment."

She pretended to do something on her computer, grabbed her tablet off her desk, then followed.

Jo led Barry on a tour of the studio. This was normally Emma's job. Emma was usually the one who charmed people with anecdotes as they moved through the building. Today, though, she stayed quiet, couldn't stop looking at Barry's face. He was perfectly nice. He didn't stand too close or say anything inappropriate. She was probably overreacting. Maybe she had misinterpreted.

On set, Chantal called for a break and Barry got introduced around. Emma let out a breath. Her whole upper body felt tight, like she'd been holding perfect posture for hours. Jo furrowed her eyebrows at Emma, but asked nothing.

Barry circled back to their side eventually. Emma shuffled a little closer to Jo.

"Feel settled in?" Jo asked Barry.

He grinned. "Feel great."

"Then I suppose I'll leave the two of you to it."

If it were any other week, Emma might have said something to get Jo to stay, might have somehow indicated she didn't want to be alone with this man. But Jo had barely looked at her since asking about her inhaler that morning. She didn't look at her then, either, just turned and headed toward her office, leaving Emma beside Barry as Chantal announced the end of the break.

"I get what you see in her," Barry said at Jo's retreating form. His eyes were glued to her ass.

Emma swallowed. "She's certainly something."

Barry laughed. Emma would have rather heard nails on a chalkboard. The quiet-on-set call went up, and Emma was grateful for the reprieve.

This happened. Of course it did. They were in Hollywood. Just because more people talked about it now didn't mean it stopped happening. Emma had dealt with plenty of disgusting, overstepping men. She knew how to handle the situation. Keep her smile polite but her nails sharp.

But this was Barry Davis.

He hadn't even done anything all that bad, she knew. A couple of rude comments that he could pretend weren't meant that way. It was nothing, really. And nothing she couldn't handle. She straightened her posture, kept her head up.

They watched filming for a while. Emma's eyes stayed on the actors until Barry took a step closer to her. She countered, stepping away, and his quiet chuckle sounded predatory, but he didn't pursue her.

He didn't try anything the rest of the morning—didn't stand too close, didn't say anything inappropriate. Emma knew she hadn't imagined what had happened, but she still doubted herself.

He hadn't meant it that way.

It hadn't been a big deal.

It was fine.

She had to win him over, anyway. He could help her career or destroy it, if he wanted.

And, really, he was fine now. He made insightful comments about the show, taught her more about directing over the course of two hours than any of the books Jo had suggested for her. They ate lunch together; craft services had set up under a tent outside on the lot today. Emma sat across from Barry at a folding table. Normally she liked to plop down in the middle of anyone eating at the same time she was, but everyone gave the two of them a wide berth. She knew it was because she was supposed to be learning from him, but all she wanted to do was sit next to Phil and steal food off his plate. Instead she picked at her salad and tried to keep up conversation.

"What was your favorite film to direct?" she asked, because asking famous men about themselves was a good way to not have to talk for a while.

Barry didn't answer the question, though.

"Look, you seem like you can handle yourself," he said as he chewed a bite of his sandwich. "If you can *handle* me, I know a guy who's looking for a second AD. I'll recommend you."

Emma rolled her shoulders down from where they'd shot up toward her ears. She looked at Jo, standing across the lot and talking to Aly by the drinks.

"If I can handle you?" she said. Maybe playing innocent would get her out of this.

"I mean, you are more than welcome to use your mouth," Barry said so casually that he could be talking about traffic, "but your hand is all I need."

Emma flinched hard enough to drop her fork onto her plate.

"What?" Barry had the gall to sound incredulous. "You're already trying to sleep your way into the business. I can get you more opportunities than her."

Emma wanted a lighting fixture to fall on his head. No, she wanted to bring it down on him herself. There was a scream inside her mouth, behind her eyes, building from a clenched fist in her chest.

"Please excuse me," she said, and hated herself for the civility.

She left her plate and fled. Saliva was thick in her mouth, her blood rushing in her ears. Jo must have finished her conversation, because Emma almost ran into her twenty yards from the table where Barry still sat.

"Excuse me," Jo said.

Emma was afraid that if she opened her mouth, she might vomit. She opened it anyway.

"Jo, I—" She didn't know if she could say this out loud. "Barry . . ." She bit down on a grimace. "He's . . ."

Jo sighed, half rolling her eyes. "Ms. Kaplan, I know you're . . ." She paused. Emma stared blankly at her, no idea what she was going to say. "If you're starstruck here, you have to get over it. I pulled a lot of strings to get him here for you. Don't make me look bad. He can open a lot of doors for you if you make a good impression."

Emma remembered telling her how much she liked Barry. Before Jo invested, before the baseball game, before everything, when they talked, when they told each other things, Emma had gushed about her favorite movies, which meant she gushed about Barry and his movies. Of course Jo thought she was starstruck. It wasn't like Jo heard or saw anything. It wasn't like Barry had been anything but pleasant to anyone but Emma. No one knew about it. Emma wished she could pretend it didn't happen, could go back to how excited she was to meet him, just this morning. She glanced at Jo, who looked more annoyed than concerned. Of course she was worried about Emma making her look bad. Of course that was all that mattered. Emma was *furious* with her suddenly, for everything.

"I'm not *starstruck*," she snarled, keeping her voice low. "I'm the opposite, in fact. Unimpressed. And I have other work to do at my desk, so if you'll excuse me—"

"Is this really what you want to do?" Jo asked, her eyebrows up by her hairline. "Throw this opportunity away?"

Emma didn't bother responding. She left without a second glance.

She wasn't sure how she made it back to her desk, only that she did, and knocked her tablet off it as she reached for her purse. It hit the ground with a crack loud enough that she spared one moment to worry it broke, but she didn't care enough to check. Instead she grabbed the purse and locked herself in Jo's private bathroom just in time for the tears to start.

She was so angry: at Jo, at Barry, at herself. She couldn't believe—or, she could. Maybe she even should. She knew people thought she was sleeping with Jo. Even though she wasn't, even though Jo was maybe with her former costar, the rumors of their being together had been around long enough that Emma should've been used to people assuming she was sleeping her way into the business. But the way Barry said it, the way he assumed she would— she felt sick, and stupid, and like she needed to get it together.

She gave herself five minutes in the bathroom, figured there was no way Jo and Barry would finish lunch in that time. She spent only half of it crying, used the rest to make it look like she hadn't cried at all. She blew her nose until nothing more came out, then cold water on her fingertips, patted gently under her eyes; a cold, wet paper towel to the back of her neck to cool herself down. She was grateful she tended toward minimalism when it came to makeup so that she didn't have smudges of dark liner and shadow everywhere. Instead it just took a little touching up, and her waterproof mascara held up like a champ. She looked in the mirror, and as long as she could ignore the hard rock in her stomach, she could almost believe she was fine.

EMMA SPENT THE AFTERNOON finding excuses to not be near Barry. The crease between Jo's eyes got more pronounced every time Emma said she was so sorry but she had to step away, but Emma didn't care. Jo could think whatever she wanted.

Avery texted a couple of times. She knew today was the day Barry Davis was going to be on set, and she knew Emma loved his movies, and she was being a good sister and checking in. Emma didn't reply to any of her messages.

She thought she was going to make it through the day. It was almost five, and they weren't shooting late. They were running through blocking for what would be filmed tomorrow. Normally, Emma and Jo wouldn't be around for this, but Barry was here to observe, and so they observed with him. It was the last thing Emma had to get through before she could go home.

The scene they were blocking was a big one. Holly's character figured out she wasn't straight, and she was saying it out loud for the first time, voicing it to Tate's character while pacing her living room. Emma was glad to get to watch the scene come together— she liked to see the actors and director and crew all working it out.

She'd almost forgotten Barry was there until he spoke up.

"Excuse me, if I may," he said. Everyone came to a complete stop to pay attention to him. "What if she was unhappy about this situation? I know she's nervous here, but maybe it's a little upsetting to her, too, to say 'I'm bisexual.'"

Emma's whole body did a record scratch, like a needle dragged across her brain.

"Are you kidding me?" she snapped.

Every person on set looked at her. For once it didn't make her nervous.

"That's maybe the worst direction I've ever heard," she said. "It fits neither the character nor the show. Have you ever even seen an episode?"

Barry had this surprised smile like it was adorable that the little assistant was speaking up. Emma wanted to hit him. She wanted an actual answer out of him, too, wanted him to explain why the hell he thought that was a good directorial choice. It was all kinds of wrong, and she couldn't believe Barry Davis, her favorite director, had turned out to be this terrible. In every way.

"Perhaps when you do more than get the coffee, people will be interested in your opinion." Jo's voice was wire taut. Emma's eyes cut to her boss, who wasn't even looking at her. "In the meantime, I could use an iced latte."

Emma felt her mouth drop open. Jo could *not* agree with this man. She couldn't possibly think that was good direction. Emma blinked at her.

Jo flicked her fingers toward the door.

It was then that Emma finally processed everyone staring at her, then she processed that she had told off an Oscar-nominated director in front of—in front of *everyone*. Tate and Holly. Yuri working on lights. Phil's eyebrows were close to his hairline. Chantal pretended to look at the script, at least, but everyone else was—Emma couldn't believe she'd done that.

She made herself walk, not run. Iced latte, coming right up.

She tried to be unimposing when she walked back onto the set. She tried to blend into the walls. It didn't work. No one looked directly at her, but they were all aware of her, it felt like. She had considered not coming back, but Jo had asked for an iced latte, and ignoring her boss immediately after talking back to a famous director was probably not a great idea.

Emma stopped at Jo's side, didn't look at Barry. Jo watched Tate and Holly run through the blocking. She reached out for her iced latte without so much as a glance at Emma. After Emma handed it over, Jo fluttered her hand again.

"You're not needed here," she said quietly.

Emma's face burned with shame. She went back to her desk.

Maybe she should've cried in the bathroom again, but she didn't actually feel like crying. She felt like fighting. She felt like *quitting*. It was an overreaction, she knew. She couldn't quit over one bad day.

But it was a bad *week*.

She couldn't make a decision like this while anger bubbled under her skin, but she wanted to anyway. She had some money saved. Maybe she could find something new over the next hiatus.

WHEN JO CAME BACK, Emma's only solace was that Barry wasn't with her. Jo's face was blank, her cheeks pinched, just slightly, but enough that Emma noticed.

"Ms. Kaplan," she said as she passed Emma's desk, "my office."

Emma pressed her lips together, held her head high.

"Door," Jo said.

Emma took her time in closing the door, tried to compose herself, tried to feel bad for what she said to Barry. She couldn't do it.

"I wasn't wrong," she said before Jo had the chance to yell at her. "You can't possibly believe she should sound *unhappy about this situation.* 'This situation'? Like figuring out she's bisexual is some horrible predicament for her to be in."

"Look, I know this is personal for you, but—"

"No," Emma said, and wow, she wouldn't have to quit, because she was going to get fired for all the bad decisions she'd made today, interrupting her boss being the most recent. "You don't get to act like this is just some personal thing for me. This isn't about me. This is about the show and the characters and the story you're telling. That direction was *wrong*, for all of it. And if it wasn't? If that's what you actually want to do? You don't get to win GLAAD

awards and give that speech and then go around making characters unhappy about their 'bisexual situation.'"

The GLAADs had been months and months ago, but it was a
good speech. It was a great speech. It was the type of speech
Emma expected from Jo, because Jo had always been fantastic
when it came to queer issues, and Emma couldn't *believe* she agreed
with Barry.

Jo dropped herself into her chair, scrubbed a hand through her
hair.

"I know," she sighed.

Emma blinked. "What?"

"You thought I *disagreed*? You thought—what? That I'm the
type of lesbian who thinks bisexuals are greedy and always going
to leave you for a man?" Jo scoffed. "Please give me more credit
than that."

"I—um." Emma wanted to hold onto her anger but her brain
short-circuited around the word *lesbian*.

"Christ, Emma, of course you were right," Jo said. "I told Barry
as soon as you left."

Emma blinked at her.

"I'm sorry I treated you that way," Jo said. "But God, people
already think we're fucking—you think me letting you talk to
Barry Davis out of turn was going to help?"

That made sense, sure. Maybe if Emma weren't having such a
terrible day, she would have figured that out herself. Except, for
months now, Jo had been all about ignoring the rumors like that
would make them go away. The rumors that could be true, given
that Jo was a lesbian. Apparently.

That wasn't the important part of this conversation, though.
Sorry or not, Jo had been treating her poorly. To do it in front of

this awful man was worse. Jo was supposed to be winning back Emma's trust, and instead it felt like she'd picked Barry over her, which was ridiculous. This was Emma's *career*, not choosing teams on the playground. But that was still somehow what hurt the most.

"I just wish you had had my back," Emma said quietly.

"I can't have your back in everything if we ever want these rumors to go away," Jo said. "I'm your boss, Emma. I have to act like it."

"There's a difference between acting like my boss and throwing me under the bus," Emma said. "And you know there is, because you've *never* done that before."

Jo fisted her hand in her hair and tugged. She looked sad, at least, which Emma liked even if she shouldn't.

"I don't know why the rumors even matter to you," Emma said.

"Excuse me?"

"I don't know why you care about the rumors anyway." Emma couldn't figure out why she was choosing this battle, except she was mad at Jo for everything with Avery, was mad at her again for telling her off in front of people, no matter the reason. She didn't want to be. She wanted to be over it all. Being mad only made things worse, but she couldn't stop. And so she stood her ground. "You're seen as getting some hot young thing. I'm the one who people think is unable to get a job without sleeping with someone."

Jo's teeth flashed into a smile she quickly bit down on. "While I admire your confidence in being some hot young thing," she said, and Emma realized that might have been a bit much, "that is not all I'm seen as. And I know I have a reputation for not giving a fuck what people think about me, but I've cultivated that. I've cultivated that because it's easier than people knowing they can hurt me."

Emma's heart twisted a little. Jo continued.

"I know you're mad at me, Emma," Jo said. "And I deserve it. Not telling you about meeting Avery was wrong, and I'm sorry."

Emma stiffened. That didn't need to be part of this conversation.

"And I'm sorry I acted like it didn't matter, like I didn't have to apologize," Jo said. "You deserve better than that."

This was exactly what Emma had wanted Jo to say this morning, before Barry ever showed up. Now, she didn't feel ready to address it.

"But you can't take that out on me like this," Jo said. "I *had* to tell you off because you were out of place. Going easy on you would've just stoked the fire of people believing we're sleeping together, and that's bad for *both* of us. Stop being mad and think about it for a second." She sighed. "You think people don't look at pictures of us and think I'm corrupting this lovely young lady? I'm a predatory lesbian in the middle of a midlife crisis. I'm a frigid bitch who just hasn't found the right dick. I'm a dragon lady who's stealing a pretty white girl from the white boys she should be dating."

Just like that, all of Emma's anger collapsed.

"Boss, *no*," she said, horrified. "You're not any of those things."

Jo stared at her for a moment, then shook her head like she was clearing it. "It's all about perception, Emma. You can't talk like that to directors, especially not to directors like Barry Davis. No matter how wrong they are."

Emma nodded. "Right. Won't do it again."

"You know you can trust me with these characters. I'll step in when someone is out of line," Jo said. She offered Emma a small smile. "You can trust me even when you're pissed at me."

"I wasn't *pissed* at you." Emma *was*, obviously, but she didn't want to admit it now.

Jo tilted her head at Emma, her smile disbelieving. "Of course you were," she said. "You should've been. I assumed Avery would tell you things, and when she didn't, I just—I didn't know how to say anything." Normally she commanded the room from her sleek white desk chair, but now she looked open—vulnerable, even. Her shoulders were down, her neck long. "The longer it went on the harder it got. Not that that's an excuse. I shouldn't have hidden it from you, and I shouldn't have pretended like it wasn't my responsibility to tell you, and I'm sorry."

"It's fine."

"It's *not*," Jo said. "I care about you, Emma, and I want you to thrive. I made a hostile environment for you, and that was wrong and not fair. You deserve to be mad at me, but I hope you can forgive me."

Emma scuffed her toe against the carpet. "Of course, boss," she said quietly.

"And I'm sorry it coincided with Barry Davis's visit," Jo said. "I know how much you were looking forward to meeting him and learning from him. I will talk to him tomorrow and hopefully, if not salvage a recommendation to potential employers, at least not get a warning about you either."

Emma kicked her foot harder into the ground, looked down at it instead of up at Jo. "No," she said. "I don't want a recommendation."

"Emma." Emma didn't have to look at Jo to imagine the incredulity on her face. "It could help you quite a bit."

"Yeah, but—" Emma tried to swallow the frog in her throat. "I don't want it from him."

Jo *hmm*ed. "He didn't live up to your expectations, did he? What with that terrible direction and all."

Emma played with the hem of her top. She glanced at Jo, who looked more at ease than she had in a week.

"That and—" Emma didn't want to tell her, didn't want to say anything, didn't want to think about it. But his set visit wasn't just about her shadowing him—there was still a possibility he could direct an episode. Emma had to do something to stop it. "He said something not great to me."

Jo's eyes flashed for a moment. "What did he say?"

"Just a couple of comments," Emma said. "I thought I was maybe overreacting but . . ." She cringed a little. "He indicated if I gave him . . . if I . . . he said he'd recommend me to a friend for a second AD position if I gave him a hand job."

Jo blinked slowly. She put both hands flat on her desk and stood. "He said that?"

By now, Emma had learned the outward signs of Jo's moods. This—eyes narrowed and fingers twitching on the desk, almost like she was shaking? This was anger. This was fury. Emma shrank, wanting to take her words back. She said nothing.

Jo took a deep breath. Emma was ready for her to yell. She didn't do it often, but this seemed like a moment it would happen.

Instead, she said softly, "Emma. Are you okay?"

It wasn't quite bursting into tears, but Emma's eyes definitely welled. She shook her head—at herself, at this stupid emotional response, not at Jo.

"I'm fine, boss," she said. "It was just—it was dumb. And I was upset and—I'm sorry I reacted the way I did."

"Emma." Jo's voice was so gentle. "You do not have to apologize for being upset over sexual harassment." She paused. "Do you want to sit down?"

Emma nodded. Jo came around her desk. She led Emma

toward the couch without coming close enough to touch her, then she sat down, too, a good two feet away.

"Do you need any water?" Jo stood back up. "Have you eaten recently? I have granola bars or yogurt or—"

"I'm fine, boss," Emma said.

Jo sat down again. Her hands started toward Emma and then stopped, ended up in fists in her lap.

"I'm so sorry this happened, Emma," she said. "I am so sorry this happened to you. And I am sorry I did not know. He will not be directing an episode nor allowed back in the building, ever."

"No, Jo, I—"

Jo held up her hand. "It's nonnegotiable. Anyone who treats you like that is not welcome here."

It made Emma want to cry harder, for some reason. A minute ago she accused Jo of not having her back, and here she was standing up for her without hesitation.

"I would also like your permission to release a statement explaining that he was not asked to direct because he sexually harassed one of my employees."

Emma's eyes went wide. "Boss, no. I don't want to cause any trouble. He's Barry Davis and—"

"And he sexually harassed you. He's the one causing trouble." Emma swore Jo's voice shook. "I won't mention your name, obviously. But I would like to release a statement."

"He'll know it was me," Emma said. "If I ever want to do anything in Hollywood, he'll make sure I can't. He said he could get me opportunities, which means he can definitely make sure I don't get them, too."

"Fuck whatever opportunities he says he can get you," Jo snarled. She took a breath, but she was still obviously angry when she continued. "I'm sorry, I'm just—he might *not* know it was you, actually, because men like that don't just pick one woman to harass. And even if he does, the statement is going to be my first step in making sure *he* can't work in the industry anymore, not you. He thinks he can come in here and treat you like that? Treat anyone like that? If he hadn't already left, I'd throw him out myself."

Emma smiled a little at that. She rubbed her nose and sniffled.

Their whole relationship felt like it had been turned on its head in the last five minutes. Emma had spent so long thinking Jo didn't care about her, thinking she wasn't important enough to her.

She didn't think that anymore.

She couldn't, not with the way Jo looked at her, worried and nervous and desperate to do something. Jo was supporting her. That wasn't always how it went in situations like these. Too often, bosses didn't believe you; people overlooked horrible things because other people were talented. To have Jo so ready to fight— Emma definitely couldn't think Jo didn't care about her. Something swooped within Emma's stomach.

Jo took a deep breath and let it out slowly, like she was trying to calm down.

"We'll talk about it more tomorrow, if you'd rather," she said. "I don't want to overwhelm you."

"I'm fine," Emma said, even though she wasn't.

Jo smiled gently at her, and more tears leaked out of Emma's eyes. She laughed at herself.

"I'll be okay, boss," she said. She sat up straighter. "Is there anything more to do today? Are they finished on set?"

"Emma." The amount Jo was saying her name made her chest feel tight, especially with how she had called her Ms. Kaplan for most of the day. "They're done on set. There's nothing you need to do today except go home and take care of yourself."

"Right," Emma said.

Jo stood, and Emma did, too. She wanted to ask for a hug. But Jo was her boss, and they'd been talking about sexual harassment, and it didn't seem like the best idea. Emma sort of shrugged at her instead.

"I'll see you tomorrow, boss."

"Have a good night, Emma," Jo said. "Drive safely. If you need anything—if you want to take tomorrow off—anything, just let me know."

Emma bobbed her head in a nod, gave a half wave, and left.

12

EMMA

EMMA WENT HOME, UNLOCKED THE DOOR TO HER APART-ment, locked it behind her. She dropped her keys and her purse on the table by the door, dropped herself in the middle of her couch.

It had been a day.

She stared blankly at her TV. Restless energy filled her body, but she couldn't bring herself to move. She flexed her calves, wiggled her toes. She thought about this morning, how she'd tried not to fidget while waiting for Barry Davis to arrive. It felt like a week ago.

Emma rubbed the back of her hand hard against her wet eyes. She was so goddamn *frustrated*. Women shouldn't have to deal with this shit anymore. No one should. Everything felt dirty now. Emma's favorite movies. Her dream to direct. Her workplace itself. She needed to shower.

She wiggled her toes more. Didn't get off the couch.

He was one of her heroes. Twelve hours ago, he was near the top of the list of people she'd like to meet in life. Now she never wanted to see him again. Never wanted to think about him. And yet he'd make more movies; people would continue to love him. If she stayed in the industry, she'd never escape him.

If she stayed in the industry.

One day, and he had her doubting her dreams, her goals. She rested her elbows on her knees and held her head in her hands. Maybe she could learn how to bake, work for Avery for the rest of her life. She'd dropped out of film school, people thought she only had her job because she was sleeping with her boss, and she'd publicly challenged a guy who could make or break her career. How the hell was she ever supposed to become a director? She exhaled hard through her nose.

Jo would never let her quit.

Jo, who she wasn't mad at anymore. Jo, who supported her immediately. Jo, who was a lesbian. Emma leaned back and kicked her feet up onto her coffee table. She bit at her thumbnail.

Jo had apologized. Sincerely. She apologized about how she hadn't apologized at first. Emma hadn't forgiven her when she'd said sorry yesterday, but today? Today, Jo had fixed all the reasons Emma was mad at her. Emma wondered if Jo was still at work. She should've stayed, made sure Jo left at a reasonable time. But Jo was an adult. She could get herself home. It was just that—well, maybe Emma wanted to take care of Jo.

No. Not maybe. Not anymore. Emma had said *maybe* she'd had feelings for Jo when her mom had pointed out how upset she was about Jo being at the baseball games without telling her, but Emma wasn't unsure anymore.

Today, Jo had made her feel safe and warm and cared for, and that was how Jo had made her feel for months now. Emma was finally ready to admit it, was finally able to see it. She wondered what her life would be like without the rumors. She and Jo had definitely gotten closer over the year, but that made sense—she had been just a props PA last year. She'd never worked closely with Jo, could hardly believe it when Aly told her Jo wanted to steal her away. But they'd been together constantly the past year, so of course they'd gotten closer. It wasn't the fault of the rumors.

Neither were these feelings. Rumors didn't make Emma feel safe around Jo. Rumors didn't make Jo gorgeous and caring and kind. Rumors didn't give Emma a crush. In fact, Emma probably would've figured her crush out earlier without the rumors. She'd been so focused on how wrong the rumors were, she'd never really considered that they weren't wrong at all. Or—they might have been off base when they began, but somewhere along the way her feelings shifted.

Not that Emma realizing this changed anything. Jo was still her boss. She might care about Emma, might be taking care of her, but that didn't mean there were feelings. This whole thing was about inappropriate behavior at work. Jo would never be interested in an employee.

Instead, she wanted to release a statement about Barry. She wanted to ruin his career. It sounded nice, maybe, getting some kind of revenge. Except he was *Barry Davis* and Emma was an assistant everyone thought was sleeping with her boss. Who'd be believed in this situation? Emma needed to be realistic.

This was something that happened. For all the men who had gone down for it, Hollywood probably had thousands more who hadn't. Who hadn't gone down for it and who hadn't stopped. They'd just moved deeper into the shadows. Even if people did believe Emma, would it be worth it? She didn't want to be in the news or the tabloids or anything anymore. She was sick of it. She was sick of people talking about her and thinking they knew her and *judging* her. She didn't want to bring any more of that on herself, didn't want to bring any more of it on Jo. A statement would be bad enough for Emma's career—a slut making false accusations about an industry golden boy. Jo didn't need to be connected to that, too. She had pulled strings to get Barry to set. Emma didn't need to damage Jo's career along with her own.

Emma leaned back into the couch cushions and took out her phone. Usually she only read stuff related to the rumors if Phil or, rarely, Avery sent it to her. Googling her name brought up way more than she expected. There were articles from *today*. She clicked one.

"How do they have this *already?*" she asked her empty apartment.

It was an article about Jo cutting her down on set. There were quotes from a source; the leak was apparently back, because they knew exactly what had happened. They knew Jo had told her no one cared about her opinions, knew she got dismissed after returning with the iced latte.

Emma clicked away from the article to text Jo.

> Somebody on set is leaking stuff to the press. There's already an article about me talking back to Barry and everything.

The article went on to talk about Jo being seen with her former costar. Emma knew now that they weren't dating, but the author of this article didn't. They posited that Jo and Emma had broken up. That was good, Emma supposed. If no one thought they were together, maybe she didn't have to worry about being comfortable in Jo's office or laughing at her jokes or whatever else people saw and decided meant more than it did.

I know. Not much can be done without it looking like I'm
going on a witch hunt for my girlfriend's sake.

Jo calling her her girlfriend made the butterflies in Emma's
stomach flutter, even though it was obviously a joke.

Didn't you see? Emma texted back. We're not girlfriends anymore.
Apparently you broke my heart.

She was quoting the source from the article, who said she'd
been sad for a week, but it felt weird anyway. The source was *right*,
was the thing, and Emma's sadness *was* because of Jo. It wasn't
actually hard to see how everything had been misconstrued.

That doesn't sound very plausible, Jo texted, just as Emma was
thinking about how plausible it was. Another text came through
quickly: Hopefully the idea that we've "broken up" sticks. It will be nice
to be rid of these rumors.

Go out with that former costar again and we should be fine.

Emma typed it but didn't hit send. It felt weird, felt jealous. It
showed she was aware of Jo's actions outside of work even when
they hadn't talked about them, and that definitely felt weird. Jo
had probably read an article by now, anyway, probably saw exactly
what Emma saw, things saying she and Sam Allen were now dating. Emma didn't need to point it out.

I'll try to look appropriately depressed at work, Emma texted instead.

The three dots showing that Jo was typing appeared for a long
time before Emma got her next message.

I meant it when I said I want work to
be a place you can thrive. Don't let any
rumors, or anything at all, prevent that.

I know, boss.

Emma kept their conversation open. The three little dots appeared on and off for almost five minutes. Jo didn't send another text.

Emma opened a new message and texted her sister that they should hang out tomorrow after work. She'd tell Avery about Barry, she would, but she was going to take care of herself tonight. That meant ordering in Vietnamese and drawing herself a bath after dinner. She kept the bathroom lights off, lay back in her tub illuminated only by candlelight. She considered getting a cat—something easy to take care of, but something she could snuggle after hard days. She couldn't keep asking her sister to bring over the rottweilers. Avery was the one who suggested it this time, actually, which meant she must have figured out things hadn't gone well today. Maybe she'd read about Emma and Jo's "breakup," and thought Emma was sad about that. Emma really hoped the breakup stuck. Anything to get her out of the tabloids.

As Emma dried off and got into her pajamas, she wondered what would happen when Jo left *Innocents*. She wasn't so naively idealistic to think that Jo could be interested in her if she wasn't an employee, but she hoped they'd end up friends.

JO STOPPED BESIDE EMMA'S desk the next morning.

"Thanks for the chai," Emma said, raising the drink in question at Jo.

Jo half smiled, but her brow was furrowed, worry lines around her eyes. Emma's stomach flipped at Jo's concern.

"I'm fine," Emma said before Jo could ask.

"If you don't want to be here today, that's okay," Jo said. "You can—"

"I'm fine, boss," Emma said again. "I'm good."

"If you need anything, you'll let me know?" It was more question than command.

"I will."

"Okay."

Emma's heart beat double time as she and Jo held eye contact. Eventually, Emma gave a roll of her eyes—both at herself and Jo—with a smile.

"Your script isn't going to edit itself," she said.

"Right," Jo said. Her smile was weak. "Okay."

She went into her office, leaving the door open behind her.

Jo was supposed to be writing all day. Only taking breaks to troubleshoot if anyone needed anything on set. Days like this, she usually stayed behind her desk for hours.

Today she came out and leaned against the doorjamb after less than an hour.

"You okay?" she asked.

Emma ducked her head in an approximation of a nod. Jo's attentiveness made her warm all over. She had to get ahold of herself. There was no way she'd survive this crush if she blushed during every interaction.

Jo went back into her office. When Emma sneaked in later to check if she needed a refill, Jo held her tumbler away from Emma's hands.

"Is there anything you need?" she said.

Emma let out an exasperated chuckle. "I need to refill your coffee, Jo," she said. "I need to do my job."

"You know if you need time—"

"You're making it weirder by asking every hour how I am." Emma wasn't lying when she said, "I really am okay, boss."

Jo smiled softly at her. Emma's stomach went wobbly. She reminded herself that the crush didn't matter. Nothing would ever happen between them, but that was okay. Being Jo's friend—and they were friends, even if Jo was her boss, that didn't mean they weren't friends—wasn't a consolation prize. Emma liked the way Jo relied on her. She liked everything about Jo, and she liked it before she figured out she had feelings. The crush didn't have to change anything between them. As long as she could pull it together and stop the swooping feeling in her stomach every time Jo looked at her.

Jo's face went more serious. "I want to do something about this."

"I *don't*," Emma said. It was easier to think about her feelings for Jo than about everything that had happened with Barry. "I don't want to cause any trouble. I just—I know I should. I know I should stand up and do what I can to make sure he doesn't do this to anyone else but—"

"His behavior is not your responsibility," Jo said. "You don't need that weight on your shoulders. I completely understand why you wouldn't want to say anything."

Emma let out her breath, her shoulders sagging.

"But I am asking—you don't have to do anything," Jo said. "But I'm asking your permission to do things on my own. I know you don't want me to release a statement about why he wasn't hired, and I won't. But what's the use of being a former child star Hollywood darling if I can't stand up for people who can't do it on their own? You can't possibly be the only person he has said something like this to. I want to bring him down."

Emma shrugged, feeling helpless. "I don't want to be a part of it."

"You don't have to," Jo said. "I was just going to do it, without asking, but . . . it seemed better to tell you."

Emma heard everything Jo wasn't saying. They'd only just—*made up* might not be the right term, but it was all she could think of. They'd just made up after a fight because Jo didn't tell her things. Emma hadn't been moved by Jo's first apology because it felt like an empty gesture. But this one was more than words—Jo was backing it up with actions. Still, Emma didn't want to be involved.

"I don't want to be a part of it," she said again. "At least not right now. I don't want to know about it. I really appreciate you telling me, but . . . I don't want to know anything else. You can do whatever, just keep me out of it."

"Okay," Jo said. "Thank you."

"Thank you."

EMMA ATE LUNCH WITH Phil, and he gave her such a pitying look that she knew he thought she was pathetic.

"How *are* things with you and Jo?" Phil asked.

"Fine," Emma said immediately. She didn't want to talk about it. Didn't want to explain how Jo's reaction to what Barry had said made her feel safe. She didn't want to tell anyone else what Barry said, but she wasn't sure she could adequately describe how things were between her and Jo without it.

"Girl, she tore you *apart* yesterday," Phil said.

"Yeah but she apologized." Emma shrugged. "She says I was right."

"So you kissed and made up?"

Chantal walked by then, and by the look she gave them, she probably overheard.

Emma smacked Phil's arm and rolled her eyes. "You know we

were never actually dating," she said. "But thank God the tabloids have decided we broke up. Now people can stop thinking I'm fucking my way into the business."

Phil bumped his shoulder against hers. "I know I tease you, but were the rumors really that bad?"

"Yeah," Emma said, no hesitation. "They were."

"I guess I'll stop selling my stories to the tabloids then."

Emma rolled her eyes again. "Hopefully whoever on set actually *is* stops. Or hopefully they're at least in the camp who thinks we 'broke up' or whatever." She thought about Chantal walking by, wondered if there would be an article about how Jo and Emma kissed and made up. But Chantal had worked with Jo for *years*; she didn't seem a likely leak. Emma looked around. No one else was close enough to hear her conversation with Phil. "I don't understand why anyone here would tell tabloids Jo and I were together. Surely people who actually see us interact know we're not?"

As soon as it was out of her mouth, she expected Phil to make a joke about the way she looked at Jo or something. It was his style, and usually it made her laugh, but she was sick of it at her expense. Especially now. How exactly *did* she look at Jo?

But Phil just shrugged. "Money makes people do dumb stuff."

Emma bumped their shoulders again and smiled as she finished her lunch.

OVERALL, THE DAY WENT well. Sure, there were a few times when someone mentioned Barry Davis and Emma's whole body went stiff, and she dealt with looks from the cast and crew that made it clear that even people who hadn't been present when Jo had yelled at her knew Jo yelled at her, but she didn't particularly care. Because Jo kept checking on her, brows furrowed with concern. Every time Jo looked at her, Emma's muscles went loose and warm. When she really thought about it, it wasn't all that different from how she always felt around Jo. She was just aware of what the feelings were now. God, she could literally never tell her sister. She'd never hear the end of it.

She was so focused on Jo all day, Emma actually forgot she had to tell Avery about what happened with Barry. She was reminded when the first thing Avery did when she arrived at Emma's apartment was open her arms for a hug. Emma sank into it, let her sister hold her up for a moment. Avery squeezed tight, the bag in her hand heavy against Emma's back and Cassius waiting patiently at their feet.

"I brought dinner," Avery said.

Dinner was a loaf of crusty sourdough bread and six different kinds of cheese.

"You didn't need to bring comfort food, Ave," Emma laughed.

Her chest was warm, though, at how much her sister wanted to take care of her.

"There's never not a time for grilled cheese, okay?"

Emma couldn't disagree.

Avery sneaked concerned glances at Emma as she got to work making dinner. Emma sat on the floor with her back against the back of her couch, let Cassius climb into her lap. She and Avery chatted about the bakery while Avery cut medium-thick slices of bread and slathered one side of each with butter.

"I kind of assume you read something about me and Jo, right?" Emma eased into her story.

"I might've," Avery said. "It didn't sound good."

"I know! It's wonderful," Emma said, and Avery gave her a quizzical look. "That people think we're broken up? I hope the story sticks, because then we'll finally be *left alone*."

"Yeah, I get that, but . . ." Avery got a pan heating up on Emma's stove. "Don't you *not* want Jo yelling at you in front of half the show?"

Emma smiled, shrugging one shoulder. "It worked out in the end."

She scratched Cassius behind the ears and stole some of his strength to explain what happened. She told Avery about yelling at Barry over bad direction and getting cut down by Jo, told her how Jo apologized afterward, for everything. She said nothing about the irony that the tabloids decided they'd broken up at the same time Emma had realized she actually had a crush.

Avery looked dubious. "So the two of you are suddenly okay now?"

"I mean, I guess it is a little sudden, yeah, but—things have gone back to normal so easily," Emma said. "I look forward to going to work again."

She didn't tell Avery about Jo coming out to her. Avery already thought Jo was queer, and Emma wasn't here to out anyone, not even to her sister, who would never tell anyone, including Dylan, if Emma didn't want her to. Plus, Emma may have had other reasons to not want to invite discussion of Jo's dating preferences. Selfish reasons.

Avery piled cheese onto a piece of bread, butter side down, in the now-hot pan. She put another piece of bread on top. She didn't say anything more as she cooked, letting Emma chatter about things with Jo and how she'd probably be able to come to the twins' last baseball game tomorrow.

When the sandwiches were ready, Avery took their plates and set up on the couch. Emma poured herself a huge glass of milk, poured her sister a smaller one before joining her in the living room. Cassius came to lie at their feet, but he knew better than to even consider begging.

"So Barry Davis wasn't the greatest guy in the world like you thought he might be?" Avery asked. She was lighthearted about it, while Emma's chest tightened in a way she'd gotten used to over the day. "You didn't fall madly in love with his talent or anything?"

"Please don't even joke about that," Emma said, disgusted. "He was very definitely not great, turns out."

"Not great?"

"Not great," Emma repeated. She tried for nonchalant, her voice breezy. She took a bite of her sandwich before continuing. "Okay, first of all, this is delicious and I love you."

Avery tipped her glass of milk at her.

"Anyway," Emma said, "he kind of acted like since of course I'm sleeping with Jo, I shouldn't have a problem, like, giving him a hand job, for opportunities. Though honestly I think if I were sleeping with someone for a job, I'd be more than an assistant at this point."

Avery didn't laugh at the joke. She stared at Emma, cheese oozing out of the sandwich in her hand and stretching toward the plate below.

"He propositioned you?" she asked.

"Eh, I guess?" Emma waved her hand, acting like he didn't very explicitly proposition her. It hadn't been a comment taken out of context. "He was a dick. And he's definitely *not* my favorite director anymore."

"Em," Avery said.

Emma knew she wanted more information, wanted to talk it out. But Emma didn't. She didn't want to talk about it or think about it or do anything about it. She was focusing on good things.

"Don't worry about it," she said. "I got to yell at him, and Jo was really supportive when I told her. He's not going to direct. I'm never going to have to see him again."

Avery set aside her plate. "Emma, are you okay?"

Emma sighed. She gave her sister a smile. "I'm fine," she said. It got truer every time she said it. "I'm going to talk to Rabbi Blumofe about it over the weekend. You don't need to worry about me."

"I'm your older sister, of *course* I need to worry about you."

Avery climbed right into her space on the couch, wrapped both arms around her. Emma held her sandwich as far away as she could so it didn't make a mess, but she didn't pull back.

After they'd finished dinner and were flipping through streaming shows to find something to watch, Emma's phone buzzed, *Mom* flashing across the screen when she grabbed it off the table.

"Hello, it's your favorite daughter," Emma said as she picked up the phone, grinning at Avery, who rolled her eyes.

"Hi, honey," her mom said. "How are you doing?"

"Good," Emma said. "Avery's over. She made me dinner."

"Oh good," her mom said. "She's taking good care of you?"

Avery was currently tearing up her napkin, rolling the pieces into balls, and flicking them at Emma, so she wasn't sure it counted as taking good care of her.

"Why would she need to be taking care of me, Mother?" Emma was fairly certain she knew the answer.

"Well . . . you know . . . I heard that you might need it."

Emma laughed. "You've been reading the tabloids and now you need to call to check in on me?"

"Sometimes it seems like the tabloids are the only way I can find out what's happening in your life," her mom huffed. "You don't call enough."

It was her standard line, even though Emma called every Saturday, and usually at least once more during the week.

"I'm fine, Mom," Emma said. "Jo and I actually are on better terms, regardless of what the tabloids say."

"Right."

Avery sent a napkin ball directly into Emma's eye. Emma cursed under her breath.

"I have to go beat up your useless eldest," she said. "I promise I'm fine. I'll call this weekend, okay?"

"Okay, okay," her mom said. "I love you."

"Love you, Mom."

Emma hung up the phone and launched herself at her sister.

Emma had three inches on Avery, long legs and a runner's body, but Avery was built like a weight lifter. She wrestled Emma from the couch to the ground and almost had her pinned—much to Cassius's distress—when Emma resorted to tickling. She didn't relent until Avery called uncle.

"I hate you," Avery said afterward, still clutching her side.

"Sure you do," Emma said. "That's why you came over with comfort food and that superworried look on your face? Super hateful."

Avery shoved Emma's shoulder but then held up her hands in defeat when Emma made to start up their battle again.

"Fine," Avery said as she got resituated on the couch. "I, like, love you and stuff."

"I, like, love you and stuff, too." Emma plopped on the cushion next to her. "And don't tell Mom about anything, okay? I don't want her worrying about me, too. I'm fine, I swear."

"Okay," Avery said quietly. "But you know you don't have to feel ashamed or anything. You can tell her, if you want."

"I know, Ave," Emma said.

She wasn't ashamed, but she didn't want to deal with it.

"So I'm not going to tell Mom or tell you how to react to this whole situation or anything," Avery said, "but if I ever meet Barry Davis, I'm gonna kick him in the nuts."

Emma giggled.

"Also," Avery said, scooching farther away on the couch. She patted the cushion between them. "Cash, want up?"

Cassius hesitated for only a second before joining them on the couch. Emma stared at her sister, mouth agape.

"You really *do* love me!" she said, snuggling into the dog.

"I do, but I'm picking what we watch," Avery said.

"Deal."

13

JO

J O DIDN'T KNOW WHAT SHE WAS GOING TO SAY TO EMMA when she handed over her coffee Thursday morning. She stopped beside her desk. Opened her mouth and—

"You're coming to the game tonight, right?" It came tumbling out. She didn't let Emma answer. "It's the last game and the team is going for ice cream after. I can drive you, if you'd like. You can't miss the last game."

Emma blinked. "I was going to go home first," she said. "I didn't bring clothes for the game. I only have this."

"This" being the navy-blue dress with white piping that she had on, that was altogether too fancy for a baseball game. Emma looked good in it. Jo noticed and then set the thought aside.

"You can go home at lunch and change, or get clothes to change into at least," Jo said. She looked away. "If you'd prefer I can avoid the bleachers. You can sit there with your sister and—"

"Don't be ridiculous," Emma said. "I'll sit by you. We're okay."

"Of course," Jo said.

She still felt like the other shoe was about to drop.

"I'll change before we go," Emma said. "I'd appreciate the ride, thank you."

She smiled like Jo was made of glass. Jo gave Emma a nod and headed into her office.

Perhaps the other shoe had already dropped in the form of Barry Davis. After Emma had left Tuesday, after she told Jo Barry harassed her, Jo stood silently in her office. She had wanted to scream. She still did, a little. Barry's assistant had called yesterday, but Jo couldn't answer the phone. She'd tear into him if she talked to him right now, and that wasn't going to help anyone. She had to get it together. Had to figure out how to turn him down and ruin his career without any fallout for Emma.

Emma didn't want to release a statement, and as much as Jo hated that, she understood. This was the industry that ostracized Jo for calling out racism, and that was when she was a household name. Emma was an assistant. But Jo was rich enough now, established enough. This was something she had to do.

AVERY CALLED JO MIDMORNING. Jo could hear the rage in her voice when she said hello.

"You're doing something about this, yeah?" Avery said, no small talk first.

"Of course," Jo said. "It may take some time but—yes. Of course I'm doing something."

"When she told me—God, I want to kill him."

"I brought him here, Avery." Jo said the thing that had been bothering her since she found out. "I invited him into our workplace. I'm the one who fucking introduced them."

"He's the asshole who did it, Jo," Avery said. "This isn't on you any more than it's on Emma, and you know it's not on her."

Of course it wasn't on Emma. But *she* should've known. She shared an industry with Barry Davis. She should have heard something.

"You're really rich," Avery said. "Surely you have enough money to have him murdered."

Jo barked a laugh at that. "I can't say I haven't considered it."

The tension broke a little. Jo could hear the grin in Avery's voice as she joked, "Is this a secure line?"

They spent fifteen minutes sharing more and more gruesome ideas about what to do with Barry Davis. If anyone *were* listening on the line, Jo and Avery would probably both be arrested.

Jo hung up feeling better than she had in a week.

EMMA RAN HOME TO change before they left. She returned in jean shorts and a thin plaid button-down over a white tank top.

Jo drove to the game, telling herself the whole ride that this didn't have to be awkward. She and Emma had been in a car together plenty of times. But it was strange to have Emma in a car that was actually hers, that didn't belong to a car service and get switched out every day so it was always perfectly clean. Instead there was a receipt on the floor beneath Emma's feet. Jo's travel mug was in the cup holder between them. The coffee Emma handed her every morning was always at least the second cup of the day, sometimes the third.

After surviving the stilted conversation in the car, they arrived, late enough that Avery, Dylan, Vincent, and Sally were all already seated. Avery and Vincent smirked at them as they climbed the bleachers.

"Your jerk boss let you take the afternoon off?" Vincent asked Emma.

Emma gave him a little smile. Jo rolled her eyes. She hugged Sally and gave Thomas, her younger nephew, a high five.

"You ready for ice cream after the game?" she asked him.

"Yeah!" he shouted. He tugged on his dad's arm. "Ice cream! Ice cream!"

"Thanks for that," Vincent muttered when he hugged her.

Jo said hello to Dylan and Avery, who slid down the bleachers a bit to make room.

Not much room, though. There were exactly two seats between Avery and Vincent. It was fine, sitting next to Emma. They went so long without really talking and now they sat close enough that their thighs almost touched. Jo edged closer to her brother, making him shuffle sideways. It gave her some breathing room. She hoped none of the parents were the type to sell a picture to tabloids. The rumors would've kicked right back up if people saw them like this, looking like lesbian aunts cheering on their siblings' kids. Emma was even wearing *plaid*.

Avery bumped Emma's shoulder.

"How are you doing?" She said it quietly. Jo was sure she wasn't supposed to hear.

"I'm good," Emma said, bumping Avery's shoulder back.

Jo took a breath and relaxed.

The game was pretty much like any other game. Emma sat with them, which was new, but she didn't change much. The parents still talked sparingly, Vincent and Avery both giving Jo more trouble than she deserved, as always. At one point, as Vincent joked about how annoying it was that whenever anyone found out Jo was his sister she was all they cared about, Emma scoffed.

"Oh yes," she said. "I'm sure it's very tough for you to have a famous sister with whom you don't share a last name. Her fame is

probably worse for you than it is for her, who has paparazzi rumi-
nate about her sex life. It sounds really hard for you."

Avery burst out laughing, and Vincent promptly shut his mouth.
Jo bit down on her grin.

"Thank God," she said. "I don't usually have anyone on my side
here."

"Siblings are the worst," Emma said, as though her sister weren't
her best friend.

Vincent would probably have argued his case, but it was Ethan's
turn at bat.

Ethan already had a double, for which Jo's whole row had
stomped their feet against the bleachers beneath them. He didn't
look over before he got in the batter's box. He used to—when he
was younger he always sought out his family in the crowd for reassurance before he went up to swing. Jo could hardly believe how
fast he was growing up. She still had a flutter of nerves every time
he was up.

The first pitch was a ball.

Vincent clapped. "Good eye!"

The next pitch was wild as soon as it was out of the pitcher's
hand. It hit Ethan right in the wrist. Jo's heart jumped to her
throat. She wanted to leap to her feet and yell at the pitcher. They
were only kids, it wasn't intentional, but the ball hit her nephew in
the wrist and he was crouched down, head between his knees,
holding the injured arm to his chest. Vincent and Sally were both
tense beside her.

Jo clutched the edge of the bleacher as the coach took a look at
Ethan's arm. He was moving it, but he was also crying, Jo could
tell from the stands. Jo had broken her arm as a kid; she still remembered that sharp, agonizing pain when she landed wrong in

the middle of trying a gymnastics routine she was obviously not talented enough for. She was ready to throw Ethan in the back seat of her car and speed to a hospital.

Emma's hand came down, not quite on top of Jo's, but right next to it. Her pinkie hooked over Jo's. Jo looked at their hands, looked at Emma.

"He's okay," Emma told her. "Look at him, so tough—he's not even coming out of the game."

Emma removed her hand to clap as Ethan jogged toward first base. Jo and the rest of the parents joined in the applause. She shared a relieved look with Sally.

THE TEAM WON, WHICH was a nice way to end the season even if they were too far back in the league to make the playoffs. Everyone went to ice cream afterward, Emma squished into Avery's back seat with the twins for the ride.

Ethan's wrist was a little swollen, but he wasn't much worse for wear. Still, Jo ruffled his hair.

"A banana split for the injured hero," she suggested.

Ethan beamed at her. His parents did not. She didn't care at all. He deserved as much ice cream as he wanted.

She didn't order anything for herself, knowing she'd be able to polish off what was left of Ethan's.

She sat on the edge of a picnic table bench, and the others joined her as they got their ice cream. Emma climbed onto the middle of the bench at first, but when Dani and Ezra followed suit, she slid toward the edge, right up against Jo. She gave her a smile of apology but didn't move away. Jo shifted, just a little, just enough to give them both some more room for their upper bodies. Their hips and thighs were still pressed tight together.

No one gave them a second glance. Not even Avery smirked at her. Ethan was at the other end of the bench, half hanging off the edge but not complaining. Then there was Dani, Ezra, and Emma, with Jo on the end. Avery, Vincent, and Sally—with Thomas in her lap—sat on the other side of the table. Dylan stood behind Avery. The rest of the team and their parents were around, too— they took up every last one of the picnic tables at this place. Everyone was loud and laughing and not paying any attention to Emma, crushed into Jo's side. Emma didn't seem to mind, either. Perhaps Jo didn't need to worry about rumors that had already passed, and could just enjoy the evening. She relaxed, her shoulder coming to rest against Emma's. Emma never even paused in her discussion of the best flurry toppings with the kids.

Ethan hadn't eaten half of his ice cream when he slid it down the picnic table toward Jo. When it passed Emma, she plucked the one leftover cherry out of the whipped cream and popped it into her mouth. She didn't look contrite in the least, giving Jo a grin before doing a long lick around the edge of her ice cream. Jo looked at the leftovers of Ethan's split.

Really, Jo didn't know how to explain how glad she was that she and Emma were okay. She *missed* her. There had been a few moments where she thought Emma might just quit, and Jo was so grateful that she hadn't. She was so grateful that instead they were smiling at each other over ice cream.

After everyone was finished, the kids tired themselves out running around and playing on the ice cream shop's jungle gym. Players and their families slowly filtered out. Jo drifted in and out of her brother's conversation with Dylan, when she overheard Emma and Avery arguing.

"I took the bus back to work," Emma was saying. "You don't have to take me to the studio, just home. C'mon, Avery."

Jo cleared her throat. The sisters turned to her.

"I drove you here," Jo said. "I can drive you home. You're mostly on my way."

Emma smiled. "That'd be great."

Jo caught the smirk on Avery's face as she turned away, but she tried not to think about it too much.

Together in Jo's car once more, there was no semblance of awkward tension. Instead, Emma launched into a play-by-play of the game of tag she'd played with half the team after ice cream. She talked about Ethan getting hit by the ball, about how Dani wanted to play catcher but her parents were worried about misread pitches, foul balls, and backswings. She was so enthusiastic. Jo couldn't do anything but let her talk the whole ride.

Jo didn't consider that it might be a bad idea to be seen personally dropping Emma off at her apartment until Emma directed her onto her street.

"I'm the third building on the right," Emma said.

Jo went tense then, trying to look for paparazzi but not look like she was doing it.

Emma noticed anyway. "Oh, right," she said, like she'd also just remembered this wasn't the best idea. "But, like, I think they've lost interest. They were around after our 'breakup' and all. But once I wasn't sobbing or dressed like a slob who'd just had her heart broken, I think they gave up."

Jo hadn't been certain they'd even found where Emma lived. She wasn't sure what to make of the nonchalant way Emma brushed the idea off. How often had they been here?

"Okay," Jo said as she put on her blinker and pulled over at the steps to Emma's building.

"Thanks for driving me, boss," Emma said. "And for telling me I had to come."

Jo chuckled.

"It was great." Emma smiled so big that Jo couldn't see anything else. "Sorry not sorry I stole your cherry."

Jo raised her eyebrows, and Emma's face went bright red.

"I mean—you know what I mean!"

Jo laughed. "I do," she said. "This was fun."

Emma ducked her head. "Yeah, it was. I'll see you tomorrow."

She looked over at Jo, almost through her lashes, before opening her door and heading for her apartment. Jo waited until she was inside before pulling away.

14

JO

J O STILL HAD THE PICTURE OF HER AND EMMA IN THE TOP right drawer of her desk. The original picture. The two of them on the red carpet at the SAG Awards, fancy dresses and shining jewelry and those smiles, bright and focused only on each other. Emma had smiled at her like that after the baseball game, too. Jo had had the picture in her drawer for almost eight months now. She didn't look at it often, but sometimes . . .

Jo looked at the picture and understood, a little, why people saw something there.

There hadn't seemed to be any paparazzi outside of Emma's apartment, nor any parents selling photos from the baseball game to the tabloids. There were no articles about the two of them, no rumors since everyone decided they'd broken up. It was good. Jo never expected it to take so long, but she was glad they'd finally died down. She wondered if denying it might have been the better route, in the end, if damage had already been done to Emma's reputation, even when she never deserved it. There wasn't much to be done about that now.

Jo was pulled from her thoughts when Emma knocked on her office door Monday morning. Her jaw was set.

"Do you have a minute?"

"Of course, come in."

Emma closed the door behind her. Jo sat up straighter.

Emma came to stand in front of her desk. She stood tall, feet firmly planted, like she needed to be in a power pose to say whatever she was going to say.

"I want you to release a statement," she said. "Not with my name, but explaining why you didn't offer Barry an episode to direct."

"Are you sure?" Jo said. "I don't want you to do anything you don't want to."

"I want to," Emma said. "I talked with my rabbi. I have to do something. I know it might not work—people won't believe it or they'll believe it and it won't matter. But I have to try."

Jo nodded. She was proud of Emma for dealing with the situation at all, but especially for wanting to stand up.

"We'll get something drafted," Jo said. "I'll make sure you get to see it before we release it."

"That'd be great, thanks," Emma said, her body relaxing a bit.

"You're—" *Amazing* was the first word that came to mind, but Jo bit it back. "—strong, Ms. Kaplan. There's no right way to handle this. You're doing fine."

Emma gave her a smile. "Thanks, boss."

Emma went back to her desk while Jo scrolled through her address book to find the number of the publicist she most trusted at the Jones Dynasty.

It had been almost a week since his set visit, but she hadn't broken the news to Barry yet. She was still too angry to even talk to him on the phone. Breaking it to him through a press release sounded much more fun.

Jo put a rush on the statement. She wanted to get this out as soon as possible. In the meantime, she wasn't sure it was the best idea, but she called Annabeth Pierce. Annabeth's first movie had been a Barry Davis movie. She was a big-name actress now, but she was a nobody then, and if Jo knew men like Barry Davis, she knew what that meant.

Annabeth's agent gave Jo Annabeth's number without a moment's hesitation. He probably thought this meant Jo wanted her for a cameo appearance or maybe a role in Agent Silver, and she let him. She had to be delicate about this.

She and Annabeth made the standard small talk for a few minutes before Jo mentioned Barry.

"Barry Davis visited set the other day, actually," she said breezily. "He directed your first big film, right?"

"Yes, ma'am," Annabeth said. "That was Barry."

Her voice hadn't changed at all, still nothing but chipper with that hint of a Georgian accent.

"It was possible that he might direct an episode," Jo said. "Though that is not what is going to happen." She paused. Annabeth said nothing. "I imagine you might know why that's not going to happen."

If Jo was wrong about this . . .

The quiet way Annabeth said, "Why would I know?" confirmed she wasn't.

"My production company will be releasing a statement, probably tomorrow morning, about exactly why he was not extended an invitation to direct," Jo said. "Based on his behavior toward a young woman in my employ—his behavior that I will not tolerate.

He does not have a heads-up about this, but I wanted you to. Just in case."

"Right," Annabeth said.

Jo let the silence hang.

Eventually, Annabeth took a deep breath on the other end of the line. "I really appreciate that, Ms. Jones," she said. "I don't mean to rush you off the phone, but I think perhaps I should talk to my publicist."

"Please call me if you need anything, Ms. Pierce," Jo said.

"Yes, ma'am. Thank you for the call."

JO HAD THE STATEMENT by the afternoon. She should've probably trusted the people whose job it was to write these things, but she made a few minor edits anyway. Then she called Emma into her office.

"I have it," she said, pushing the printed statement across her desk. "I thought you might want to read it in here."

Jo wanted to give Emma the space to have whatever reaction she needed to.

"I'm going to get a refill," Jo said. "I'll close the door behind me and you can open it whenever you're ready?"

Emma nodded. She looked sick to her stomach. Jo took her tumbler and headed out. She wanted to offer Emma some form of comfort, squeeze her hand or pat her on the back, but she didn't think it was appropriate, didn't *ever* want to touch Emma in a way she didn't want. Instead she gave Emma the room, closing the door gently behind her.

The door was open by the time Jo returned. Emma was sitting on her couch, working on her tablet, which she set aside when Jo came back into her office. Emma smiled, and the tension in Jo's shoulders eased.

"It's a good statement," Emma said.

"Good," Jo said. "I agree." She sat in her desk chair. "It'll be released tomorrow, first thing in the morning. Probably before you even get in."

Emma got up to stand in front of Jo's desk.

"Tonight, set your phone so it goes straight to voicemail," Jo said. "Record a new voicemail reminding people who they should contact if asking for a comment. You don't need to deal with any calls tomorrow. Maybe not the next day, either."

"Okay." Emma nodded. Her eyebrows pinched together.

"We don't have to do it if you don't want to," Jo reminded her.

"I want to," Emma said immediately. She took a deep breath. "I'm nervous. But I want to."

"I wouldn't be surprised if it's the talk of the crew tomorrow," Jo said. "Cast, too, maybe. Make sure you're ready for that. I don't want you to be caught off guard."

"Thanks, boss."

Jo didn't know who else Emma had told. Avery, of course, but perhaps that was it. Jo hoped no one figured out who it was from the statement. She didn't want Emma to have to reveal it to anyone if she didn't want to. It was a vague statement, no names but Barry's and Jo's, but still. Jo worried.

THE PRESS RELEASE WAS live by the time Jo woke up in the morning. She made herself an espresso from the machine next to her bed and read hot takes while she sipped it. There was a lot of dissecting her background, discussing how she'd never shied away from controversy, the way she called out *The Johnson Dynasty* all those years ago, how she went to bat for her crew in her own contract negotiations. Her history meant most people believed the statement, thankfully.

By the time she got to work, there was a new article. An article with quotes from Annabeth Pierce and three other actresses detailing further harassment from Barry Davis. Jo felt like she should have a bucket of popcorn as she scrolled through the news. She shared a secret grin with Emma when she came into Jo's office to ask a question about the filming schedule. Once Annabeth Pierce came forward, no one bothered trying to find out who Barry harassed on the *Innocents* set—they had bigger fish to fry now.

Jo had to say something to the cast and crew. She was right that it was all anyone was talking about, and it was both distracting and not something she wanted to make Emma relive in conversation after conversation.

She went to the soundstage as everyone returned from lunch. All she had to do to get quiet was raise her hands.

"I'm sure you've all heard the news about Barry Davis." She breathed through her nose, decided to show most of her cards. "I am furious about this situation. That he thought he could do this to a member of the *Innocents* family. I don't have words for how angry I am." They could probably tell anyway, the way her voice shook. "I know this has been established from day one, but behavior like his will not be tolerated. Not from Oscar-nominated directors, not from Emmy-winning writers, not from a gaffer or a deliveryman or anyone. If you have ever been sexually harassed or assaulted by anyone on this set—" She took a steadying breath. "I'm not telling you you have to come to me, because you can deal with it however is right for you. But I am telling you that if you come to me, anonymously or otherwise, I will stand by you. I will have *zero* tolerance."

Everyone stayed silent.

"Okay," Jo said. "Back to work."

EVELYN CALLED THAT NIGHT while Jo ate takeout.

"It was Emma, wasn't it?" she said as soon as Jo picked up. "No wonder she talked back to him."

"Hello to you, too," Jo said. "And I didn't say it was Emma."

"You didn't," Evelyn agreed. "But it was. Wow, okay, so that gives a lot of context to the whole you and her suddenly being okay with each other."

It did, Jo supposed. Would Emma have forgiven her if this other terrible thing hadn't cropped up? She'd rather still be fighting, as much as she hated that, than have Emma forced to deal with this.

"I'm surprised the rumors haven't kicked back up about the two of you," Evelyn said. "Given how white knight you're probably going for her."

Jo scoffed. "I'm not going *white knight* for her."

"Releasing a statement and—and I'm just guessing here, but I know you, and you're a badass, so I'm probably right—contacting and forewarning other actresses you figured he harassed? A coordinated effort to fuck up his career? Seems pretty white knight to me."

"Fine," Jo said, "but it's not *for* Emma. I'd do the same regardless of who he harassed because he is a disgusting excuse for a—"

"Yeah, yeah," Evelyn said, and Jo could picture her in her apartment, waving Jo off. "Down, girl."

Jo picked up a piece of chicken with her chopsticks and popped it into her mouth. When she finished chewing, she said, "I need lawyers."

"You mean for after you kill Barry Davis?"

"We both know I could make it look like an accident," Jo said. "But seriously. Sexual harassment lawyers. Libel lawyers. Any type of lawyer that could help a victim come forward if a celebrity harassed or assaulted them."

"What are you planning?" Evelyn asked.

"I'm not sure yet," Jo said. "I've got to talk to people. Figure it out. I know it's not your specialty, but you have contacts. Put me in touch with the right people."

"God, you're a bulldog," Evelyn said.

It wasn't an actual solution—it wasn't changing the Hollywood culture, the *societal* culture of the way men treat women. Support after the fact wasn't as good as prevention. But it was something.

"You'll get me names?" Jo asked.

"I'll reach out to some people tomorrow," Evelyn said.

"Good people."

"As if I associate with anyone else."

EMMA TURNED HER PHONE back on Thursday morning, but even then she was so inundated with calls that Jo had her turn it off again. No phone made for a quiet week. Not many people had Jo's direct line, for good reason, but it rang Friday afternoon. Jo didn't recognize the number, which at least meant it was neither *Innocents'* network nor Agent Silver's studio.

Instead, it was Annabeth.

"I hope your week hasn't been too hard," Jo said.

"Lord, it's been a *disaster*," Annabeth said, but she was laughing. "In a good way, if that's possible."

"I've had good disaster weeks," Jo said. "Though I doubt any of them were particularly like your week."

"Probably not."

"You've done well," Jo said. "Handled it well."

"Thank you," Annabeth said. "I'm actually calling to thank you anyway. For the heads-up. For the kick in the behind to make me step forward."

Jo didn't like that phrasing. "Ms. Pierce, I didn't mean to push you into anything you didn't want to do."

"First of all, call me Annabeth," she said. "And I know you didn't. You *not* pushing me is what I needed to finally decide to do it. Which was the right choice for me. Thank you."

"You're welcome."

"And bless his heart, Barry didn't know what hit him," Annabeth laughed.

Jo chuckled. Barry's people had attempted damage control all week, not to much avail. More women had stepped forward. If it had just been about discrediting Jo and the anonymous employee from *Innocents*, he might have been able to do it, but this? He was drowning, and it was beautiful. It reaffirmed Jo's desire to do it to every scumbag in Hollywood.

"I'm thinking of funding a group of publicists and lawyers," she told Annabeth. "To help women who want to speak out. Get their statements organized, protect them from any lawsuits or threats."

"That's great in theory," Annabeth said, "but there's more to it than that. I wouldn't have said anything back during my first movie even if I had lawyers and publicists. That's not really going to help a teenage actress on the edge of stardom—she's going to put up with a lot because she thinks it's the price of fame. I tell you this from experience."

"It shouldn't be," Jo growled. She was quick to anger on this subject, but she tried to reel it in. "I want to do something to stop the perception that women have to put up with this as the price of fame."

"You'd have to connect the victims with other job opportunities. Somehow ensure they wouldn't end their careers by saying something." Annabeth paused, changing tack. "And victims shouldn't have to speak out. That's not always the best choice for them personally. You don't want to be forcing this on people not ready for it."

Jo rubbed her forehead. "I want to make a safe space," she said. "Where victims have access to everything that could help them, no matter the path that's right for them."

Annabeth was quiet for a moment. When she spoke again, there was a spark in her voice.

"You need counselors, as well as the publicists and lawyers," she said. "Counselors and other actresses, who have been through it—like mentors. Who can help you through it professionally."

"Not just actresses," Jo jumped in. "Any job in Hollywood."

"And there'd be records," Annabeth said. "Even if someone didn't want to come forward, there would be records on each abuser. If a later victim comes forward, the organization—or whatever this is we're dreaming up—can say, 'Three other women have made such complaints about this man.'"

"That's good," Jo said. "Smart."

"God, this thing would have to be huge," Annabeth said. "It'd take so much money."

"Good thing there isn't exactly a dearth of that between the two of us."

"Are you serious?"

"Absolutely," Jo said with no hesitation. "I'd love to have you with me on this, but I'll be doing it regardless."

"I'm with you."

"A friend has already put me in touch with lawyers who may be interested," Jo said. "It's going to take a lot of logistics, but we'll get there."

Her adrenaline pumped. She'd never been one to sit on the sidelines. Being productive was how she worked through every-thing. It was a lot easier to focus on starting this organization than on how angry she was.

SHE TOLD EMMA ABOUT the project the next week.

"I'm doing more about this situation than just releasing the state-ment," Jo said. "I'm happy to include you in that or work on it sepa-rately from you. Your level of involvement is completely up to you."

Emma looked apprehensive. "What more are you doing?"

"It's not clear yet," Jo said. "Some sort of foundation, nonprofit—some kind of organization to support people facing sexual harass-ment and assault in Hollywood. It's in the idea stage right now, but the plan is to include trained counselors, publicists who can work on the process of releasing statements and everything in-volved with going public, and lawyers to protect victims from threats and retaliation."

Jo tried not to shift under the way Emma stared at her.

"Boss . . ." Emma trailed off. "Are you serious?"

"Of course," Jo said. "It's something that needs to exist, and I have the money and influence to build it. I have to."

"Jo, that is amazing," Emma said. Jo looked away. "That is just—it's such a good way to use your money and celebrity. It's a really great idea."

"I wish it was something I came up with before this happened to you," Jo said quietly.

"Well, I'm glad you've come up with it now," Emma said. "It makes me feel like something good is coming out of this whole thing."

Jo didn't know how to take the compliment, so she moved on.

"There will be a lot of phone calls and meetings as this gets started," she said. "I can deal with everything directly, if you don't want to be a part of it, or——"

"I want to be a part of it," Emma said. "And c'mon, I'm not going to make you set up your own schedule while you try to create a foundation from nothing. Even if I didn't want to be a part of it, I wouldn't stop doing my job."

"You could," Jo said, and Emma gave her a look. "Sexual harassment is a serious issue. If a part of your job made dealing with it worse, I would completely support you not doing that part of your job."

"Jo, that's ridiculous," Emma laughed. "I'm your assistant. I'm going to answer your phone calls and schedule your meetings. I appreciate how much you're willing to work with me on this but I'm not that fragile."

"I don't think you're fragile, Ms. Kaplan."

Emma shrugged at her. "Just let me do my job, boss. Especially because it sounds like you're going to be pretty busy. Let me know whatever you need me to take care of for the organization, or whatever it's going to be."

Jo nodded. She should have known Emma would want to be a part of it, wouldn't want to back down.

EMMA WAS RIGHT; WORK was busy. Chantal mostly ran *Innocents* as things picked up with Agent Silver. Jo's script—the second draft, of course, as the first was a trash fire—was out with other writers, for critique and revision. Jo bounced back and forth between scripts, dealing with the production side of things, too. Beyond that, she had the Cassandra Project, as they called it for now. They named it after the figure from Greek mythology to acknowledge that for too long women hadn't been believed when it came to sexual harassment and assault. With how busy Jo was, making time for dress fittings for the Emmys was even more annoying than usual.

Emma was there through it all, smoothing out issues with Jo's schedule, making sure she ate, making everything easier, as usual. Friday, after Jo's final dress fitting, Emma was in her office. She gave Jo a brief rundown of the following week's shooting schedule, then asked if there was anything else.

Jo chewed her bottom lip. "Do you want to come to the Emmys?"

The ceremony was Sunday. She was basically doing what she'd done with the SAG Awards, inviting Emma days before. Except she was actually inviting her this time, not simply demanding she come.

Emma laughed at first, but swallowed it back when she saw Jo was serious.

"We just got these rumors to stop," Emma said. "You really want to get into them again?"

Jo sighed.

"No," she said. "But I don't want to go to the damn Emmys, either."

"Why not?"

She gestured vaguely. "Things like the GLAADs and the Golden Globes can be fun," she said. "The GLAADs are important and everyone gets drunk at the Globes. But for the most part, awards shows are people in uncomfortable clothes thinking too highly of themselves, giving each other awards."

"You didn't seem to have too terrible a time at the SAGs," Emma said.

"Yes, well, you were there," Jo said. She realized that shouldn't have been enough to be an explanation, and went on. "You were a good buffer and a good distraction." She wasn't sure she was helping her case. "When I go alone, people think they can just come up and talk to me whenever they want. You may not have known it, but at the SAGs you saved me from at least five conversations with people I hate."

Emma giggled. She tucked her hair behind her ear.

"I mean, I could come with you to the Emmys, I guess," she said, not sounding certain of it. "If you wanted."

Jo looked at her. She did want. She wanted so much. Emma stared back, blinked those big brown eyes. Jo forced out a chuckle.

"Nah," she said. "You hated the red carpet. And you're right—we just got out from under the rumors. How stupid would we be to stoke them again?"

"Right."

"Thank you, though," Jo said. "For the thought."

"Of course, boss," Emma said.

She gave her a lopsided smile. Jo closed her eyes and took a breath.

"Sometimes I think I should apologize for not disputing the rumors," she admitted.

"What?" Emma blinked at her, incredulous. "No, boss, you've never commented on your love life. In no way should you have commented on it just because I was involved."

"Except it wasn't just about people thinking they knew my sex life," Jo said. "People think you slept your way into this job, which is wrong, unreasonable, and not fair to you. And I don't know if saying something would have prevented that, but I think I should have tried."

"We've both survived," Emma said. She shrugged. "And I love

my job. I love it even if people think I slept my way into it. I love this show and I love being your assistant." Emma scuffed the bottom of her ballet flat against the carpet. "I'm excited to move to associate producer. I know it's a step toward directing. But . . . I'm going to miss this."

Jo took a deep breath, warmth radiating out from behind her sternum. "Yeah," she said. "Me, too."

Emma smiled and returned to her desk. Jo went back to work. Before she left for the weekend, she looked at the picture in her top drawer. She sighed, wishing the Emmys would be as good as that night.

SUNDAY AFTERNOON, AS JO was getting her hair done, her phone buzzed. She hadn't checked it since before lunch; no one needed her on days of awards shows. But she made Jaden stop curling her hair for a moment so she could reach for it.

There was a missed text from the morning, from Emma: I hope Kelli et al are treating you well.

Then the recent message: Is Jaden talking your ear off?

Jo bit down on her grin. She texted back: He's in the middle of a very in-depth story involving a distant relative's cat.

"What are you smiling at?" Kelli asked.

Jo locked her phone. "Nothing."

Her attendants shared a look.

"Did the girlfriend text?"

Jo rolled her eyes. "I thought we broke up."

Kelli grinned like she was baring her teeth. "So you're not denying she texted."

"I'm keeping her updated on Jaden's mother's cousin's daughter's cat," Jo said. "She's very invested."

The conversation shifted to teasing Jaden, and Jo relaxed.

She kept her phone in her hand, and Emma kept texting. Nothing important. She was watching an arrivals show with her sister. Jo couldn't imagine who would be arriving this early before the ceremony. She was going earlier than usual herself, taking time to do an interview or two about the Cassandra Project.

I have a real hankering for pigs in a blanket right about now, Emma texted, and Jo had to swallow her laugh. Emma immediately followed it up with: Actually, I made Avery make us some so I'm literally eating them right now.

You have a pretty good sister, Jo texted back.

She's not terrible.

Eventually, Jo had to actually go to the theater. She let herself be handled on the red carpet a bit more than usual, went where she was supposed to go, and ended up doing *four* separate interviews. As soon as she was off the red carpet and inside, she checked her phone. She'd missed three messages from Emma.

Wow. You look really nice, boss.

The interview with E! was great!

Seriously if you're not on a best-dressed list, they're wrong.

Jo grinned to herself and found her table next to Chantal and the cast.

She didn't turn off her phone during the ceremony. She kept it in her clutch and checked it on commercial breaks. Emma worked just as well as a buffer through the phone as she did in real life, though it was less fun texting. Jo much preferred the SAGs, muttering things under her breath with Emma beside her, trying not to laugh. Laughing emojis and *lol*s weren't the same as the way Emma bit the corner of her mouth to keep a chuckle in.

15

JO

A FEW WEEKS AFTER THE EMMYS, THERE WAS A QUIET KNOCK on Jo's door. She looked up to see Emma, and Jo smiled until she registered the look on her assistant's face.

"What's wrong?"

"Your father called," Emma said. "He's planning to stop by around lunch."

Jo's spine straightened of its own accord. She sucked in a breath.

"Excellent," she said, though her jaw stayed clenched. "Thank you for letting me know."

"I told him you had a busy day," Emma said. "But when I suggested he schedule a better time, he said he was sure you could fit him in and hung up the phone."

That sounded like her father.

"Thank you, Emma," Jo said again. "I'm sure it'll be fine."

It wasn't, of course. But there was nothing to be done about that now. When her father decided something, it was decided.

Jo sent Emma on fifteen different errands at eleven and told her she could stop for lunch while she was out.

"Should I grab you lunch, too, boss?"

"No, I'll be fine."

"Are you sure?"

"I'm sure."

Honestly, Jo was nauseated at the thought of her father visiting, and annoyed at herself for it. She was forty-one years old and a multimillionaire, and she got nervous at the thought of her father disapproving. Worse still, she already knew he disapproved, had known that since she was a kid. She should've been over it by now. Instead, her stomach roiled too much for her to eat anything. She waited in her office, one foot tapping, unable to get any work done.

Eventually, her father appeared in her open door, ramrod posture and stern expression. He knocked on the doorjamb as though she hadn't noticed him. Jo took a breath and affected something approximating a smile, standing to greet her dad.

"Father," she said.

"Josephine."

She didn't cringe at her full name. She offered her cheek for him to kiss. It was that or a handshake—her father did not hug. She left her office door open. There weren't many people around, but her father didn't know that. Maybe it would keep him from making a scene.

It did, at first. He asked after her—he didn't seem particularly interested, but the fact that he asked at all was something, she supposed. He talked about Vincent, proudly, as usual. Jo was fine with that. When she could think rationally about it, she really didn't mind disappointing her father.

His good behavior only lasted about ten minutes. Then: "The debacle with Barry Davis," he said. He shook his head. "You could have handled that better."

"I'm handling it just fine," Jo said. "And I'm not discussing it with you."

Her father's lips pursed. He glanced at the door, then looked back at Jo. "I'm glad you've gotten rid of that assistant girl."

Jo rolled her eyes. "Her name is Emma. She's a lot more than *that assistant girl*, and I haven't gotten rid of her. She's running some errands for me."

"She still works for you," her father said. "But I was referring to that dating nonsense that thankfully appears to be over. Honestly, Josephine, what a disgrace."

Jo's throat went tight. Her breath shuddered through her nose. She was not going to rise to the bait.

It wasn't bait, though. Her father wasn't saying it with the intent to get a rise out of her; it was simply what he believed. She couldn't fucking stand him.

"You could fire her," he continued. "At the end of the season. People move on from shows."

He said this like he knew anything about television, like he had ever cared about her career. It was her mom who had first put her up for auditions, and it was her mom who had known the ins and outs of the business when Jo was growing up. She doubted her father had seen a single episode of *Innocents*.

"I would never fire Emma because of rumors," Jo said.

She shouldn't have conditioned it. She would never fire Emma. Period. Rumors or not.

"Perhaps at the end of this season you should let her go," her father said as though she hadn't spoken. Jo bristled further. She was *promoting* her midseason, not firing her. "If you're not even sleeping together, surely she's not worth keeping around when it damages your reputation."

Of course, that moment was when Emma arrived.

Emma stood in her doorway with a bag from Jo's favorite burger place in one hand and a drink in the other. She was looking at Jo's father with sharp eyes that softened when she looked to Jo.

"I know you said you didn't need me to get lunch," Emma said, as though Jo's father were not there. "But I thought you could use something."

Jo swallowed. "Great. Thank you."

Emma came into the office and set the bag on Jo's desk. She held out the drink.

"Strawberry milkshake."

Jo must not have kept her nerves in check that morning. A strawberry milkshake was her go-to on stressful days. Emma knew that.

Jo took the cup from her. "Thank you."

"Do you need anything else, Ms. Jones?" Emma asked, holding eye contact.

Jo heard her father cough, but she didn't look away from Emma.

"No, Emma," she said. "I'm fine."

Emma turned to go. On her way out, though, Jo's father opened his mouth.

"Honestly, you're going to throw your reputation away on this slut?"

He said it in Cantonese. Emma couldn't understand him, didn't break stride. She hadn't given him the time of day. Perhaps if Jo could think straight, she'd be proud of Emma for ignoring him. As it was, her head was filled with television static. She couldn't think at all. She was *furious*.

"Shut the fuck up," she said.

That froze both Emma and Jo's father, and they turned to stare at her, wide-eyed.

"Excuse me?" her father said.

"Shut the fuck up," she repeated, each word its own sentence. She was standing now, leaning over her desk toward her father. "You do not get to talk about her like that."

"You do not get to talk to *me* like that," he said. "I'm your father and—"

"And you've always been a complete jackass," Jo said. "Apologize to Emma or get out."

"You're willing to treat your father this way over some *girl*?" He said the word with such derision he might as well have been cursing.

Jo had left her door open so her father wouldn't make a scene. She made it instead, slamming her hands against her desk.

"This *woman* is fantastic at her job and is the only reason I survive most days," Jo snapped. "And that's true whether or not we're *fucking*, and whether or not you approve."

"Josephine!"

"You'll find that not only can I speak to you however I damn well please, I can also have you removed from the premises." She picked up the phone on her desk and dialed Mason in security. "Yes, Mason, could you send someone to my office to escort my father from the building? And please make sure he is not allowed entry again without my prior, explicit approval. Great, thank you." She faked a smile in her father's direction. "Security will be here in a moment to make sure you can find the door with your head so far up your ass."

Her father stared at her. She didn't blink.

"I'll find the way out myself, thank you," he said, and left without sparing Emma so much as a glance.

As soon as her father was out of sight, Jo crumpled, resting on both hands on her desk, all of the breath out of her in a harsh sigh. She hung her head. She heard Emma close her office door and was grateful; she needed a moment to get herself together.

Then Jo heard movement. She looked up to find that Emma hadn't left her alone after all. Emma had stayed on this side of the door when she closed it, and she was now hesitantly rounding Jo's desk.

"Boss," she said. "Are you okay?"

Jo nodded. "It's fine."

"Jo," Emma said.

She caught Jo's hand where it was clenched around the edge of her desk. Jo let Emma uncurl her fingers.

"What can I do?" Emma said.

Jo wasn't lying when she said Emma got her through most days. She did it because of things like this, because of the way she had Jo's back, the way she took care of her. It was her job, sure, but Emma went above and beyond on a regular basis.

Jo squeezed Emma's hand. "Nothing," she said. "It's fine. The milkshake will help."

Emma glanced at the milkshake and bag of food still on Jo's desk, then looked back to Jo. Her hand came up to cup Jo's cheek, and Jo didn't think before letting her eyes slip closed, leaning into the touch.

"Are you sure you're all right, boss?" Emma whispered.

Jo opened her eyes. She nodded, Emma's hand still on her face.

God, Emma looked so beautiful, her brows furrowed, her eyes full of concern and shining like dark honey. She brushed her thumb over the apple of Jo's cheek before sliding her hand back to tuck Jo's hair behind her ear. Jo swallowed. Emma let out a breath and Jo could feel it, soft across her face. She blinked slowly, and when she opened her eyes again, Emma was even closer, too close. Jo should've known better, Jo should've pushed her away, should've leaned back, but she leaned forward instead, her nose brushing against Emma's and—

Jo's desk phone sounded shrill, too loud.

It rang again before Jo forced her eyes open. Emma was on the other end of the desk by that point, fingers twitching at her sides. Her face was bright red.

"Yes?" Jo answered the phone.

"I wanted to let you know your father is out of the building and won't be allowed back without your say." It was Mason, the security guard.

Jo breathed. "Thank you."

"You're welcome, ma'am."

Jo hung up her phone.

Emma was still there. Jo could see her throat work as she swallowed.

Jo wanted to—she wanted to talk about this and wanted to ignore it in equal measure. What she wanted more than anything was for her phone not to have rung.

"You should eat your lunch before it gets cold," Emma said. "I'll be at my desk if you need me."

She turned to leave and Jo couldn't—she couldn't let her go.

"Emma," she said.

Emma looked back at her, eyes apprehensive. Jo looked away.

"Thank you," she said. "For bringing me lunch."

"Of course, boss," Emma said softly.

She closed the door behind her when she left.

When Jo blinked, her eyes were wet.

AT THE END OF the day, Emma hovered at the door to Jo's office. It was only five o'clock, but Jo was *exhausted*. Emma looked at her, looked away.

"Is there anything else, Ms. Jones?" she asked.

Jo thought about when Emma had been mad at her, how she stopped calling her *boss* for a week.

"Emma," Jo said. She wanted to apologize. Wanted to thank her. Wanted to kiss her. She sighed. "No, thank you. I'll see you in the morning, Ms. Kaplan."

16

EMMA

EMMA UNLOCKED HER APARTMENT DOOR.

She didn't remember the drive home. She didn't even remember where she had parked her car. Everything was on autopilot: keys on the hook on the wall, shoes toed off and left by the door. In the kitchen, she got herself a glass of water, took one sip, then set it on the counter.

She almost kissed her boss.

She leaned over the sink and thought she might throw up.

She almost *kissed* her *boss*.

But—well—that wasn't a big deal. It didn't have to be, anyway. She *had* kissed her boss, months ago by this point. If that wasn't a big deal, this was even less of one.

Except this time hadn't been an accident.

She hadn't been drunk, hadn't had bad depth perception. She'd been completely sober and aware of what she was doing. And it was all her—she stayed in Jo's office, she rounded Jo's desk, she cupped Jo's cheek, she leaned in. But Jo had leaned forward, too—Emma was pretty sure.

Maybe she'd imagined it.

Last time, Emma would've done anything to avoid talking about it. Her primary feeling after the wrap party had been mortification. Now she just felt . . . *want*.

She wanted to talk about it. She wanted to do it, to actually kiss Jo. Not drunkenly, not in the heat of the moment. She wanted to kiss Jo hello and goodbye, to kiss her with garlic breath and in the morning before either of them had brushed their teeth.

But none of that was possible. Jo was her *boss*. Jo had created an entire organization against harassment in the workplace. Emma couldn't go into their own workplace and tell Jo she wanted to kiss her.

Though Jo had probably figured that out by this point, given what happened today. Jo shrank around her father, always had. Jo— a towering giant no matter how short she was, Emma's *hero*—was made small by this man. Emma *hated* him. Jo was the sun. Jo was gravity. Emma wanted to take the weight off her shoulders for a minute.

Avery's voice popped into Emma's head, asking how *kissing* Jo was what Emma came up with to take the world off her shoulders. Emma didn't know. But she'd been desperate to do something, and there was a longing in her chest that hadn't left, like a string was wrapped around her heart and connected to Jo. It pulled hard enough that she wanted to go to Jo still, drive to her house to tell her all the ways she was wonderful.

Emma picked up her glass and drained it. Left it sitting in the sink.

It hadn't mattered before, her little crush. Jo was beautiful and brilliant, and she was fiercely protective of Emma after the whole Barry Davis debacle. Who wouldn't have a crush on her? It had been weirdly normal when Emma had figured out her feelings. Nothing had really changed. Sure, she noticed the way her heart sped up and her face warmed in Jo's presence more than she used to, but it wasn't a big deal. It was like having a crush on a celebrity. No matter how gorgeous or smart or kind Jo was, there was no chance. Not to mention the fact that Emma had thought Jo was straight for so long, it had really seemed impossible.

Today, though, Jo had leaned in. She did. Emma hadn't imagined that. She could still feel the satin soft skin of Jo's cheek beneath her thumb. Her fingers buzzed. They'd been close enough to breathe each other's air. Emma could count Jo's eyelashes as they fluttered.

She should've been frightened of these feelings, maybe, but the memory was too intoxicating to be terrifying. Emma pulled out her phone and sat on the couch. Her finger hovered over her sister's name in her list of favorite contacts. Avery would be able to help her figure this out. Avery helped her figure everything out. But Avery also teased her. She couldn't tell Avery about this without getting laughter and an *I told you so*. It would be well meaning, sure, but Emma couldn't. Not when the walls of her heart felt thin, like they might collapse in on themselves at any moment.

Because none of this could work.

Even if Jo wanted to kiss her, too, it was too complicated. Jo was her boss. Her boss who was already being undermined by people who didn't think a woman could write an action movie. This would just give them something else to complain about, to point to and say women had too many feelings, weren't focused on what mattered. Of course it was men sitting on the sidelines who decided what mattered.

As Emma's anxiety explained how this would never work, her pragmatism kicked in. She was a problem solver, a planner. If anyone could figure this out, it was her.

A few months from now, Jo would be working full-time on

Agent Silver. Emma would be an associate producer on *Innocents*. Different projects, different hierarchies of supervision. She could move up the hiring process for Jo's new assistant, if Jo agreed, and move to associate producer earlier. The optics of a relationship might not be excellent. Maybe they'd get dragged through the mud in the tabloids, but Emma had been through enough shit in the tabloids this year. She could take it. This could work.

Of course, it all hinged on Jo actually wanting her back. Just because she'd leaned in today didn't mean she wanted more. What did Emma have to offer Jo freakin' Jones?

Except—didn't Jo always say how important Emma was to her? Wasn't that what the whole fight with her dad was about? How much Emma helped her get through each day.

If Jo was interested in her—it made Emma reexamine their whole relationship. She knew better than to wonder if that was the reason Jo had hired her. Jo was too professional for that. Emma hadn't had a crush on Jo then, either. So when had things changed for Jo? Was it possible that Jo *had* taken her to the SAGs because she liked her? Emma couldn't believe that.

But she remembered Jo's panic at upfronts, the way Jo touched her back. Emma had been the one worried about the rumors then. She'd had to remind Jo about them. Jo was willing to miss a panel for her. Jo canceled plans for her.

Over the summer, Jo had said Emma was hiring her next assistant, not her next Emma. Emma hadn't thought much about it at the time, but now her heart leapt at the idea of being *Jo's Emma*.

Maybe this wouldn't work. Maybe saying anything was a terrible idea. But these feelings mattered now. The chance that they might be mutual mattered. Emma didn't know what she was going to say the next day, but she had to say something.

SHE STOOD NEXT TO her desk when Jo arrived. Indoors, and Jo had huge cat-eye sunglasses on. Emma held on to the coffee cup as Jo's fingers closed around it.

"Can we talk?"

Emma felt Jo grip the cup tighter.

"Of course," Jo said.

Emma swallowed and let go. She knew that tone of voice. That was Jo's network voice. If you didn't know her, her voice sounded agreeable and warm. But Emma knew her. She knew it was distanced and fake.

She followed Jo into her office anyway and closed the door behind them.

"What can I do for you?"

Emma closed her eyes. Her breath hissed out of her nose. She pressed her lips together, planted her feet, and opened her eyes. Jo hadn't taken her sunglasses off.

"We need to talk about yesterday."

Jo nodded, jaw set. "We do."

This was it. Emma was going to tell her—well, maybe not everything. She'd test the waters before she told her *everything*. Emma took a breath and—

"My father has always made me behave in ways I shouldn't," Jo said. "I was unfocused and not thinking, and the situation it led to was inappropriate."

The *situation*. Emma blinked.

"That's not—"

"I apologize." Jo smoothed her ponytail. "I won't let it happen again."

"No, it was fine." Emma shifted from one foot to the other. "That's what I wanted to say—I didn't mind."

Emma wasn't done, but Jo acted like she was. "I appreciate that," Jo said. "Not many people would understand my relationship with my father. If what happened yesterday had to happen with anyone, I'm grateful it was with you."

She made it sound like it had been bad. Like she was embarrassed. Emma herself flushed at the thought. If Jo was *embarrassed* over the almost kiss, Emma couldn't tell her how she felt. She tried one more time anyway.

"I'm here for you," Emma said. "I *want* to be here for you. With your dad or the network or anything. Whatever you need."

Whatever you need. She willed Jo to understand. Jo took off her sunglasses, smiled with no teeth.

"I assure you, nothing of the sort will happen in the future." She wasn't using her network voice anymore. Emma had never heard this voice—like a blank white wall. "Is there anything more you want to discuss?"

If this was what happened when Emma tested the waters, she sure as hell wasn't going to say anything more.

"No, Ms. Jones," she said quietly.

Jo's jaw twitched like she was clenching it.

17

JO

J O HAD SPENT THE PREVIOUS NIGHT STARING MINDLESSLY AT cooking shows on her TV. She ate three dinner rolls dipped in oil and vinegar and drank a glass of room-temperature water. She hadn't allowed herself alcohol—she could hardly think as it was.

She wasn't going to do better tonight, but she at least made herself dinner—frozen homemade enchiladas popped into the oven. She stuck with water while she ate, but it was staving off the inevitable.

Getting drunk was not something she did often, but it was something she would do tonight. She couldn't stop feeling the ghost of Emma's hand on her cheek. She blinked and saw Emma's big brown eyes, deep and open and yearning. She put her leftovers in the refrigerator, put her dishes in the sink, then skipped wine and went straight to scotch.

It did the job.

It did the job of getting her drunk, anyway. It did not help with forgetting the way Emma had looked at her right before they almost kissed. They almost kissed. She almost kissed Emma, and despite knowing what a bad idea it was, sprawled drunk on her couch, what she wanted more than anything was to *actually* kiss Emma. Oh, she was in trouble.

Jo hated herself for putting Emma in that position. Emma, who had already been sexually harassed at work. Emma, who suffered through half a day of awkwardness before having to be the one to say they should talk about it. They did talk about it, which was good, even if the memory was like nails against the chalkboard of Jo's brain. They'd addressed it, and Jo promised it wouldn't happen again, no matter how much she wanted it to. She was humiliated. Emma shifting awkwardly in front of her, saying she was okay with it like it was part of the job. If the workplace hadn't been hostile to Emma during the rumors, it sure was now, knowing her boss had tried to kiss her.

The rumors. They had to be to blame for Jo thinking about Emma like this. Jo had never been interested in someone she worked with, not since she was a teenager and Jane Fonda guest starred on *The Johnson Dynasty*. Jo loved work, but it was work. She had never looked at a coworker with romantic intentions.

She thought of that picture that was still in her desk at work, thought of the way she was looking at Emma back in January. Sure looked like there were romantic intentions there. Or did she just think that because everyone else did? Did she only see Emma this way because it was how people thought she saw her?

Except the rumors were gone. The rumors went away two months ago. No one tricked Jo into thinking of Emma like this. Emma was strong and smart and so damn loyal. She was beautiful and kind and Jo wanted to kiss her. Emma deserved so much better than anyone thinking she'd sleep with someone for a job. She deserved better than being Jo's assistant. She deserved better than Jo's father calling her a slut.

Jo wanted to tell her. It was late, but not *too* late, and Jo's head was swimming too much for her to consider this might be a bad decision.

She opened a new message to Emma, didn't pause to think before typing, *I meant what I said yesterday. You are magnificent.*

She sent it, and poured herself another glass of scotch. She'd barely recapped the bottle when her phone rang. Her phone rang, and she didn't understand.

It was Evelyn, but it was almost three a.m. in New York. Why was Evelyn calling her?

Jo picked up. "What are you doing awake?"

"My best friend texted me I'm magnificent."

Oh.

It was better, probably, that she'd texted Evelyn. Emma didn't need weird, cryptic late-night texts from her boss.

"What's going on?" Evelyn asked.

Jo sighed. Rubbed her forehead. Took another sip of her scotch.

"My father came to visit set yesterday."

Evelyn let out a breath full of the kind of understanding only a best friend could give.

"You deserve to be drunker," she said, and Jo chuckled. A beat, then: "What happened, Jo?"

"He called Emma a slut, acted like she was *worthless.*" Jo wanted to punch something just thinking about it. "God, Evelyn, is this what everyone thinks of her? How have I not contradicted these rumors if this is what people think of her? I should release a statement tomorrow."

"Okay, honey," Evelyn said. "You should absolutely *not* do that."

"I should! I—"

"—will sober up and realize that releasing a statement this long after the rumors started—this long after the rumors *ended*, even— is going to do more harm than good," Evelyn said. "Remember that according to the tabloids you aren't together anymore. Most of the world thinks you dumped Emma for Sam."

"I would never."

"Yeah, because you're a big lesbian, I know."

That was part of it, obviously, but there was something else. The idea of dumping Emma was—they weren't dating, of course, but Jo would *never*. The idea of leaving Emma behind, of finding someone to replace her. It was impossible. She was *Emma*.

"Look, Jo, it's almost three in the morning. Can you drink some water and go to bed? I'm going to call you in the midst of your hangover and bother you about this, but I'm really fucking tired right now."

"Yes, yes," Jo said, waving the hand holding her drink around and almost spilling it. She set it on the table. "Go to sleep."

"You promise not to do anything stupid tonight?"

Jo rolled her eyes but promised anyway.

When Evelyn hung up, Jo did as she was told: got water, went to bed. She looked at her phone as she settled under her sheets. It would be easy to send the text to the right person. But it was past midnight by now, and she did promise Evelyn, and she was sober enough to know she was still a little drunk. She set her phone aside and turned off the light.

18

JO

EMMA MADE A VALIANT EFFORT TO ACT LIKE EVERYTHING was normal between them the next day. But her smile when she offered Jo coffee was stiff, and Jo knew her too well to think it was real. Jo practically collapsed into the chair behind her desk. She remembered the way Emma had pulled her clenched hand off said desk, and burned her throat with a gulp of coffee.

Emma was the one to lean in, Jo reminded herself. Emma was the one to start the whole thing, to almost kiss her. The excuse sounded thin. Jo was in a position of authority over Emma. She held the responsibility for anything that happened between them, and something almost did. Jo wanted to apologize again. Wanted to kiss her again.

She *did*. God, she thought about it too much last night, drunk and texting the wrong person, but she was sober now and she was still thinking about it, still thinking about just how true everything she said to her father was. Emma was her *rock*. Every bad day she'd had this year was because she and Emma weren't on good terms. When things were going well between them, Jo had gotten through everything—the stupid rumors and the morons at the network and the writer's block. Emma *was* magnificent, and Jo was an *idiot*, just seeing all of this now.

Emma was in Jo's office, discussing location scouting for the spring arc of *Innocents*, when Evelyn texted.

How's the hangover, sweetheart?

Jo ignored her. A minute later, her phone buzzed again.

How's Emma today? Still magnificent?

Emma paused and looked at Jo expectantly, giving her time to respond to her phone if need be. Jo was grateful that Emma had stopped avoiding all eye contact. She responded to Evelyn.

Absolutely.

Ev typed back immediately.

You're such a lesbian.

Emma looked away. How long had it been since Jo had taken her last ibuprofen? Her head still ached.

I'm a hungover midlife crisis of a person in love with my assistant. Give me a break.

Jo's phone rang. She should have expected that. She declined the call and gestured for Emma to go on.

"Calgary is looking like a good option," Emma said. "Cheaper than Vancouver, and—"

Jo's phone rang again. She declined it again. Emma paused for a moment, then continued.

"There are good outdoor opportunities, of course. There is some interest in—"

The third time Jo's phone rang, she gave Emma a clenched-tooth smile.

"Can we go over this later?"

Emma nodded and started gathering her things as Jo picked up her phone.

"Hello?"

"Are you *serious*?" Evelyn's voice was so loud that Jo worried Emma might overhear.

"This actually isn't a great time." Jo kept her own voice steady.

"She's in your office, isn't she?"

"Yes."

Emma had all of her papers and her tablet by now, gave Jo an awkward half smile, and headed for the door.

"We need to go over what happened when your dad visited," Evelyn said.

"We don't," Jo said, even though she needed to go over it with *someone*. She wished she could've been honest with Emma about it, could've told her just how much she wanted to kiss her—and not as a drunken accident or in the heat of the moment. "And we can't right now. I'll call you later."

"If you don't, Jo Jones," Evelyn said, the threat clear in her voice. "If you do not call me back and tell me everything, I am going to fly to LA myself."

Jo believed her.

"Mm-hmm," Jo said. "Okay, talk later."

She hung up. Emma was gone by now. She had pulled the door closed behind her in case Jo needed privacy. Jo dropped her forehead onto her desk. The impact just made her head hurt more.

EMMA STAYED DISTANT ALL DAY. After Jo had sent her home, she dialed Evelyn. Ev had said she'd fly out if Jo didn't call her back, and Jo knew it wasn't an empty threat.

"I've got a bowl of popcorn ready," Evelyn said when she picked up. "I'm ready for all the dirty details."

Jo sighed. She was used to Evelyn's teasing, but she'd had a terrible day. Evelyn seemed to figure that out.

"Okay," Ev said, all traces of mocking gone from her voice. "Tell me what happened."

Jo took a breath. She could tell her what happened without getting into feelings. Her hands shook, but she kept her voice steady as she told Evelyn about her father's visit, about what he'd said to Emma, about what Jo had said to him.

"Then I had him thrown out of the building."

Evelyn let out a whistle. "Damn, girl, it's about time. We'll get to this Emma stuff but honestly—I'm proud of you. Tossing your dad was long overdue."

Jo knew.

"The Emma stuff," she said, her voice still so quiet. "There's more than that."

"Yeah?"

"We almost kissed." It was barely louder than a breath. "We would've kissed, Ev, had my phone not rung."

Jo's breath shuddered. She leaned back in her chair, exhausted though all she did was tell a story.

"Then what happened?" Evelyn's voice was quiet.

"Then Emma fled and barely looked at me the rest of the day," Jo said. "We talked about it yesterday morning. I made it clear nothing like that would ever happen again. I'm just—"

"Overwhelmed with emotions you didn't know you had?" Evelyn said. "What—your dad insults Emma and suddenly you realize you're in love with her?"

It was more than that. This had been building for longer than Jo wanted to admit. Emma had made the Emmys bearable even though she hadn't attended. Jo had flushed at Emma pressed up against her on a picnic bench after the baseball game, that tongue curling around her ice-cream cone. Emma had calmed Jo, her pinkie hooking around Jo's when she was worried about Ethan. Before that, Jo had been crushed every day that Emma didn't speak to her more than necessary. Even dress shopping for the SAGs, Jo hadn't been able to look at Emma because she was so beautiful.

It took her father's revulsion to put everything together, but Jo had long been a mess for Emma.

She told Evelyn none of that. It made her feel too soft right now, too fragile.

"So what did Emma say when you talked about it?"

"She acted like it was fine. Like she was okay with it as a requirement of her as my assistant. It was awful."

"Emma's not an idiot," Evelyn said. "I'm sure she does not think it's a job requirement. She knows you a lot better than that."

Jo ran a hand through her hair. Emma had said she wanted to be there for Jo. She had to mean it in an assistant way. Because if she meant—the thought made Jo's breath catch. But Emma couldn't want to *be there* for her as more than an assistant, and even if she did, it didn't matter. It was inappropriate. Jo knew that. She knew that, even if, thinking about it, she couldn't come up with anything she'd do differently.

"Tell me about your day, will you?" Jo said. She was done thinking about her own life, thank you very much. "Distract me."

Evelyn was Jo's best friend for a lot of reasons, not the least of which was that without so much as a pause, she launched directly into a story about one of her clients. She didn't mention Emma again for the rest of the conversation.

THE NEXT DAY, EMMA continued her efforts to act like everything was normal, and Jo joined her. They were all forced smiles and *Is there anything else, Ms. Jones?* and *No, Ms. Kaplan, that's all.* Jo took herself to lunch to escape the suffocating cloud between her and Emma's desks.

She returned from lunch to find Emma standing in her office door, blocking a woman from getting inside. The woman was Evelyn, because of course it was.

"Terrorizing my employees, are you?" Jo said.

The other two women stopped their stare down and noticed Jo.

"No, darling." Evelyn grinned. "You still have a monopoly on that."

Jo laughed and hugged her best friend. Jo's eyes closed when Evelyn squeezed her tight. When she opened them, Emma, who was looking at her with some kind of frustration on her face, quickly looked away.

"I can't believe you're actually here," Jo said.

"Of course you can," Evelyn said.

"Of course I can," Jo laughed. She already felt lighter than she had since Emma told her that her father was coming to visit. "I see you've already met my assistant? Emma, this is Evelyn. Evelyn, Emma."

Jo could see Emma trying to figure out exactly who Evelyn was for a moment, before she put on a smile and offered her hand.

"Nice to meet you, Evelyn."

Evelyn shook her hand, grinning. "Same to you. Sorry if I was too much trouble."

"She's not sorry at all," Jo laughed.

Emma looked confused by the whole interaction, and Jo left her to it. She gestured Evelyn into her office.

"Hold any calls that aren't urgent," Jo told Emma, and she closed the door behind her.

A small part of Jo felt bad closing the door on an obviously perplexed Emma, but most of her didn't care. She didn't care, because her best friend had flown across the country for her with less than twenty-four hours' notice. Jo hadn't even asked her to, but she was here.

Evelyn squished Jo into a tight hug, then tugged her over to her couch.

"I can't believe you're here," Jo said again.

"Start believing it," Evelyn said. "Because you have to entertain me for six days."

"Evelyn!"

Ev grinned at her. "I had some vacation to use." She shrugged. "And your birthday's coming up."

Jo hugged her again.

It was Jo's biggest problem with fame, the lack of sincerity in the way other people treated you. For almost all her life, she was never sure what people's motives were in their interactions with her. Evelyn up and flying across the country to spend a week with her, though, had nothing behind it. Jo would say it meant more than Evelyn realized, but Ev knew her well enough that that was probably not true.

"You really do basically have a guard dog out there," Evelyn said. "She was *bodily* blocking me from entering your office. I thought she was going to tackle me."

"Be nice to her," Jo said.

"Yes, of course I'll be nice to your girlfriend."

Jo's face flushed immediately. She felt like she was a teenager. "If you'll remember, according to the tabloids, we broke up months ago."

"If I remember, according to our conversation last night, you almost kissed three days ago," Evelyn said.

Jo gave her a pleading look, and Evelyn laughed but didn't push.

"So, you going to give me a tour of this place, or what?"

"I can't believe this is your first time visiting," Jo said, making no move to get off the couch and start the tour.

"I'm a terrible friend, I know," Evelyn said. That was categorically not true. Before Jo could refute it, Evelyn continued, "But let's focus on this tour thing. I have to meet Tate and decide if I want to beat him up for giving you so much trouble or if I want to help him."

"Oh God, if you're going to team up with him, I'm not introducing the two of you."

She did, of course. She showed Evelyn to set, kept her quiet while they watched filming for a while, and then introduced her around on a break.

As soon as Tate shook her hand, he turned to Jo.

"Is she single?" he said in a faux whisper.

"She's saving herself for Sam Allen," Jo said without missing a beat.

Tate looked confused, and Emma's brows furrowed, but Evelyn cackled. Jo didn't care that no one else got the joke.

Having Evelyn there was probably not helping Jo's relationship with Emma, who continued to keep her distance, but overall it was definitely helping Jo. It made her feel young, honestly, shut away in her office and giggling with her best friend. The fact that Evelyn loved her enough to board a plane just because Jo was upset over a girl helped, too.

"Why is she still out there?" Evelyn whispered. "It's past five; when does she go home?"

"Oh," Jo said. She hadn't thought about it. "Emma!"

Evelyn's eyes went wide, but Jo ignored her. Emma came to stand in the doorway.

"Yes, Ms. Jones?" she said.

"I'm all set here," Jo said. "You can go home for the night. I'll see you in the morning."

Emma gave her a nod and offered a smile in Evelyn's direction. "Have a good night."

Evelyn waited a reasonable amount of time for Emma to get out of earshot before saying, "Does she not have regular hours? She doesn't leave until you dismiss her?"

"Well, usually she checks in," Jo said. "She probably didn't want to interrupt us, or something."

"Do you think she'll be that submissive in bed, too?"

"Evelyn!" Jo snapped because, no, they were not going to talk about Emma like that. As though this whole thing weren't inappropriate enough.

"I'm teasing," Evelyn said. "C'mon. Let's talk about this."

"You don't want to talk about it, you want to make fun of me." Jo felt petulant.

"Ā-Jo," Evelyn said quietly. "I'm serious."

Jo sighed. "What is there to say?"

"How are you feeling? How do you think she's feeling? What do you want to do? What are the next steps for getting whatever it is that you want?"

The questions all seemed too big to fathom. What were the next steps? There were no steps. She couldn't have what she wanted. Even if she could, she didn't deserve it. What did she bring to a relationship? Money, fame, scrutiny. Nothing substantial.

"I'm feeling stupid," Jo said. "I'm feeling like a cliché. Middle-aged boss and her assistant, how unique. It's all made worse by the fact that the paparazzi seemed to figure it out before we did."

Jo opened her desk drawer, rooted around under some folders to find the magazine with that first picture, and tossed it across her desk toward Evelyn.

"I used to look at this and wonder," she admitted.

Evelyn looked at the picture for a moment.

"You're allowed to want her," she said.

"I'm *not*," Jo said. "I'm not, Ev. She's more than a decade younger than me and she's my assistant. Talk about a predatory lesbian."

"You're not a predatory lesbian," Evelyn insisted. "You're not treating Emma like *prey*. You have feelings for her. You're allowed to. You're allowed to tell her that. Maybe not right now. But she's going to stay on *Innocents* when you move on, right? Maybe tell her then. You're allowed."

Jo was forty-one years old and there were tears in her eyes over a girl. It was embarrassing.

She deflected.

"*In love* was strong language," Jo said, referencing her text from the previous day. "An overreaction."

Evelyn cocked an eyebrow at her.

"I can't *love* her," Jo argued. "I don't even know her outside of work."

"Oh right, I'm sure she's a vastly different person than the one you've gotten to know over the past year," Evelyn said. "The one who worked in your office all summer, who goes on business trips with you, who—what was it? Gets you through every day?"

Is the only reason I survive most days was what Jo had actually said to her father, but she didn't think Evelyn really needed correcting.

Jo was fighting herself on this. Loving Emma seemed like too much, seemed too ridiculous. How could she love her and not realize it until they almost kissed?

"Maybe the rumors have twisted my thoughts," Jo suggested.

Evelyn scoffed at her. "Jo, those rumors are long over—you're the one who keeps this picture in your desk. This isn't about how people think you feel about her. This is about how you do feel about her. I'm not saying you do or do not love her. But don't talk yourself out of it if it's how you feel."

Jo made a face but held back from grumbling under her breath like she wanted to.

"I'm in the process of creating a safe space for women in this industry who are harassed, and I almost kissed my assistant," she said. "What kind of hypocrite—"

"Okay, but you didn't kiss your assistant," Evelyn cut in. "And you won't, even if she obviously wants you to, because when you aren't under the stress of your asshole father visiting, you wouldn't. You wouldn't kiss your assistant. You wouldn't base any professional or employment decisions on whether or not she kissed you. You're not harassing her. You're not abusing her."

Jo knew that, rationally. Knew all of that. But her feelings for Emma felt *wrong*, and she didn't know how to fix that.

"C'mon, Jo," Evelyn said. "Let's go order takeout and maybe get you drunk."

"I don't need to be drunk two nights this week, and I was already drunk Tuesday."

"Yes, I remember," Evelyn said, and Jo rolled her eyes.

They didn't get drunk, in the end. They ordered takeout from the restaurant they'd gone to since they were children growing up together in Chinatown and ate it on the floor of Jo's living room.

Evelyn talked mostly. Told Jo about New York and her firm and how her parents were doing. Jo sat cross-legged and ate rice noodles and smiled a lot.

They were on to the fortune cookies by the time Evelyn brought Emma back up.

"You have to figure out what you're doing about it," Ev said. "Because I did not fly out here to spend six days with you moping about it. I am *definitely* teasing you about it, and that's only fun if it annoys you, not if it depresses you."

"It doesn't depress me," Jo said. "But there's nothing to figure out. I'm going to move to Agent Silver soon enough. Emma will be associate producer and I'll be working elsewhere and I'll move on. It won't be an issue."

"Good idea," Evelyn said. "Promote her and then work elsewhere and then *ask her out*, you idiot."

Jo rolled her eyes. "I'm not going to ask her out."

"Fine, whatever," Evelyn said. "But you at least won't be sad when I tease you about it?"

Jo would've liked to promise that. She'd have loved to not feel bad about the way Emma made her heart race. She didn't think she could guarantee it, though.

"I'll try," she said.

THE NEXT MORNING, EMMA smiled when she offered Jo her coffee.

"Is Evelyn not joining us today?"

"She'll be by sometime this afternoon," Jo said. She told herself she imagined the way Emma's smile wobbled.

Evelyn may have flown across the country for Jo, but she had other people to visit while she was here. Not to mention that Jo had work to do; she didn't need Evelyn in her office bothering her all day.

Jo considered inviting Emma in, instead. Extending some kind of olive branch to make sure they were okay. But she didn't want it to be misconstrued. She left her door open, though, just in case.

"WE'RE GOING OUT TONIGHT." Evelyn breezed into Jo's office that afternoon.

Jo didn't look up from her work. "Are we?"

"Of course," Evelyn said. "Early birthday celebration."

Jo finished the paragraph she was reading before turning to Evelyn.

"I hate celebrating my birthday."

"You hate celebrating it with your family," Evelyn corrected. "You hate celebrating it publicly, with people who only care it's your birthday because you're a celebrity. Good thing you've got your best friend here to celebrate with instead."

Evelyn wasn't wrong, no matter how much Jo would like to say she was.

"Come on." Evelyn dragged the words out. "Let me take you

out and get you drunk and make you forget about how you hate yourself for—"

She cut herself off but glanced toward the open door, outside of which Emma worked at her desk. Jo glared at Evelyn, but there was no real heat behind it.

"Plus," Evelyn said, "I had a great idea. We'll go out with Sammy."

Jo had to admit that was actually a good idea.

"Fine," Jo said. "But you're not telling anyone at the restaurant it's my birthday."

Evelyn rolled her eyes. "That's a terrible condition, but I accept."

Sam was thrilled to go to dinner with them. It was more fun than Jo had had in weeks. Evelyn flirted her heart out the whole time, and still all the tabloids talked about the next day was how Jo and Sam were dating.

JO AND EVELYN SPENT the weekend kicking around their old haunts, realizing they were both probably too old for most of them. It was a great time anyway.

Evelyn came back to work with Jo Monday morning. Emma smiled sweetly at her.

"I would've gotten you a latte if I'd known you'd be here," she said.

Evelyn chuckled.

"She'll live," Jo said before Evelyn could say anything rude.

She closed the door behind them. She wondered what Emma thought of Evelyn visiting. Was Jo being obvious—needing her best friend after she and Emma had almost kissed? Maybe it was tipping her hand, but it was keeping her sane.

"You picked a good one, you know?" Evelyn said, lounging across what Jo had come to think of as Emma's couch. "Loyal, obviously. And certainly not bad looking."

"Shut up."

It wasn't like Jo didn't know Emma was attractive. She'd always known, really. Since back when Emma was hired on props. She was a beautiful woman, objectively. Jo knew that, and it never used to matter.

She hated that it mattered now. Hated that she noticed it, at random times, even before her father's visit. Emma would be telling her about a meeting later, and Jo would get distracted by the way her hair fell in front of her face. It made Jo feel dumb, and inappropriate. Emma was still her employee. Emma was her employee who had already been sexually harassed. She didn't need her boss creeping on her.

Evelyn spent the whole last day of her visit teasing Jo about how great Emma was. Jo couldn't exactly disagree.

"YOU'RE NOT GOING TO take me to the airport?" Evelyn acted outraged.

"My car service will," Jo said, sorting papers on her desk. "I, however, have a job I've been slacking on during your entire visit."

"As though you've ever slacked in anything in your entire life," Evelyn muttered.

Jo came around her desk to stand in front of her best friend.

"Thank you for coming," she said.

Evelyn grinned. "I'm really glad I did."

"I'm really glad you did, too."

Evelyn hugged her, tight. "There's nothing wrong with your feelings," she said right into Jo's ear. "You're great, and she's great, and if things work out, that will be great."

Jo tried not to roll her eyes, because nothing was going to *work out*, but she appreciated the sentiment.

"Get out of here, okay?" Jo said. "Don't miss your flight."

"I'll be back if you need me, you know?"

Jo's heart felt full. "I know."

WITH EVELYN GONE, JO had nothing to distract her from Emma, whose smiles still never reached her eyes. Jo wanted to give Emma a way out, if she was uncomfortable. She called to her from behind her desk.

"What's up?" Emma asked. She hovered at the door to Jo's office.

"Come in."

Emma did, her eyes shifting around the room, nervous. Jo hated that she made her feel that way.

"How is the search for my next assistant coming?" Jo asked.

Emma scratched the back of her neck. "Fine. Good. I'm still narrowing down résumés."

"I was thinking, if you wanted to, you can move to associate producer earlier than midseason. As soon as you hire your replacement, we can make your promotion official."

"I know," Emma said slowly, like she didn't understand. "And it's on track for that to happen at midseason."

"Right," Jo said. "If you wanted to move on sooner, I meant. You're welcome to speed up the process."

Emma stared at her. Jo adjusted some papers on her desk. She sighed, didn't say what she really meant. *I'd understand if you're desperate to get away from me.*

"I'll move on at midseason," Emma said. "As I said, I'm still going through résumés. I want to take my time and make sure I hire the right person. There's no need to rush, is there?"

"Of course not," Jo said. "If you don't want to—of course there's no rush."

If Emma wanted to get away from her, Jo wouldn't stop her. But she didn't, apparently. Jo felt marginally less terrible about the whole thing.

JO DIDN'T LIKE TO make a big deal of her birthday. Evelyn was right about why; it never felt like people were making a big deal for *her*, so much as because she was a celebrity, they thought they were supposed to. She didn't need to be the center of attention any more than she'd already been for most of her life.

Last year, a cupcake had appeared on her desk when she wasn't in her office. She knew it was Emma, of course, even if she hadn't seen her actually do it. A cupcake appeared, and at the end of the day, Emma had quietly wished her a happy birthday. That was all Emma did, and Jo liked it. It felt like she did it for her, her specifically, not just because that was something you did on someone's birthday, but because she wanted Jo to feel special on her birthday. Jo appreciated it.

This year, even after the almost kiss, even after all of the awkwardness between them, there was still a cupcake on her desk when she came back from a meeting. It was huge, as it was last year. Dark cake and a tower of white frosting with crushed red-and-white mints on top. From the smell, Jo guessed it was a cupcake version of a peppermint mocha. She immediately unwrapped it. It was so big she had to find a plastic fork in her desk to eat it; otherwise she'd end up with frosting all over her face.

Jo savored that first bite. The mint was sharp and the cake was deep and rich and delicious. Emma was too good to her. Too good for her. Emma was smart and kind, and sometimes it seemed like she worked even harder than Jo. Jo ate the cupcake Emma bought her, and inexplicably felt like crying.

That evening, after Jo told Emma she could go home, Emma hovered in her doorway for a moment.

"Happy birthday, boss," she said quietly.

Jo wanted to tell her she loved her. Wanted to tell her she was sorry for everything.

In the end, all Jo said was, "Thank you, Emma."

19

EMMA

EMMA HAD NARROWED DOWN THE POOL OF CANDIDATES for Jo's next assistant to four. It was weird, picking her own replacement. Weirder still doing it in the wake of . . . everything.

Of realizing she had a crush on Jo and then almost kissing her and then imagining how things could work, only to have Jo invite her *girlfriend* out for a week. Jo and Evelyn had gone out to dinner with Sam, Jo's former coworker, and the tabloids might have taken it as confirmation of Jo and Sam's relationship, but Emma knew better. She knew those weren't the two dating at that dinner.

Of course Jo had a girlfriend. Why wouldn't she? She was gorgeous and successful, funny and kind. All the reasons Emma was interested in her were all the reasons she obviously already had a girlfriend. It made sense, even if it hurt.

Emma wished Jo would've just said she wasn't interested in her. Instead, Jo had her girlfriend visit like she was pointing out she was off-limits without having to have the conversation with Emma. What was worse was how Jo offered to promote her early—like Jo wanted to put distance between them, like she no longer trusted Emma to be professional.

But whatever. Emma was being professional. Things between her and Jo were fine—normal, almost. Emma was hiring her replacement.

All of the candidates she found were qualified. Any of them would probably do fine. But she wanted better than fine. Jo deserved better than fine. If Emma hired the perfect assistant for Jo, it would prove this stupid crush didn't affect any of her work. Her palms sweat every time she looked over the candidates' résumés.

The only interview Emma had left was Phil. She was surprised he'd applied. He'd been on the show a year longer than she had and had never switched departments or, really, shown any desire to advance. When she was on props with him, he was the jokester. They'd gotten along because he made her laugh, but he was always more likely to go for a joke than to volunteer for extra work. Jo could use someone laid-back, though, so Emma set up an interview.

Phil grinned as he shook her hand.

"Let's get this over with so I can get my promotion," he said.

Emma bristled. "Phil, I've interviewed three other really strong candidates. This isn't a formality. You don't automatically have the job just because we're friends."

"Of course I shouldn't have the job because we're friends," Phil said. "But you know I'd be great at it."

"And why is that?" Emma tried to pivot to a serious interviewer tone. She sat at the conference table and gestured for Phil to sit across from her. "What do you think you'd bring to the job?"

"Emma, it's just an assistant position. I think I can handle it."

Emma raised her eyebrows. "You think my job has been *easy* the past year and a half?"

"No, of course not," Phil backtracked. "It's just not like you're guarding nuclear launch codes."

Emma chuckled along with him, but seethed inside. People always acted like being someone's assistant wasn't hard, like it was all ordering lunch and picking up dry cleaning. Phil should've known better. Emma folded her hands on the table in front of her.

"How would you deal with the more difficult aspects of the job?"

Phil must have recognized the frustration in her voice—he seemed to flip a switch, taking everything more seriously. It ended up being a pretty good interview. Emma was going to have a hard decision ahead of her. After, they slipped back into their roles as friends, chatted about nothing important—Emma and Jo's upcoming trip to Calgary and what Phil was doing over the winter break.

"Do you have any questions for me?" Emma asked before officially ending the interview.

"Can you give me tips to keeping her happy, you know, *behind the scenes*?" Phil waggled his eyebrows at her. "I want to make sure I get as good a recommendation out of this as you got."

It was a joke. Emma knew that. But the words chafed against her skin.

"I appreciate you taking the time to interview," she said, straightening the notes in front of her. "Unfortunately we're going to be going in a different direction."

Phil guffawed at her. "You're kidding."

"I don't think it's appropriate to insinuate that your interviewer has been sleeping with her boss," Emma said. "I can't imagine any situation where you'd expect to get the job after that. I'm sure Aly will appreciate not having to find another PA for the second half of the season."

"You're unbelievable," Phil said. "It was a *joke*."

"A joke that demonstrated you're not ready for a position like this," Emma said. "You're a good PA, Phil, but this isn't the right job for you."

Phil left. He just left the room with a scoff and nothing more. Emma's skin tingled, her heart raced. Phil was her best friend on set, but friend or not, that had been completely inappropriate. No, her job wasn't guarding nuclear launch codes, but that didn't mean it wasn't important. That didn't mean it could go to someone who couldn't read a room and understand when a joke might not be a good idea.

She gave him a few minutes' head start to get away from the conference room and maybe blow off some steam before she headed back to her desk. Thankfully, there was no sign of him.

"How'd the interview go?" Jo asked as soon as Emma returned.

Emma tried to smile at her. "Fine," she said. She didn't want to think about it. "I'll have a decision made by the time we go to Calgary."

"Great," Jo said. "Our last business trip together."

Emma didn't want to think about that, either. She was nervous about the promotion. Rationally, she knew she already had plenty of production duties. She knew she had stepped up, done more than she needed to as an assistant. But staying on *Innocents* in a new position while Jo left? Something about it made her skin crawl. It wasn't her crush—she had no chance with Jo whether they worked together or not, clearly. But not working with her directly . . . except for the week they were fighting, Jo had always had her back. She had this unwavering belief that Emma would succeed. No matter what happened between them personally, Jo had always been there for her professionally. Emma was nervous to lose that, especially at the same time she was stepping into a new position.

"Don't forget to bring your inhaler," Jo said with a wink.

Emma half laughed at her. "Of course not, boss."

Moments like this, everything felt normal between them.

"Hey." Emma started at the voice behind her. She turned to find Chantal, whose approach she hadn't noticed. Chantal was just as small as Jo, but without heels to add height or announce her arrival.

Chantal looked between Jo and Emma, eyebrows not quite raised. "Got a question for you," she said to Jo.

"Come in," Jo said, giving Emma one last smile before retreating to her office.

Chantal followed.

Emma wished she could ask Jo if they were really okay. Wished she could tell her that she was sorry for almost kissing her, that she understood Jo was with Evelyn and it didn't matter even if she wasn't. But of course she couldn't. Better just to make sure she didn't look at Jo too long, didn't stand too close, didn't let their fingers touch when she handed over papers or Jo's coffee. Better to make sure she didn't call Jo *boss* where anyone else could hear.

THE TRIP TO CALGARY was the final step of location scouting for an arc of *Innocents*. It had been well vetted, approved all the way up the ladder to Jo. All that was left was for her to fly out and take a look at various sites to give her own approval. She and Emma were scheduled for a quick two-day tour, flying out Friday morning and back on Saturday evening, the day before Emma's birthday. Normally, Emma might have minded going on a weekend or so close to her birthday, but *Innocents* only had one more week before breaking for the holidays. The trip felt like Emma's last adventure in a job she wasn't quite ready to leave. She wasn't going to complain about any part of it.

On Thursday, Emma went to Avery's for dinner to see her before heading off on her trip. Dylan was picking up the twins from a friend's house, so it was just Avery and Emma as Avery prepared dinner. She was using turkey stock from Thanksgiving to make soup. Emma sat on a stool and watched her, not allowed to help.

"So who'd you hire to replace you?" Avery asked as she sautéed carrots, celery, and onions.

"A woman named Marlita," Emma said. "She'll do well."

"Is Phil gonna be pissed it wasn't him?"

Emma rolled her eyes. "I'm the one who's pissed at him. I told him he didn't get the job at the end of his interview."

Avery added broth into the pot and stirred it quickly before joining Emma at the kitchen island.

"Tell me everything."

Emma did. She felt vindicated when Avery announced, "Fuck Phil, then."

"Right?" Emma said. "My job is important. If it weren't important, why'd Jo say—"

She cut herself off. Avery didn't know that story.

"Why'd Jo say what?"

Emma shook her head. "It's nothing."

Avery narrowed her eyes. "Sounds like something. The way you're blushing says it's something."

"I'm not blushing," Emma said, and blushed harder.

"What did Jo say?"

Emma would've buried her head in her hands, but that was worse than blushing.

"She said I was the only thing that got her through her day," she mumbled.

She expected Avery would make her repeat it, just to be a jerk, but her sister just blinked at her instead.

"When did she say this?" Avery asked.

"A while ago."

"And to whom?"

Emma could feel exactly how red her face was. "Her father."

Avery's eyebrows went up. "Explain."

Emma hadn't told Avery about Jo's father visiting. It was too fragile. Too real. Plus, then Evelyn flew in and Jo turned almost girlish, giggly and happy. Emma spent the week complaining to Avery about Jo's girlfriend. Avery had called her jealous and hadn't known just how true it was.

But Avery had said *explain*. So Emma did. She told her about Jo's father, about the milkshake, about Jo telling him off and looking so broken that Emma had to do something.

"And what you had to do was kiss your boss?"

"We didn't kiss!"

"And why was that again? Was it because you didn't want to, or was it because a security guard called?"

Emma hung her head.

"That's what I thought," Avery said. "Did you want to kiss her?"

Emma closed her eyes. Nodded.

"Do you still?"

Emma cracked one eye open. "Your soup's going to bubble over."

Avery went back to the stove to stir the soup and let Emma get away with not answering. "So let me get this straight. You're telling me that Jo Jones yelled at her father about how great you are, about how you're the *only reason she gets through most days*, and then you almost kissed her, and you're claiming this isn't a big deal?"

"Well, see—"

"No," Avery said. "There is no 'well, see' here. You almost kissed her! You would've if you weren't interrupted! Right?"

Emma picked at her fingernails. "Right."

"Yeah. That's a big deal."

It *wasn't*. It didn't matter. Jo was dating Evelyn and that was fine; Emma was fine with it. It didn't matter that she'd wanted to kiss Jo then, wanted to kiss her still. What she really wanted was to go back to her normal relationship with Jo, like over the summer, where they got along and made each other laugh and worked together well. Where Jo didn't think she had a crush on her. Where there was none of this awkwardness. Where Emma wasn't so damn unsure about everything.

"It's not that big of a deal," she said. "I'm just worried because after Evelyn left, Jo told me we could make my promotion official as soon as I hired the replacement, even if it was before midseason. Like the promotion was because she was trying to get rid of me instead of because I deserved it."

Avery gaped at her. "Emma, she decided on this promotion at the end of last season. It has nothing to do with you guys almost kissing."

Emma shrugged. "Plus, we're going on this trip and—I don't want things to be awkward, is all. I want things to be normal again."

Avery kept staring at her for a moment. Then she shook her head and put rolls in the oven.

"And what's normal?" she asked.

"Like this summer," Emma said. "When it was easy."

"So normal is you guys getting along so well people think you're dating?" Avery said. She seasoned the soup.

"No," Emma said immediately. "No, that's not what I mean."

"It kind of sounds like that's what you mean."

Emma leaned her elbows on Avery's kitchen island and dropped her head into her hands.

"I just want things to be easy," she said. "I don't want to have to *worry* about all of this."

"Things aren't always easy, Em," Avery said. "Especially when you're taking steps forward."

"I'm not *taking steps forward* with Jo." Emma paused, then grumbled, "Especially not since she has a girlfriend."

"I meant that you're moving on to a new job, but way to be totally not convincing about not wanting to date Jo," Avery said, and Emma cringed. "You're moving to a new job and Jo is moving to a new show, and that's going to make things different and weird between you and Jo, even if you hadn't almost kissed."

Emma rested her chin in one hand and looked up at her sister.

"You've got a work trip," Avery said. "Focus on work."

"And just ignore the almost kiss?" Emma asked quietly.

"Sure."

"Because it's not a big deal?"

"It is a big deal," Avery said. "I'm just letting it go because I'm a good sister. I'll bother you about it after your trip."

"You're an okay sister," Emma said.

Avery pointed the wooden spoon in her hand at Emma. "If you're going to be like that, I'll bother you about it right now."

Emma giggled. "No, no, you're a *great* sister, the best sister."

"Better."

Dylan and the twins arrived then, and Emma was glad to put the discussion aside to greet them and help Dani and Ezra set the table for dinner.

AFTER THEY ATE AND Emma got her fill of cuddling both the twins and the dogs, Avery walked her to the door and brought up Jo again.

"I know I've teased you about it forever, but you're allowed to have a crush on her, you know?" she said.

Emma admitted nothing. "She has a girlfriend. And she'd never date an employee anyway."

"You're not going to be an employee soon," Avery reminded her.

"Exactly," Emma said. "Any crush I might have on her doesn't matter. She's going to move to Agent Silver and I'll stay with *Innocents* and we won't even see each other. It'll be fine."

"How do you feel about that? About not seeing each other?"

Awful.

When Emma didn't actually reply, Avery sighed.

"Have fun on your trip," she said. "Try to get some work done instead of just making out the whole time."

"This is why I didn't tell you," Emma said.

"I know," Avery said. "But you still love me."

"Do I?" Emma asked. She immediately felt bad, threw herself back over the threshold for another hug. "I do." She squeezed her sister tight. "Okay, I'm going now."

20

EMMA

EMMA SPENT HALF THE FLIGHT TO CALGARY GOING OVER her notes for the trip: their itinerary, the locations they were scouting, the restaurants she'd researched. She only stopped when Jo leaned over and touched her shoulder gently.

"How's the trip look?" Jo asked.

"Oh, everything's set, boss," Emma said. "The car service will be waiting by the time we get our bags, and we'll head immediately to the hotel to check in. We'll have to grab lunch pretty quickly before . . ."

She trailed off, noticing Jo looking at her with something like a smirk on her face.

"Did you not want to know about the trip?" Emma asked.

"You've been going over everything for an hour, Emma," Jo said. "Take a break. It's a two-day trip. I know the itinerary. I know everything's going to be fine and you don't need to go over it for the fifteenth time."

Emma colored slightly. She liked to be prepared was all.

"I appreciate you being thorough," Jo said. "But balance that against stress, because I promise there's nothing to be stressed over. It's going to be an easy trip."

It was their last trip together. Emma's chest clenched, and she remembered their most recent trip, to upfronts. Remembered her asthma attack and the way it had kicked up rumors about them. It had been months since she'd seen an article about herself. Emma didn't know why whoever was leaking had suddenly stopped after Barry Davis's visit, or if maybe they just really thought Jo and Emma had broken up.

Did the leak notice how Emma and Jo sometimes seemed like they were on eggshells around each other now? She didn't know if anyone else could even tell, but she could. They were good, for the most part, but when they talked about Jo moving on, Emma getting promoted, there was always this undercurrent of something Emma didn't really understand.

But whatever. Emma could relax. For the rest of the flight, she and Jo watched sitcoms on the TVs in the backs of the seats in front of them. Jo's nose crinkled when she laughed. Emma wasn't stressed at all.

AS EMMA HAD SAID there would be, there was a car waiting to take them straight to their hotel, where their rooms were across the hall from each other. Emma unpacked her suitcase and changed into warmer clothes. December in Calgary had her happily bundled into layers.

Not much later, there was a knock on her door. Emma checked the peephole to see Jo, her hair in a thick braid over one shoulder. When Emma opened the door, Jo grinned at her.

"Lunch?" she said.

She was dressed for the weather, too, a scarf around her neck and knee-high boots. She held a herringbone coat folded over one arm.

"Sure," Emma said. "Let me grab my coat."

"I know you're all about the food when we go on trips," Jo said as Emma retrieved her coat. "Did you run across that Vietnamese place a few blocks away?"

"Absolutely," Emma said, too excited at the prospect of Vietnamese to be embarrassed about her restaurant-researching habit she'd thought was private. "I wanted to try that one the most."

Jo led the way out of the hotel, Emma at her side. When they found the restaurant, the smell from the sidewalk had Emma's mouth watering. It only got better inside.

Emma had never eaten out with Jo like this without staying eagle-eyed, ready to avoid cameras or push through a crowd to get Jo back to the car. Today, she didn't have to worry about paparazzi. No one in the restaurant glanced their way.

Instead, Emma got to focus on how delicious the spring rolls were, how absolutely wonderful the pho broth was. It was a perfect meal for a day that probably didn't count as blustery by Calgary's standards, but was colder than it ever got in LA. Jo added a hefty spoonful of hot oil to her pho, but Emma declined.

From the moment she'd knocked on Emma's door, Jo had been calm and loose. It took Emma the whole day to fully let her guard down. Jo was never recognized. There were never any cameras in their faces or peeking out across the street. While they worked, Jo asked Emma questions, took her opinion into consideration at every site they visited.

It was easy, just like Emma had hoped.

They scouted out places and met people who would be involved if Calgary were chosen as the shooting location. Jo explained the production difficulties of filming in two places—on location in Calgary and in studio in LA. Emma took notes, brainstorming possible solutions to problems that had yet to arise.

THEIR FLIGHT OUT WAS scheduled for early evening on Saturday. For their last hurrah in Calgary, Jo took Emma to a late lunch at a deli. They were seated at a booth in the back corner.

"This place is supposed to have the best Montreal smoked meat," Jo said. "It's like Canada's pastrami."

Emma grinned. She hadn't found this restaurant in her research, but—"It's perfect."

Jo got a Reuben. Emma couldn't resist the latkes.

"As a kid I'd eat these until I puked," she said, dunking a forkful into applesauce before raising it to her mouth.

"I hope you've outgrown that," Jo chuckled. "My overeating food of choice as a kid was Evelyn's mom's bee hoon—rice noodles with veggies and chicken, shrimp, and pork."

In the moment, Emma wasn't jealous of Evelyn at all, just happy Jo had someone who made her smile like that.

"How long have you two been together?" Emma asked.

The smile fell off Jo's face and she just stared at her, mouth open.

Emma backtracked. "I'm sorry. I shouldn't have asked. You don't have to—"

"No, Emma, no, God, it's not—" Jo pressed her lips together like she was swallowing laughter. "Evelyn and I are not and have never been dating."

Oh. Emma thought it before she said it aloud. "Oh."

"Ev has been my best friend since I was a kid," Jo said. Her cheeks were red. "She would die laughing if she knew you thought we were dating."

"Right."

Emma took another bite of her latke. Evelyn was Jo's best friend. Evelyn, who stayed for a week after Jo and Emma almost kissed. Avery was Emma's best friend, and she didn't even know about it until this week. Did Evelyn? The idea of Jo talking about Emma seemed unrealistic.

Jo pushed her plate toward Emma, pulling her from her thoughts. Half of Jo's sandwich was untouched.

"Try the smoked meat," Jo said.

Emma's stomach fluttered. She used her fork to get a piece of meat off Jo's sandwich. It was like pastrami, but not exactly the same. It tasted good, but when she swallowed, it felt like she hadn't chewed enough.

She smiled at Jo, her cheeks tight.

"Amazing," she said. "But I can't eat another bite."

She set aside her fork. Jo picked up her own and poked at the second half of her sandwich.

"Are you excited to move to associate producer?" she asked.

Emma swallowed. "Sure."

Jo looked up at her, eyes searching. Her face softened. "Did you pick me out a good assistant?"

"Of course, boss," Emma said, even while she doubted herself.

Marlita was great. Qualified. Kind. Seemed hardworking. But Emma didn't trust her to take over the job. When Jo was on deadline, would Marlita know she had to not only bring Jo lunch, but also make sure she stopped writing long enough to eat it? That after two p.m. her iced lattes needed to be decaf unless they'd be working late?

And then it clicked.

Emma suddenly understood the reason she'd been nervous about the promotion. It didn't have anything to do with the promotion itself.

The reason was sitting across the table from her.

The reason was the way Jo was smiling at her, gentle and almost shy, like Emma was a wild animal that could spook. The reason was the way Jo worried about her, took care of her. The reason was Jo's voice every morning, thanking Emma for her coffee. Emma always knew how the day would go, based on how Jo said thanks. She could tell when Jo hadn't gotten enough sleep, or when she was too busy and already thinking about tasks she had to accomplish that day. Emma liked starting her day with Jo. Emma liked spending her day with Jo. The idea of moving on from that was terrifying.

The amorphous dread Emma had whenever she thought about her new job was coming into shape. It wasn't about her job. She liked her job—loved her job, even. But associate producer would be better, in the long run, she knew that. The thought of not getting to see Jo every day, though—her stomach clenched.

Her chest felt tight. Jo caught her hand across the table, squeezing quickly before letting go.

"Are you okay?"

Emma nodded. "Sure, yeah," she said. "I'm just going to—I'm going to run to the restroom real quick."

She consciously moved slowly toward the bathroom, but it still felt like she was fleeing. Her heart pounded in her chest.

It wasn't a one-person bathroom, so it wasn't necessarily private. There was no one in the stalls, but Emma couldn't lock the door like she wanted to. She splashed some water on her cheeks.

She stared at herself in the bathroom mirror.

When people first thought Jo and Emma were together, Emma

told herself Jo was probably straight. When she found out Jo knew Avery and had lied to her about it, Emma told herself she was just upset because their relationship was different than she thought it was. When she almost kissed Jo, Emma told herself she got caught up in the moment. When Jo turned her down afterward—not directly, not explicitly, but enough—Emma told herself it didn't matter. Now here Emma was, her heart racing, terrified at the thought of not seeing Jo every day. Everything she told herself, and now she was hiding in the bathroom while her gay, single boss waited for her at their table. Her gay, single boss who wouldn't be her boss soon.

This was their last business trip together. There was only a week of work left before Emma wouldn't be Jo's assistant anymore. What happened then?

Emma took a deep breath, put some more water on her face. She didn't know how long she'd been in the bathroom.

When she returned to the table, Jo looked at her with such concern she *had* to be interested in her. She had to, right?

"Are you okay?" Jo asked. "I didn't mean to upset you."

"I'm not upset," Emma said.

"I'm sure Marlita will do fine," Jo said. "She won't be as good as you, but that's a given."

Emma stared at Jo.

"You're the best assistant I've ever had, Emma," Jo said quietly. "Before that you were the best props PA Aly had ever had. I hope, at some point in the future, you'll be the best director I've ever worked with."

"*Boss*," Emma said, awed. The response was reflexive, but suddenly the word felt like a term of endearment.

Jo never broke eye contact. Emma felt like she should. She didn't know what to say. It wasn't just Jo's belief in her—Jo wanted to work with her whenever she became a director. That would be years from now, could be decades. Jo still imagined they'd be in each other's lives. Emma didn't look away.

"All finished here?" The waiter appeared then, shocking them both out of their reverie.

Emma blinked a few times. She looked at the waiter, who didn't seem to have noticed he'd interrupted anything.

"I am," Jo said. "Emma?"

"Yeah," Emma said. "Yes. All finished. Thank you."

They didn't speak while Jo paid the check. Out on the sidewalk in the cold, they waited for their car to arrive. Emma's blood thrummed. Jo stood close enough to touch. Emma watched her own breath fog in the air. She could see Jo looking at her out of the corner of her eye. She told herself she shouldn't look back—whether because it would give away her feelings or lead to something happening, she wasn't sure. She looked back anyway.

She looked back, and as soon as she made eye contact, Jo stepped closer, stepped into her space. She was right in front of her, reaching her hands up toward Emma, and Emma couldn't breathe as they curled around her scarf. They didn't pull her in, though, just tugged on the scarf itself, adjusted it tighter around Emma's neck.

"Emma," Jo said, her voice like she was fighting to get the word out, and Emma wanted to say yes. Whatever came next, *yes*. But then Jo swallowed, blinked, and she sounded less strangled when she said, "Do you have your inhaler?"

Emma nodded. Jo's hands were still on her scarf.

"Yeah, boss," Emma said. "Don't worry."

Even if Emma could have breathed, she'd be holding her breath. She didn't want to do anything to shatter the moment.

Jo looked at her mouth. Emma wanted to lean down, to lean

into her. She and Jo had almost kissed more than a month ago, and she'd mostly blocked that out in the time since, but maybe she shouldn't have. Maybe she was an idiot for it. Maybe she wanted to kiss Jo now as much as she did that day, and maybe she should listen to those emotions for once.

Jo finally dropped her hands as the driver pulled up in their car. Her cheeks were pink, from the cold, probably.

WHEN THEY ARRIVED AT the airport, their flight was supposed to be on time. Security moved quickly, but by the time they were through it, the flight was delayed by an hour. Emma groaned when they saw the delay on the departure screens.

"It'll be fine," Jo said. "We can get a drink."

Emma could use a drink. They were already not set to arrive in LA until past ten. She wasn't looking forward to getting in later.

Jo took her to the Vin Room. It was fancy enough that Emma was surprised it was in an airport. She and Jo sat across from each other at one end of a long curving table with other diners.

"What kind of wine do you like?" Jo asked, looking over the menu Emma swore had hundreds of types.

"Uh, red?" Emma half grimaced. She didn't know wine well enough to make this decision.

Jo smiled at her and ordered a bottle of something Emma couldn't pronounce.

There was a silence between them when the waiter left, and it was more awkward than it had been all trip. Emma bounced her leg. She wondered if there was a less convenient time she could've picked to learn Jo was single, was—dare Emma even think it?—*available*. They had to be together for hours more, and Emma wasn't sure how she was supposed to handle that. Jo was quieter than usual, too, which meant she could tell Emma was uncomfortable. It was all a mess.

Jo let Emma pour her own wine when the bottle came. Emma probably took more than she should've, only just remembered to sip instead of gulp.

"I know we just ate," Jo said. "But do you want to look at the dessert menu?"

"I would *love* to look at the dessert menu," Emma said.

Alcohol and dessert—it was how she'd deal with this situation were she at home, so it seemed like a good enough way to deal with it now.

They got a menu and eventually put in orders for tiramisu and strawberry cheesecake. Jo poured them both more wine.

"Are you . . . ," Jo started quietly. She was looking at the wood of the table. "You were upset, or something, at the restaurant. Are you nervous about your promotion?"

What happened at the restaurant had little to do with her promotion, but maybe if Emma could act normal about it, she could throw Jo off the scent. Plus, she *was* nervous about the new job.

"A little," she admitted. "I guess maybe I like my job so much I'm scared to move to something else for fear it won't be as good."

Emma felt vulnerable, saying that, but it was better being vulnerable about her career than about her heart.

"You're going to be fine," Jo said. "We'll both be fine. We're branching out, moving on, and we'll do okay."

Emma breathed. It sounded like a promise, and with it, the tension lifted. Emma and Jo drank and talked and ate dessert and Emma felt okay, felt good. She had a brief moment of panic when Jo made a noise of pleasure over her tiramisu, but besides that, she was fine.

They were both done with dessert and the end of the wine was poured when Jo brought up work again.

"You're going to be a great director," she said. "Lord knows advancement takes forever. But when you get there, you'll be great."

"I don't know about that," Emma said.

"I do," Jo said. "You're smart, and you've got a knack for bringing out the best in people." Her hand fell to Emma's on top of the table, and she squeezed it. "You could do *anything*, and I don't want you to let doubt or anything else hold you back."

Drinking might not have been a good idea. Emma wasn't close to drunk, but her stomach swooped at Jo's smile. Jo's hand burned her skin, even after she pulled it away. Maybe drinking with her boss an hour after realizing her feelings for her actually mattered wasn't the best idea.

"I dropped out of film school," Emma said. Jo already knew, but there was a part of the story she didn't. "My boyfriend at the time told me I wasn't any good. And I don't think I was. And I'm afraid that's just going to happen again, when I try to do something other than be your assistant."

Jo let out a breath. "Your boyfriend saying you weren't good doesn't mean you weren't good. It means he was an asshole."

Emma couldn't help but laugh.

"Sometimes things are hard," Jo said. "Really hard. Sometimes you have to work at them. Sometimes you have to fail first. But that doesn't mean they're not worth doing." She gestured wide enough that Emma pulled her wineglass closer on the table, just in case. "Go for what you want. No matter what anyone says, no matter what anyone thinks. I know you, Emma, and if you put your mind to it, you can do *anything.*"

Emma grinned. "Good pep talk, boss."

Jo beamed at her. Emma's heart did a somersault.

Jo had been in Hollywood for so long, she was probably quite used to modulating her behavior and expressions. Emma didn't get to see Jo smile like this often, full and wide and without a self-conscious bone in her body. With it directed right at her, Emma couldn't look away.

21

EMMA

THEY FOUND THEIR SEATS AT THE GATE, THOUGH THE FLIGHT was delayed further, and they still had time before boarding. Emma buzzed a little, pleasantly warm. She slouched in the chair next to Jo. Neither said anything. It seemed they'd finally talked themselves out. Emma people watched while Jo scrolled through her phone.

EMMA VAGUELY REGISTERED HER name being said, but it was too quiet to pay attention to.

"Emma, wake up."

Emma turned her head. There was something soft against her cheek.

"We're boarding soon." It was Jo who was talking to her, she was pretty sure.

Emma blinked awake, realized she'd been leaning against Jo's shoulder. She jerked herself into an upright position and rubbed at her mouth. She drooled when she slept sometimes, and if she'd drooled on Jo, she might have to kill herself. There didn't seem to be any drool on her face, though, and Jo was smiling at her instead of looking disgusted.

"I'm sorry," Emma said immediately. "I didn't mean to— I shouldn't have—I'm sorry I fell asleep on you."

"It's fine," Jo said. She glanced toward the desk at the gate. "We're boarding soon."

"Right," Emma said.

She didn't feel quite awake yet, still sleep warm and drowsy. The smile on Jo's face was so soft Emma couldn't stop staring at it. Jo caught her.

"You okay?" she said.

"What? Yeah." Emma sat up straighter. "Yeah, I'm good."

Their zone was announced for boarding. As they gathered their bags, Emma noticed Jo flexing her left hand, stretching the fingers wide, then closing them into a fist, like she was trying to get blood flowing to it again. Emma didn't know what time it had been when she fell asleep. How long did she sleep on Jo's shoulder? How long did Jo let her? She wondered if it meant something, or if she was just reading into it because she wanted to see her feelings reciprocated.

She kept quiet all the way through takeoff and hoped Jo assumed it was because she was tired.

"You won't mind if I fall asleep, will you?" Jo asked. "Not all of us got our nap in yet."

Emma gave her a smile. "Of course not, boss."

"Wake me up if you get too bored," Jo said, like that was a thing Emma would ever do.

Jo put on an eye mask and reclined her seat. Emma looked at her, glad she couldn't be caught.

Jo was beautiful. Emma had always known that. Everyone thought so. It wasn't strange to look at her boss on the red carpet and think she was gorgeous, because she was—like, objectively. But it felt different now. Emma looked at her, saw her long hair gathered over one shoulder and thought about how Jo only ever put it in a ponytail when she was stressed. Like when she was on deadline, at the office on a weekend wearing a crewneck sweatshirt but still in her skinny jeans, heels discarded next to the couch. Emma looked at Jo's face and thought of the different ways she smiled, close-lipped mostly, but every once in a while that face broke into a true grin, toothy and glad. Emma looked at Jo and thought she was gorgeous in a way that had nothing to do with objective standards of beauty. Watching her sleep felt too intimate, suddenly.

This whole trip had a strange kind of intimacy. Maybe it was in all business trips. Emma remembered upfronts this year, Jo's hand on her back as she struggled to breathe. She remembered Jo marching into her hotel room with pizza. The previous year's trip to upfronts wasn't like that, though. She'd explored half of Brooklyn by herself that first year, Jo nowhere near to feed her or comfort her or worry about her.

And even this year's upfronts weren't like this trip. This trip, where she and Jo explored Calgary together. Where Jo tightened her scarf and looked at her mouth. Where Jo let her sleep on her shoulder even though it was cutting off blood supply. Jo was casual with her the whole time. Jo smiled and laughed and asked Emma's opinions on everything from the shooting location to what she should order for dinner.

Single Jo, who didn't want to be Emma's boss anymore. Emma wondered if she wanted to be more.

If Jo were interested in her, how would Emma know for sure? Jo would never make a move. Not on an employee, and especially not on an employee who had been sexually harassed in the workplace. Jo would never do anything to make Emma uncomfortable. She hadn't even been the one who initiated the almost kiss. That was all Emma. If anything was going to happen between them, Emma was pretty sure it was going to have to be her. And with Jo's speech about going for what she wanted—yeah, that was about her job, her career, but Emma knew what she wanted.

She wanted to go back to that day in Jo's office after her father left, to have Mason not call and interrupt.

She wanted to go back to that moment on the sidewalk with Jo's hands on her scarf.

She wanted to kiss Jo, more than anything, and Jo had told her to go for what she wanted.

BACK IN LA, CHLOE picked them up from the airport. It was past midnight as they headed toward Emma's apartment first.

It was late and maybe Emma was sleep deprived and imagining things, but the ride home felt tense. Like the moment was a bowstring pulled taut. Emma's hand rested next to Jo's on the middle seat. She would have had to move it only a few inches and they'd be holding hands. Chloe had the privacy divider up; Emma didn't know why. It was closed when they got into the car. It was probably because it was late, and Chloe thought Jo might want to rest, might want the privacy to sleep, but it felt like it meant something more. Jo looked out the window and Emma looked at Jo's hand on the seat next to her and this was their last business trip together. This ride felt like the end of something. Emma wondered if it could be the beginning of something else. Her heart thudded in her ears.

Jo broke the silence in the back of the car. "I had a good trip. I hope you did, too."

"I did, boss," Emma said quietly.

Jo glanced at her, glanced away. Emma pulled her hand back to her side of the car. She swore Jo watched her do it.

When they pulled up to Emma's apartment, Chloe hopped out to take Emma's luggage out of the trunk. Emma stood on the sidewalk, slightly uncomfortable, the way she always was when someone did something for her she could've done herself. The rear window was rolled down and Jo smiled out at Emma as Chloe got back into the driver's seat.

"I'm glad we didn't have any asthma incidents," Jo said. "Like last trip."

Maybe Jo was only talking about her asthma. Maybe Emma shouldn't have read into this.

It was just that asthma had been a stand-in, of sorts. For when Jo wanted to talk about something more, something bigger.

It was fitting that asthma should be the metaphor for whatever was between them. Because sometimes Jo looked at Emma and Emma felt like she couldn't breathe. Jo smiled and Emma's chest clenched. Right now, Emma felt like she needed to kiss Jo more than she needed oxygen.

"Happy birthday, Ms. Kaplan," Jo said. "I hope it's a good one."

Emma had forgotten it was her birthday.

It was her birthday. It was her birthday and Jo told her to go for what she wanted. Still, she couldn't believe what she was doing even as she did it. She took a step closer and put one hand on the car door, holding where Jo's window was rolled down. Jo looked up at her and Emma leaned over, leaned closer.

It was the buildup of the trip, of Jo adjusting her scarf in front of the restaurant and letting Emma fall asleep on her shoulder. It was the buildup of the past year, even. Emma leaned closer and Jo straightened up, maybe unintentionally, maybe out of surprise, but she straightened up enough that Emma's mouth could land easily on hers. It was just the soft press of their lips together, no desperation, no tongue. Jo pushed herself closer. A shiver ran through Emma's entire body. She wanted to capture this moment, take a picture in her mind so she could never forget it.

As quickly as she leaned over, she stood back up, hand still clutching the door. Her eyes stayed closed for a moment.

"It's pretty good so far," she said, and turned to climb the stairs to her apartment building.

Her skin tingled everywhere. Her mouth was numb without Jo's against it. It took her two tries to get her key in the door, and she didn't look back when she went inside.

When she got to her apartment, she looked out the window. Jo must have had Chloe wait to see the lights go on in her apartment— her car was only just pulling away. Emma rubbed her fingers over her lips and couldn't believe herself.

THE FIRST THING EMMA did when she woke up was check her phone. She scrolled through a huge variety of birthday messages and found nothing from Jo. That was . . . good, probably. She'd see her tomorrow at work. They could figure things out then.

Jo had kissed her back. Of that Emma was sure. There wasn't tongue or anything; it wasn't a big kiss, but she had kissed her back. She'd leaned closer. Emma shivered just thinking about it. Maybe Jo would change her mind, maybe she wouldn't want whatever Emma wanted—though Emma herself wasn't sure what that was yet, not really. But she'd kissed back. Emma was always going to have that.

She was still thinking about it when Avery showed up at her door with cinnamon rolls and a cupcake with a candle in it.

Avery grinned and sang all of "Happy Birthday" to her.

Emma closed her eyes. As she blew out the candle, she wished for Jo to want to kiss her again.

"What'd you wish for?" Avery asked.

Emma busied herself with taking the cinnamon rolls to the kitchen so her sister couldn't see her blush.

"You know I can't tell you—then it won't come true."

"I can't believe you follow the same rules as my ten-year-olds," Avery said.

"Well, they've always been precocious," Emma said. "Should I pop two of these in the oven? You want yours warmed, yes?"

"What am I—a heathen? Of course I want it warmed."

Emma put two of the cinnamon rolls in her oven. Her sister had brought her a dozen—she was set for breakfast all week.

"So how was the trip?" Avery said.

"Good," Emma said, going for nonchalant. "She approved everything. So that's officially where we'll film."

"And how was the kissing?" Avery asked.

Emma startled. "What? There was no—why do you think—" She cringed, knowing she'd given herself away.

Indeed, Avery's jaw dropped. "Oh my God. I was just teasing, but you actually kissed, didn't you?"

"Um, maybe?"

"Emma Judith Kaplan!" Avery smacked her on the arm. "This is amazing. I need details. What was it like? How did it happen?"

Emma flushed and couldn't stop her smile. Avery sounded as excited as she was about the whole thing. The oven timer went off then, and Avery waved Emma away.

"I'll get them," she said. "You talk."

Emma tried to explain what it was like at the restaurant. How the thought of leaving Jo had suddenly pummeled her in the chest. She tried to explain the tension on the sidewalk or in the car on the way home for the airport. Like there was electricity in the air. Like the part in a movie where the soundtrack lets you know something important is about to happen.

"And then she said she hoped I had a good birthday, and I just—I—I leaned down and she leaned up, just a little, and I kissed her."

Avery put a plate with a cinnamon roll on it in front of Emma, but Emma couldn't be bothered right now.

"I kissed her," she said again. "And she kissed back. And it wasn't even that big of a kiss but it was *amazing*, Avery, gosh, it was so good. She *kissed me back*. And then I just pulled back and said my birthday had been pretty good so far, and then I came inside."

Avery clicked her tongue. "*Damn*, my sister's smooth."

Emma giggled and rubbed a hand over her face. She finally picked up a fork and attacked her cinnamon roll. Avery had made it, so of course it was delicious.

"So, yeah," Emma said. "She kissed me back. And now I can spend the whole day freaking out about it and we'll see what happens when I go into work tomorrow."

"You're not going to text her or anything?" Avery asked.

"No," Emma said immediately. "What would I even say? No. No. Definitely not."

"So, that's a no then."

"Yeah. No."

They ate their cinnamon rolls in silence for a bit, Emma's heart still pounding over the retelling of the kiss.

"Dylan owes me a hundred bucks," Avery said.

"Hmm?" Emma asked around a bite. She swallowed. "Why?"

"I bet you and Jo would kiss before the end of the year," Avery said.

Emma frowned. "You bet on when Jo and I would kiss?"

"Yeah. He had a lot more faith in you—thought it'd be over summer hiatus."

"What?" Emma stared at her. "When did you make this bet?"

"Uh, the day after the SAGs."

"Avery!"

Her sister just grinned.

"That's mean," Emma said.

Avery laughed. "It's not *mean*. It was fun and had no effect on you."

"It's mean in spirit," Emma insisted. "Making a bet on when we're going to kiss just because of some rumors."

"Oh no, Em, that's not what it was," Avery said. "We knew you had a thing for Jo before the SAGs even happened. That just sped it along a bit."

Emma blinked. The last two bites of her cinnamon roll sat on her plate, long forgotten.

"Avery, *I* didn't even know I had a thing for her," she said. "I'm not sure I *did* have a thing for her until this summer, maybe."

"Okay, maybe it wasn't that you had a thing for her," Avery hedged. "But you know when you're watching a show and two characters interact, and you're like, 'They're going to fall in love,' and it takes three seasons but eventually they do? It was kind of like that."

Emma went red. "We're not *in love*."

Avery smirked and said nothing. Emma thought her sister probably wasn't done betting on her love life.

EMMA WOKE UP AND went for a run before work on Monday morning. She cut a full minute off her usual pace, full of nerves.

She showered and spent half an hour trying to make her hair look nice, but not so nice that it seemed unusual. From her closet she picked navy tights and a gray sweaterdress. It was her most comfortable professional outfit, felt like she was snuggled up on her couch but looked like she could run a meeting. If the day didn't go well, at least she would be cozy.

At the coffee shop, there was a chai latte waiting for her along with Jo's regular order. Emma didn't know if that was a good thing or not. Maybe it was an "I'm sorry I'm going to break your heart later today" latte. She told herself she wasn't going to worry about it, but then she immediately began fretting over how to greet Jo when she came in. Was *morning, boss* too casual? Should she act like nothing was different? She couldn't even remember how she usually greeted Jo in the mornings.

When she heard Jo's footsteps down the hallway, Emma got up, stood next to her desk. She held Jo's latte and put a real, albeit nervous, smile on her face.

22

JO

J O DIDN'T LOOK AT EMMA WHEN SHE HANDED OVER HER coffee. She couldn't stand to see the smile fall off Emma's face, the hope drain from her eyes. Jo closed her office door behind her.

She had no idea what she was going to do about Emma. She had spent yesterday writing forty-seven different text messages and sending none of them. She'd typed declarations of love and curt dismissals and everything in between. When it finally got so bad that she was going to cave and call Evelyn, she got an email from a photographer.

Care to comment? it read, with pictures attached.

Pictures of Emma, bending over on the sidewalk in front of her building, of Jo's face through the open car window, of their mouths pressing gently together.

Jo had wanted to throw up.

She still wanted to. Took one sip of her coffee and choked on the bitter flavor. She'd throw it away if she didn't need the caffeine to make it through the day. She opened her laptop and looked at the pictures again.

This was what she had to offer Emma: scrutiny, invasion of privacy, scandal. This was all she'd given Emma for the past eleven months.

Jo let out a shaky breath. She called Evelyn.

Ev picked up on the second ring. Jo barely let her say hello.

"I need you to react as a lawyer right now, not as my best friend," she said.

Evelyn didn't hesitate. "Okay," she said. "Hit me."

"Emma and I kissed Saturday night," Jo said, and ignored Evelyn's intake of breath. "A photographer sent me pictures of it, asking for comment. I need an NDA."

There was a pause.

"I can get it to you in an hour," Evelyn said.

Jo heaved a sigh. "Thank you."

The only sound was the clacking of Evelyn's keyboard.

"Can I react like a friend now?" she asked.

"Evelyn . . ."

"I want to know how you are."

Jo scrubbed a hand through her hair and didn't know how to answer. "I need to handle the photographer."

"Okay," Evelyn said. "I'll get back to you."

Jo continued to listen to Evelyn type for a few minutes before ending the call.

JO KEPT HER DOOR closed. She asked Emma for nothing. Evelyn, true to her word, called back in an hour.

"I emailed it to you," she said. "How much money is he asking?"

"Doesn't matter," Jo said. It wasn't like she wasn't going to pay.

"Your contract ensures there's no other copies? No chance it will get out?"

"I know you're stressed, but you know better than to underestimate me."

"You're right." Jo pressed her palm to her forehead. "God, Evelyn, this is . . ."

"Fucked?" Evelyn offered. "How does Emma feel about it?"

Jo steeled herself for Evelyn's frustration. "I haven't told her about it."

"What?"

"I haven't talked to her today except to thank her for my coffee."

"Aiyah." Evelyn dragged out the last vowel. "What are you doing?"

"She doesn't need this, Evelyn," Jo said. "She doesn't need any of this."

"How is ignoring her helping?"

"I'm not ignoring her," Jo said. Avoiding her, yes. Ignoring her, no. "I'll talk to her after I figure this out."

Jo could tell Evelyn was annoyed by the way she breathed over the line. Her exasperation didn't bleed into her tone when she talked, though.

"What happened?"

"She kissed me." Jo's voice was so small she wished it weren't her own. "And that would be confusing enough without someone having pictures." She sighed, then continued before Evelyn could cut in. "She just has to get through the week. Then she'll be associate producer when *Innocents* comes back and I'll be on Agent Silver. We'll both move on. It will be fine. She won't have to deal with any more of this paparazzi shit."

"Please, dear God, talk to her before you decide that," Evelyn said. "I know you're not used to feelings and have no idea what you're doing, but don't make the decision for her."

Jo promised nothing.

THE PHOTOGRAPHER CAME TO Jo's office. Best to treat it as a business deal. Jo finished a meeting with Chantal to find the man beside Emma's desk, grinning cheek to cheek.

"Please, come in," she said with more grimace than smile.

He greeted Chantal and told Emma to have a good day and Jo wanted to punch him.

She got his signature and showed him the envelope full of cash, then watched him delete the photos before handing it over.

He grinned. "Pleasure doing business with you."

Jo absolutely wanted to punch him.

He shouldn't have been at Emma's apartment. The rumors had ended months ago. No one should have suspected anything enough to stake the place out. He *had* to be tipped off. Chantal and Emma were the only two Jo was aware of who knew enough specifics of their trip to leak it. Emma must have told someone. Jo couldn't stomach the thought of anything else. She and Chantal had worked together for more than a decade.

There was cake at lunch to celebrate both Emma's birthday and the end of the year. Jo stood in the corner and watched. She watched everyone who wished Emma a happy birthday, analyzed their facial expressions, their body language. Chantal was subdued, Tate was gregarious. Nothing unusual. Jo's heart thundered at the smile on Emma's face. Nothing unusual.

Toward the end of the break, Chantal tipped her head at Jo, and Jo followed her out of the lunch area. She expected a conversation about the show, didn't expect how low Chantal kept her voice.

"It's not my business," she said, "but I saw an exchange between the man in your office earlier today and a PA."

Jo let out a harsh breath. "With me," she said, and quickly led Chantal to her office, closing the door behind them. "What kind of exchange?"

"Manila envelope."

Jo all but collapsed onto her couch, rubbing a hand over her face.

"This leak is so bad, I thought it might be you," she admitted.

"That'd be a cold day in hell," Chantal said.

Jo knew. "Which PA?"

EVERY YEAR JO GAVE everyone on set holiday cards. They were nondenominational and included a Visa gift card and a generic thank-you. When Emma had been in props, she'd gotten the usual *Thank you for your hard work* with the big swoosh of Jo's autograph. Her first year as an assistant, Jo wrote something about how quickly and easily Emma picked up her new job. She signed it *boss*, and Emma's gift card was twice the amount of everyone else's.

Jo hadn't written hers this year yet.

She had written the rest of the cast and crew's letters weeks ago, but kept Emma's set aside. It was white with blue sparkling snowflakes on the front. Intra-office mail was delivering the letters today. Emma's was still on Jo's desk. Jo opened it, tried not to think too hard.

Emma, you don't just make my job easier, you make my life better. I am so grateful to have you in it.

She should have thought harder. Should have made it generic. She imagined Emma's face if she had just written *thanks*, and knew every option she had was a bad one.

She held the pen just above the card for a moment, hesitating on her signature. *Jo.* Not *Jo Jones*, the looping autograph most people got. Just *Jo*, small and messy, with a blob of ink at the start of the *J*.

Emma had meetings all afternoon, coordinating to ensure the set was shut down correctly. Jo waited until it was almost the end of the day before dropping the card on Emma's desk while she was away. She retreated into her office and closed the door.

Five minutes later, her door flew open. Emma marched in, swung the door shut behind her, catching it right before it slammed and closing it more gently.

She rounded on Jo, her eyes blazing.

"You don't get to do this," she said. "You don't get to not even *look* at me all day and then drop *this* on my desk when I'm away from it." She waved the opened envelope containing her holiday card. "I never took you for a coward, Jo."

Jo loved Emma for this, for her fire, for her refusal to back down. She loved her and she wanted to be with her and she knew she deserved so much more than Jo could offer. So Jo didn't tip her hand.

"I've been busy," she said calmly.

"You haven't done anything but shut yourself in this office all day," Emma snapped.

"Yes, well, I had some calls to make," Jo said. "Someone had to take care of the photographer who was outside of your apartment Saturday night."

The color drained from Emma's face. "What?"

"He was set to make quite a lot of money for photos of Jo Jones kissing her assistant in front of her apartment building at one in the morning," Jo said. "It's been taken care of."

She fluttered her hand like it was nothing.

"What did you do?" Emma's voice was wary.

"Oh, for Christ's sake, Emma, it's not like I had him killed." Jo rolled her eyes. "I bought the photos. And the contract he's signed means if he still has any copies and they show up anywhere, I take basically everything he owns. Including his dog."

Jo didn't want his dog, but Evelyn had added a little levity to the NDA.

"How much did you pay for them?" Emma asked.

That wasn't something Jo would ever tell her.

"You're asking the wrong questions," she said instead.

Emma's brow furrowed. It took her a moment, but she got there.

"Why was a photographer in front of my apartment at one in the morning?"

"There it is," Jo said.

"Why was a photographer there?"

"I let your friend Phil go earlier this afternoon."

Jo kept her voice detached. She watched a wave of emotions cross Emma's face: confusion, understanding, anger. Emma glowered.

"Why does it even matter?" she asked. "It never mattered when people thought I was fucking you for *months*, but *one* picture of us kissing and you ignore me for the entire day trying to deal with it?"

Jo gaped at her. Was it possible Emma truly didn't understand how far over her head Jo was when it came to her? Emma didn't flinch. Jo pinched the bridge of her nose.

"Are you serious?"

Emma crossed her arms, chin held high. Jo should've taken the out, should've pretended it was nothing to her—she was just protecting Emma's reputation. Instead, she snapped.

"Of course it matters now," she said with more emotion than she'd shown Emma all day. "It didn't matter when it was a stupid rumor that meant nothing. This means something, okay? It meant something to me, and I don't think the entire world should see it."

Her chest heaved. Emma's arms dropped to her sides.

"It meant something to you?" she asked, voice small.

Jo's voice was just as small when she replied, "Of course it meant something to me."

She wasn't supposed to admit it. She was supposed to send Emma into a new position with nothing holding her back. A clean break.

She took a breath and moved on. "Which is why I gave Phil an excellent severance package, provided he also signed an NDA."

"Right," Emma said.

She looked at her feet, scuffing them against the ground. Jo had no idea what was going on in her head. When Emma looked back up, her eyes shone. Jo pressed her lips together.

"I—" Jo stopped. Swallowed. Wished this were easier. "Why . . ."

This time last year, Emma would've finished the sentence for her. Would've answered the question without it being asked. Even now, if this were about work, Emma would've already solved it. Jo knew she couldn't make Emma be the one to deal with this, though.

"It's past five," Jo said, her voice flat. "I'm fine here. You can go home."

Emma turned on her heels and went. No *Bye, boss.* Not even a *Good night, Ms. Jones.* The door closed behind her, and Jo dropped her forehead to the edge of her desk.

It was the right decision, she told herself, to let Emma go. To not explain just how much the kiss meant to her. But her heart felt like it was trying to get out of her chest, like it was connected to the woman who'd walked out the door and it was stretching to reach her.

Jo stayed facedown on her desk and called Evelyn.

"Hey." Evelyn's voice was as gentle as it got.

"Tell me what to do, Evelyn," Jo begged.

"What have you done so far?"

Jo sighed and sat up. She leaned back in her desk chair.

"I bought the pictures and paid off the photographer," she said. "I fired the leak on set—paid him off, too. And I told Emma all of that. And then I told her to go home."

"Seems like you've made your decision then," Evelyn said, like she didn't know Jo was agonizing over this. "What part do you need help with?"

"The part where I want to go after her."

She did. Desperately. But Emma deserved better.

"Go, then," Evelyn said.

Jo groaned and put her forehead back down on her desk.

"Chasing her solves nothing," she said. "It doesn't matter if I want her, if she wants me. Just rumors of a relationship led to her being sexually harassed. Actually dating me would taint all of her accomplishments from now on. Everyone would think she only got them because of me. It's not worth it."

"Talk to her about this, Jo, not me."

"I *can't*," Jo insisted.

Emma could have convinced her of anything right now. Jo had to look at this with her head, not her heart.

"For God's sake, Evelyn, I'm not even out."

Ev scoffed. "You're not *out* out, but come on. The media already thought you were dating."

"Yes, they did, and look how that worked out. Barry Davis sexually harassed Emma because he assumed she was already trading sexual favors for a job."

"Barry Davis sexually harassed Emma because he is a disgusting creep. You don't get to blame yourself for that."

Jo would never stop feeling guilty about it, though.

She changed tactics. "What do I bring to a relationship? I don't even know how to be in one. Why would Emma want to date a fortysomething who has no experience? I've *never* had a long-term relationship."

"Why don't you ask Emma what you offer? See things from her eyes instead." Evelyn sighed. "Jesus, Jo, you basically just admitted you want to be in a long-term relationship with her. Can't you at least give yourself a chance?"

But if she ended it before she began, she could mitigate the hurt.

"If you wanted to be talked out of it, you wouldn't have called me," Evelyn said. "You knew my opinion when you dialed. You knew you were going to get nothing but encouragement. Are you sure you want to be talked out of it? Or do you think you're lying to yourself?"

Jo closed her eyes. Breathed.

"Jo, you've had thirty years in Hollywood and forty-two on this bitch of an earth," Evelyn said. "People are going to find any way they can to dismiss Emma the way they dismiss every woman. You know that."

She did.

"This is a bad idea," Jo said.

"So was calling out the show that made you famous, but you could do that when you were just a kid," Evelyn said.

"That's a low blow."

Evelyn had read every draft of Jo's essay for *The Johnson Dynasty*'s ten-year anniversary. She'd never let Jo quit on it.

"What are you so afraid of now?"

Heartbreak.

Jo was afraid of hurting Emma. Afraid of hurting Emma's career. But mostly she was afraid of Emma realizing Jo wasn't worth it and breaking her heart.

She said none of this, but Evelyn seemed to know.

"Stop making excuses," Evelyn said.

"I have to go," Jo said.

23

EMMA

EMMA CALLED AVERY AS SOON AS SHE GOT HOME.

"So Phil was the leak," she said instead of hello. "Phil was fucking leaking stuff to the tabloids, and he apparently gave our flight information to a photographer and so this guy was outside my apartment late at night when we got back, which means—"

Avery sucked in a breath.

"Yup," Emma snapped. "There were pictures of us kissing."

"What are you going to do?" Avery asked.

Emma waved her hand around vaguely. She was pacing her apartment. "Jo already bought them or whatever, so it's fine."

"Yeah?" Avery said. "And how did Jo feel about the kiss?"

A whole day at work, and Emma still wasn't sure. Jo had said it meant something. Or maybe only the pictures of the kiss meant something.

"Whatever," Emma grumbled. "I don't want to talk about it."

"Em."

There was a knock on the door. It was probably Raegan, her neighbor who locked herself out on a regular basis. She was the only person who knocked on Emma's door.

"One sec, my neighbor's here," Emma said as she grabbed Raegan's spare key off the hook she kept it on and pulled her door open.

It wasn't Raegan.

It was Jo.

"Hi," Jo said, a coffee cup in each hand, shoulders curled in on herself.

"Avery, I gotta go," Emma said. She ended the call. Swallowed. "Hi."

"Chai," Jo said, thrusting one of the drinks toward her. "If you want."

Emma wanted to be mad. She wanted to ignore Jo the way Jo had ignored her all day.

She took the chai instead.

"Do you want to—"

"Can I—"

They both started, stopped. Jo laughed nervously.

Emma looked down the hallway like there would be paparazzi inside her apartment building.

"Come in," she said then, taking a step back and pulling the door open wider.

"Thank you," Jo said.

She only came far enough inside for Emma to close the door behind her. Emma had no idea what she was doing here. She was so used to making things easier for Jo, she almost wanted to start the conversation herself. But she deserved better than that. Better than Jo ignoring her all day, then randomly showing up at her apartment with nothing to say.

"I haven't stopped—since Saturday night—all I can think about—" Jo started three different sentences and didn't finish a single one.

"Come," Emma said. "Sit down."

She led Jo to the kitchen island, and they sat on stools next to each other. Emma took a sip of her drink, then set it down. She swirled liquid around instead of looking at Jo.

"This is a terrible idea," Jo said.

Emma's heart did a swan dive. She thought if Jo was here, it meant—she'd been moping since she handed Jo her coffee this morning, and she thought Jo being here was going to change that, but—

"I kept telling myself all the reasons it's a bad idea," Jo said. "Since Saturday. Since my dad visited. You're too young and I'm too old and I don't even have any idea how to be in a relationship and you work for me and, and, and."

"Right," Emma said. She hopped off her stool. She had to get Jo out of her apartment before she cried. She took three steps toward the door. "Well, thanks for the chai. I'll see you—"

"Emma."

Jo caught her by the wrist, slid off her stool, and came to stand in front of her.

"Can I kiss you again?"

"Wh-what?"

Emma's eyes bounced from Jo's gaze to her lips to her eyes again. Her breath hiccupped and she didn't have any words, but she nodded, so suddenly that she might've pulled a muscle, and then Jo was kissing her. Jo was kissing her and it was just like last time in how soft and *perfect* it was, but it was also nothing like last time, because Jo put her hands on Emma's hips, held on when Emma's knees went weak.

When Jo pulled away, she didn't go far. They were still close enough to breathe each other's air.

"So you don't hate me for kissing you?" Emma said.

Jo chuckled, bumping her nose against Emma's. "Not much chance of that, no."

She kissed her again.

This kiss was longer, deeper. Jo's tongue brushed Emma's, and asthma really was the best metaphor for their relationship—Emma wasn't sure she was ever going to be able to breathe normally again. Her arms were draped over Jo's shoulders. Even still in her heels from work, Jo was shorter than Emma.

"Do you . . . we could order food or something?" Emma said.

Jo looked like she was going to say yes, like she was saying yes to the *or something*, the way she had to drag her eyes from Emma's lips.

"I shouldn't stay," she said instead. "This *is* a bad idea, you know? We have to do everything right with how we frame it, or it's going to be a disaster. It's probably going to be a disaster anyway, coming after the rumors."

"Hey," Emma said. She dropped a hand down to catch one of Jo's. "We're not going to be a disaster."

Jo smiled up at her, all soft and beautiful. "No," she said. "We're not."

God, it was surreal. To be holding Jo and talking like this, like they were a *we*.

Jo did stay, for a while. They sat next to each other on the couch and talked about things, their drinks sitting forgotten. Jo admitted she'd had feelings since her father's visit; Emma admitted she wasn't sure hers mattered until Calgary. Jo asked four separate times if Emma was sure, if she knew her promotion had nothing to do with Jo's feelings, if she really wanted to do this.

Emma said, "More than anything," and all the tension bled out of Jo's posture.

They did agree Jo shouldn't stay. They didn't want to be in the tabloids again, and she'd already had to pay off one photographer.

Emma kissed Jo one last time within the safety of her apartment before sending her on her way.

Once Jo was gone, Emma raced down her hallway and hurled herself onto her bed. She lay spread-eagle, staring at the ceiling, a grin on her face she couldn't get rid of if she tried.

But she didn't have to get rid of it. She could smile as much as she wanted because Jo *liked* her. Emma's whole body twinkled. She thought about calling Avery back, but didn't. This was just hers for the moment. Emma wondered if Jo's heart felt as fluttery as hers did right now.

THE THING ABOUT KISSING Jo the last week of work before hiatus was that now it was hiatus. Now they had four weeks off work. Now Emma didn't have an excuse to see Jo every day.

She got up early on Saturday and went to services. She called her mother after, endured some questions about Jo, and discussed their plans for the first night of Hanukkah. Avery was hosting, as usual, and Emma couldn't wait for all the food. She'd feel bad that her favorite part of most holidays was the food, but her sister loved making it as much as Emma loved eating it.

Emma lasted until about four in the afternoon before her palms itched so much she picked up her phone. It had been less than twenty-four hours since she'd last seen Jo, and yet she had this *need* to talk to her, text her, something.

Is it uncool to miss you already?

As soon as Emma sent it, she decided *yes*, it was *incredibly* uncool, and Jo would probably think she was an idiot. Instead, her phone rang.

She stopped herself from picking up immediately. Took a breath and brushed her hand over her shirt like there were wrinkles she needed to smooth out. Answered the phone.

"Hey," she said quietly.

"I don't think it's uncool," Jo said.

Emma released her breath, smiled. "No?"

"Or if it is, I'm uncool, too, I guess."

Was smiling into the phone in silence for a good ten seconds uncool? Because that was what Emma did next.

"How was your day?" Jo asked eventually.

"Good," Emma said. "Nothing special. You?"

"Nothing special," Jo parroted. "I feel ridiculous, how much I want to see you."

Emma felt like her chest burst open.

"It's not ridiculous," she said.

"It is," Jo said. "It's Saturday. It's not like we would normally see each other on a Saturday."

"We did last Saturday, though."

Calgary was only a week ago. The flight and the drive home and the kiss in front of Emma's apartment. Emma felt warm all over.

"We have to be able to go more than twenty-four hours without seeing each other," Jo said. "We have to go this whole hiatus."

Emma knew. They weren't supposed to see each other over *Innocents'* hiatus, were not supposed to appear to be dating. Emma was pretty sure they could totally get away with seeing each other, but Jo wanted to be careful. For as much as she hadn't cared what people thought during the rumors, she cared now. She didn't want to get in trouble, didn't want to do anything that might jeopardize Emma's new job. Which was nice and good and Emma appreciated it—Emma just also wanted to see Jo.

"What about New Year's?" Emma said.

"We can't go out on New Year's, Emma," Jo said. "Do you know how many photographers lurk on New Year's Eve, waiting to catch someone in a compromising position?"

"I didn't say *go out*. I'd suggest you come here, but I'd guess it's easier to catch you coming into my building than it would be me going to your house."

Jo was quiet for a moment. "Did you just invite yourself over for New Year's Eve?"

Emma was glad Jo couldn't see her blush over the phone. "I mean, yes, but only because it makes sense. We'd be—"

"Yes," Jo said. "You should come over. I like that idea."

"Okay."

"Okay."

Emma grinned like a fool.

New Year's was two weeks away, but they could make it.

HANUKKAH ARRIVED FIRST.

Emma was already at Avery's when her parents got there. Hugs abounded, and just like at Passover, when her dad hugged her, he asked about Jo.

"You didn't bring her this time, either? When are we going to meet her?"

"When I can trust you not to be obnoxious," Emma said. "So probably never."

Emma loved Hanukkah because she loved any holiday she got to spend with family. Her mom lit the candles, like she did every year. They all sang together, and Ezra was especially careful as he carried the menorah to the window. Then it was on to latkes and jelly doughnuts. Emma really loved the food.

The entire family was piled into Avery's living room, Emma on the floor with the dogs and the twins both. The pile of food on the coffee table was so big you wouldn't know they had all already eaten more than enough.

Emma's phone buzzed.

Can I call the first night of Hanukkah or is that family time?

Emma couldn't help her smile at Jo's text. She claimed to have eaten too many latkes, said she needed a break.

"There's no such thing as too many latkes," Dani said, dunking another one in applesauce and putting it in her mouth.

Emma laughed at her and slipped into the privacy of the laundry room. She called Jo.

She could hear the smile in Jo's voice when she picked up. "Hi."

"Hi," Emma said back. She smiled into the phone herself. "You're allowed to call on Hanukkah."

"Okay, good," Jo said. "I didn't want to interrupt anything."

"All you're interrupting is everyone stuffing their faces with latkes," Emma said. "We haven't made it to dreidel yet."

"Are you having fun?"

"I am."

Even more fun now. Emma felt like she was a teenager, sneaking away from a family event to talk to a girl on the phone in a hushed voice. Her stomach was doing swoops.

They both stayed silent, Emma pressed the phone tight to her ear and tried to tamp down her grin.

"I didn't have much of a reason to call," Jo admitted. "I was just thinking about you. Wanted to wish you a happy Hanukkah."

"I appreciate it."

It was all so new. It didn't feel fragile, but Emma knew they were both being careful anyway, both unsure of what came next. It was too important to rush into and mess up; she hoped Jo thought so, too. It was nerves but not nervousness, anticipation but not apprehension. Everything between them was a big ball of potential, and Emma couldn't wait to see how it turned out.

"I should probably get back to my family," Emma said.

"Yes, of course," Jo said. "Tell them hello from me, if that's not weird."

"Oh, my parents would *love* it. They're probably going to be totally obnoxious when you meet them."

"Meeting the parents already, huh?"

Emma knew Jo was teasing, but it worried her a bit anyway.

"I'm kidding," Jo said quickly. "I can't wait to meet them. I'm incredibly charming and can do a good enough job teasing both of their daughters, they're sure to love me."

They really were, was the thing. Kind of like how Emma thought she might feel about her. Not that she'd said it.

Jo kept talking when Emma didn't say anything. "You've already met my father, anyway. Seems like meeting your parents will probably be more fun."

"It will," Emma said. "You're right—they'll love you. I promise."

Emma definitely felt like a teenager, butterflies in her stomach and perpetual grin on her face.

"Okay, now go," Jo said. "You can call me later if you want."

"Okay."

"Go," Jo said again, laughing this time, and Emma hung up with her skin tingling everywhere at the sound.

"Where have you been?" Emma's mom asked when she returned to the living room.

Emma hadn't put her phone away yet, and that was a mistake, she realized, as Avery laughed.

"Were you talking to your *girlfriend*?" Avery said.

The whole family ganged up on her.

Emma wanted to be annoyed by the teasing, but it was hard. The jokes were overshadowed by everyone gleefully calling Jo her girlfriend.

ON NEW YEAR'S EVE, Emma tried on seven different outfits. She videochatted with Avery, did a fashion show of sorts. Avery picked out her two best choices. Emma changed back and forth between them three more times before settling on one.

She bought daffodils on her way over, hoped it didn't seem too cliché. They reminded her of Jo's dress at the SAGs, and she thought they'd make Jo smile.

Emma had seen Jo's house before—the entryway mostly. Though she had even seen Jo's bedroom before, once having to pick up a change of clothes when Jo spilled coffee before a meeting with the network and her spare office set was at the dry cleaner. Emma mostly remembered Jo's closet, remembered it being as big as her entire apartment, though that was probably an exaggeration.

It was new, being shown into the house for the first time instead of simply being there for work. Jo answered the door in her usual black skinny jeans. Her feet were bare. She was so small, Emma immediately wanted to wrap her in a hug. Her shirt was thin and loose, a wide scoop neck. The pop of Jo's collarbones made Emma blush.

"Come in," Jo said with a grin. "Can I take your coat?"

"Yeah, thanks."

Emma shucked her coat, which Jo hung in a closet by the door, and took off her shoes.

"Are those for me?" Jo gestured to the flowers in Emma's hands.

"Um," Emma said. "Yes."

She thrust them toward Jo. Her nerves were getting the best of her, but she had no control over it. She was in Jo's house for a *date*, and Jo wouldn't stop smiling at her. Jo didn't stop smiling when she took the flowers, either. Instead, she put a hand on Emma's wrist, and Emma remembered, with blinding clarity, their moment on the red carpet almost a full year ago, Jo making Emma laugh so she forgot about her anxiety.

"Emma," Jo said, still with a smile. "I think this will work better if we're both a *little* nervous instead of you being *crazy* nervous."

"I'm not crazy nervous," Emma said immediately. Jo tilted her head and raised her eyebrows, and Emma sighed. "I might be crazy nervous."

"I know," Jo said. "And it's adorable, but unnecessary."

Warmth expanded out from Emma's chest. She couldn't help the way her mouth broke into a grin. Jo squeezed her wrist.

"Come help me get these in water," Jo said.

She slid her hand down, locked her fingers with Emma's, and tugged her farther into the house. Emma felt warm all over by this point. Her nerves settled down a bit.

Jo's kitchen was huge, opening into an equally huge living room. Emma hadn't seen this part of the house when she'd been there before, had turned down a hallway to get to Jo's room before making it this far inside. There was an enormous refrigerator, two ovens, and a big farm sink set into the counter.

"God, Avery would *kill* for this kitchen," Emma said, eyes wide. "How do you even have time to use it?"

"I don't have enough, certainly," Jo said.

She let go of Emma's hand to pull out a cutting board from behind some ceramic jars labeled *flour* and *sugar*. She set the flowers on the cutting board and pulled a knife from a knife block.

"Cut these while I find a vase?"

Emma was happy to have a task.

"I cook most weekends," Jo continued, answering Emma's earlier question. "I keep trying to get Avery to give me her recipe for chocolate babka so I can try it out myself."

She set a vase beside the cutting board Emma was using.

"Good luck," Emma said. "She changed something from the recipe our mom gave her for it, and she didn't even tell *our mom* what the change was for, like, three years. She guards recipes with her life."

"Maybe once I meet your mom, I'll charm it out of her instead."

Emma stopped cutting the stems, just for a moment, took a breath, and smiled to herself. Sure, they had talked about Jo meeting her parents during Hanukkah, it was just—it was hard to believe she was standing in Jo's kitchen while Jo talked about charming family recipes out of her mother.

"Or," Jo said, standing sideways next to Emma and leaning her hip against the counter. "Can I charm the recipe out of you?"

Emma grinned at her. "I hate to break it to you, but I don't have it."

Jo laughed. "How do you not have a family recipe?"

"Because I don't make things right, apparently," Emma said. "Even though I always follow recipes exactly, nothing ever turns out quite right. Avery says I don't have the touch."

"Following recipes exactly is your first mistake," Jo said. "Everyone knows the recipe is just a suggestion."

"No!" Emma huffed at her. "People put effort into making a cookbook! There are recipe testers and everything. The recipe is literally tested so you can re-create what they've made. How is it a suggestion?"

Jo got a wooden spoon full of the sauce that was simmering on one of the gas burners. She held it to Emma's lips.

"The original recipe for this called for one clove of garlic, which is ridiculous," Jo said. "I used three tonight."

Emma *mmm*ed around the burst of flavor on her tongue.

"Do you think I should've followed the recipe instead?" Jo asked.

"No, boss," Emma said, then froze.

Jo raised her eyebrows at her, smirking.

"I'm going to go die in a hole now," Emma said, burying her hands in her face, and Jo broke into laughter.

"Come on," Jo said. "It was cute!"

She tried to tug Emma's hands away from her face. Emma only put up a little fight before relenting.

"It was not *cute*," she said. "You're not my boss anymore. You're my—my—"

She panicked then, unsure what she was supposed to call this. Her family called Jo her girlfriend, sure, but they hadn't said it to each other.

Jo smirked at her again, and Emma turned even redder. She put the daffodils in the vase on the counter.

"You can call me your girlfriend," Jo said quietly. "If that's something you want to do."

"Yeah," Emma said, maybe too quickly. She tried to tone down her eagerness. "Yeah, like, I think that'd be nice."

Jo smiled at her, and Emma definitely wanted to call her her girlfriend.

For dinner, Jo had made her salmon with a lemon butter sauce and roasted butternut squash on the side. It was delicious, and

Emma told her so at least three times as they ate. Their nerves had settled now, and conversation flowed easily.

Emma insisted on helping clean up afterward. She loaded the dishwasher while Jo washed the pans. It felt, somewhat embarrassingly, like work felt over the summer, just the two of them, getting things done, occasionally making each other laugh. Emma understood a bit more about why Avery bet on her love life. This felt like an inevitable conclusion to the year, even as it was also the start of something completely new.

They moved to the couch once the dishes were done. There were still almost two hours until midnight, but Jo turned on a New Year's Eve show anyway. She sat right up against Emma on the couch, their whole sides together, and even this far into the night, it was surreal to touch Jo like this. Emma paid no attention to the TV. She couldn't pull her eyes away from Jo's face.

Jo smiled when she noticed Emma looking, gave her a half roll of her eyes. But then she didn't look away, either. Emma leaned in.

They kissed slowly. Gently. Like they couldn't believe they were allowed to. That was how Emma felt, anyway. This felt off-limits. It was like Avery teaching her to drive in an empty grocery store parking lot when she was fourteen. She hadn't gone over fifteen miles per hour that first time, but it still felt like flying. That was what this felt like, exhilarating and terrifying and easy to crash.

Jo never made a move. She kissed Emma, so, so softly, but she never pushed for more. Emma was the first to open her mouth. Emma was the first to brush her fingers through Jo's hair, to clutch at her hips and pull her closer. Jo always reciprocated, but she never made the first move.

"Is this okay?" They both asked it at the same time as Emma pulled away to nip at Jo's jaw.

They froze in their synchronicity for a moment before dissolving into giggles. Jo was leaning into Emma, not quite in her lap but almost, and Emma buried her face in Jo's neck and laughed.

"It's okay with me," Jo said, stroking her fingers through Emma's hair.

Emma grabbed Jo by the waist and tugged her closer, so Jo was actually in her lap, straddling her. "Still okay?"

Jo smiled. "More than okay."

They made out like teenagers. Emma didn't move things along now that she had Jo in her lap, and Jo herself still seemed content with whatever Emma wanted. What Emma wanted was exactly what she had: Jo on top of her and kissing her and kissing her and kissing her. Emma's hand barely slipped under Jo's shirt, her fingers resting against the skin of Jo's back.

It really did feel like learning to drive. Felt like something that, objectively, Emma knew people did—every day people did this. But her heart was in her throat anyway. She knew it was just kissing but it felt like everything.

"Actually," Emma said, pulling back a little. "Can we—can we take a break?"

"Of course," Jo said.

She pulled back farther, trying to climb out of Emma's lap. Emma's hands tightened on her hips.

"No, don't go," Emma said. "I just—the kissing is a lot. My heart is—fast."

Jo's concern melted into a bright smile.

"Good fast?"

Emma nodded. "Too-good fast."

"You know, you are breathing kind of heavily," Jo said, a teasing lilt in her voice. "You're not going to have an asthma attack on me, are you?"

Emma poked Jo in the side. "Be nice to me."

"Always," Jo said immediately, and Emma couldn't help but kiss her again. Jo laughed into her mouth. "I thought we were taking a break."

"Break's over," Emma said.

She moved things along this time. She bunched the hem of Jo's shirt in her fists before leaning back to check in. Jo nodded. Emma pulled the shirt over her head.

And now Jo was in her lap in jeans and a bra. A black lacy bra. Emma had to take another break, just for a moment. Jo used the time to take Emma's shirt off her.

"You're beautiful," Jo said, and Emma kissed her.

There was so much skin to explore. Emma ran her hands up Jo's bare back, and they both shivered. She held Jo's waist, ghosted her hands over Jo's chest until they were up on either side of Jo's neck, holding gently. Jo scratched her fingers over Emma's abdomen.

Emma moved her mouth to those collarbones she had blushed over when she arrived, kissed at first, then bit.

"Maybe we should move to the bedroom?" Jo's voice was mostly breath.

"We'll miss seeing the ball drop," Emma said. She wasn't doing a great job of putting thoughts together.

"I think we'll live."

Jo pulled Emma off the couch and tugged her down the hallway. Emma didn't care about the ball dropping at all.

"Stay here," Jo said at the door to her bedroom.

Outside the sky could have been falling—meteors or atomic bombs. The world could have been ending. Even then, Emma wouldn't have taken her eyes off Jo, moving darkly through the room until clicking on a lamp by the side of the bed. It glowed, soft and warm, and Jo returned to Emma's side. Her bedroom was a cocoon. Still and silent from the outside but the two of them within, growing and changing and—

Kissing. So much kissing. Like they were making up for lost time. Like the world really was ending, and if this was their last moment, they wanted to spend it as a tangle of skin and mouths and tenderness.

Jo, who had followed Emma's lead thus far, walked backward to her own bed, pulling Emma along with her. She hopped up to sit on the edge of the mattress and wrapped her legs around Emma's waist.

Emma bent to suck at the soft skin of Jo's neck. She tried to keep her voice level.

"Please tell me I can take off your pants."

"That's the idea," Jo murmured, sounding way more composed than Emma felt.

Emma's hands practically tore at the button of Jo's pants. The skinny jeans were tight enough that Jo's underwear came off, too. Emma froze. Swallowed. Stared.

Jo smirked and reached behind herself to unclasp her bra.

Emma stared some more.

Jo wore dark sunglasses in public. She ducked her head away from the flashes of paparazzi cameras. In interviews, when asked about her successes, Jo always pivoted to discussing people who had helped her accomplish them.

Yet here she was in front of Emma, shoulders back and head high, preening. Emma wasn't sure she'd ever seen Jo so pleased to be the center of attention.

She deserved to be proud, though. All smooth skin and perfection. Those infernal collarbones. Emma was going to combust.

She stepped closer to the bed, but before she could get her

hands on Jo, she was instead flat on her back, looking up at the ceiling. Jo pressed a knuckle against her through her jeans, and Emma's hips came up off the bed.

"I want to—"

"I know," Jo said, undoing Emma's pants and pulling them down her legs. "You'll get to."

Emma's bra and underwear were a matching set, the sexiest she owned. Jo's fingers played with the lace at Emma's waist. Those potential meteors outside? It was clear they would never distract Jo, either.

"It's my turn first," Jo said.

This time, it was intentional when Emma said, "Yes, boss."

Lightning flashed through Jo's eyes. Emma tucked that knowledge away for later use.

Later use. Because she would get to do this again and again. It barely felt real that she got to do this now; it was unbelievable that sometime later she'd get the chance to use the fact that Jo liked being called *boss* in bed.

Jo rid Emma of the last of her clothes with alarming efficiency. One moment she was standing beside the bed tracing the lace patterns of Emma's underwear, and the next there was a pillow under Emma's head somehow. Jo had gotten her naked and maneuvered her more fully onto the bed. She slid a smooth leg between hers.

Emma tried to focus, tried to remember everything. She could barely think, but she didn't want to miss anything. Jo kissed her deep and hard, and Emma tried to memorize the wet muscle of Jo's tongue.

She had plenty of time for memorizing, because Jo just kept kissing her. Which was good. It was really fucking good. It was just—well, when Jo said it was her turn, kissing wasn't exactly what Emma thought she meant.

Emma's hands were on Jo's hips, so it really didn't take much work to slip one around and grab her ass. Jo broke their kiss with a huff of breath and pulled away a bit to look down at her.

"I thought I said it was my turn." Even if Emma weren't looking at her face, she would've known Jo quirked an eyebrow just from her tone.

Emma stuck out her bottom lip. "But you're not *touching* me."

"I'm covering your entire naked body with mine."

"First of all, not my entire body. You're much too small." Jo rolled her eyes at Emma's teasing. "But also, are you touching me, like, where it *counts*?"

Jo ground her thigh against Emma's center, and Emma gasped. "I'll show you where it counts."

Jo adjusted to sit on her knees between Emma's legs. Emma spread them, wide, too ready to be embarrassed. But Jo ignored her. Instead, she drew a fingertip down Emma's nose. Emma giggled. Jo traced down Emma's arms, just enough pressure not to tickle. She interlaced their fingers for a moment, then brushed back up Emma's arms. When Jo's palms covered Emma's breasts, Emma sucked in a breath, back arching without her permission. Jo didn't stay anywhere for long.

It wasn't what Emma expected, wasn't what she'd thought she wanted, but it was everything.

Jo's hands on her felt like the culmination of every time Jo had ever touched her, a hand at her elbow or Jo's thumb against Emma's back at the SAGs, Jo's mouth at the wrap party, shocked and frozen but warm against Emma's lips. The first day they met, Emma a frazzled and terrified PA, starstruck shaking the boss's hand. They say hindsight is twenty-twenty, and looking back, it seemed like it was always going to lead to this: Jo's fingers on Emma's skin an inevitability. Not like fate—not like they didn't have a choice, but like in a thousand different universes they would always make the choices that led them here.

By the time Jo had settled lower on the bed, Emma felt like she was vibrating.

"It's been a while." Jo's voice was low. "Forgive me if I'm rusty."

Emma was accustomed to supporting Jo when she felt vulnerable. She could have taken a moment to do that here. Could have reassured Jo that everything was fine, everything would continue to be fine. Could have admitted it had been a while for her, too, actually, and the first time didn't have to be perfect. They'd have plenty of chances to learn each other.

Instead, she twisted her hips toward Jo's breath and clutched at the sheets.

"Oh my God, I don't care, just *touch* me."

Jo did.

Fuck, did she ever.

After so much buildup, there was no preamble now, just Jo's tongue licking a stripe up Emma's center and fluttering against her clit. It seemed like Emma's entire body came off the bed to meet Jo's mouth.

It all got hazy after that. Emma simultaneously wanted to close her eyes to revel in the feeling and wanted to keep them open forever, wanted to *watch*, to have visual proof that Jo was touching her this way. But looking made everything feel so *big*, made it feel like she was going to shatter from the inside out, and she was going to do that anyway, she was entirely certain, but she didn't want it to happen so quickly, didn't want this feeling to stop so soon. Didn't want it to stop ever.

But Jo seemed determined to take her apart *now*. She was relentless and so, so good, and Emma's hips were jumping in fits and starts. Emma pulled a pillow over her face to muffle her moans, but as soon as she did, Jo pulled back, bit at her thigh.

"Let me see," she murmured. "Please."

Emma threw the pillow off the bed. She stared down at Jo, who slid a finger into her like it was a reward, and leaned back in.

Fuck.

They could never have sex in Emma's apartment if Jo wasn't going to let her bury her orgasm in a pillow. Emma's walls were too thin, but at Jo's the nearest house was half a mile in any direction, and so it didn't matter when Jo made Emma scream.

EMMA DIDN'T OPEN HER eyes at first when she woke up. She was in Jo's bed. The sheets were cool and smelled of fabric softener; the pillow was like a cloud beneath her head.

And Jo.

Jo was curled up half on top of her. Emma's arm was asleep where it was under Jo's neck, but she didn't mind, with Jo's palm resting flat on her sternum and one leg thrown over Emma's. Her breath fanned across Emma's chest. Emma finally opened her eyes and looked at Jo.

She knew it was too soon, and she knew Avery would tease her relentlessly, but she was pretty sure she loved her.

She also knew how Jo liked her coffee every morning, and thought it might be sweet to wake her up with a cup. When Emma tried to ease her way out of the bed, though, Jo's leg pushed down, her hand slid from Emma's sternum across her body to her ribs, and it held on tight.

"No," she said, voice thick with sleep.

"I was going to make you coffee," Emma murmured.

"I like this more than I like coffee."

"You must like this a lot." Emma smiled even though Jo's eyes were still closed.

"I love this," Jo said, and Emma *melted*.

WHEN THEY DID EVENTUALLY get up, Jo made her own drink, and Emma's, too. Emma beamed but didn't comment when Jo pulled an unopened box of chai concentrate out of her refrigerator.

"What does Evelyn think about all this?" Emma asked over her mug. "About us?"

Jo chuckled. "I believe her exact words were 'Thank God you finally got your shit together.'"

Emma laughed. "At least she didn't bet on us," she said. "Avery's husband owed her a hundred dollars because we didn't kiss over the summer hiatus."

"Did the wrap party not count?" Jo smirked.

"No." Emma blushed. "If it didn't count for us, it didn't count for the bet."

"Yeah, I'd say our actual first kiss was better than that one."

Emma's face went redder.

"I can't believe they bet on us at all. It's embarrassing." She didn't feel particularly embarrassed anymore, though. Who cared if the world figured out their feelings before they did? They'd figured them out now. "They made the bet the day after the SAG Awards."

Jo's eyes flashed. "Speaking of," she said. "You should come with me again this year. If you'd like. As my actual date this time."

Emma beamed and agreed without a single worry about the red carpet.

Epilogue

THEY GOT READY FOR THE CEREMONY TOGETHER. KELLI smirked at them and Jaden talked too much and there were kosher pigs in a blanket for lunch. Emma couldn't stop smiling the whole day.

Jo bought her a dress again, this time a one-shoulder red gown Emma adored. Jo refused to tell Emma what she herself would be wearing, and Emma almost passed out when she first saw Jo in the black suit, top button open on her white dress shirt, bow tie hanging undone around her neck.

"Are you trying to kill me?" Emma asked in the car on the way over, gesturing to Jo's outfit.

Jo grinned. "Look who's talking."

Emma was as far as she could be from Jo while sitting in the same back seat. She couldn't trust herself to be closer. Back at the suite, Kelli had already had to fix both their lipsticks. Twice.

They got out of the car, and just like last year, Emma was overwhelmed by all the people and all the cameras and all the attention. Her adrenaline spiked, anxiety-induced fight or flight.

Then Jo caught her hand, interlaced their fingers, and smiled at her.

"You ready?" Jo asked.

Emma was.

ACKNOWLEDGMENTS

They say writing is a solitary activity, and it is, in some ways. But this book would've never existed were it not for the help of a *lot* of people.

First of all, to the reason for my existence: Bonnie Raitt. My mom used to love telling the story that I was conceived after a Bonnie Raitt concert. I finally got her to stop when I took to telling people I was conceived *at* a Bonnie Raitt concert. The day I was born, Bonnie took home four Grammys. And here we are thirty years later, where I name my debut novel after a Bonnie Raitt song. It feels like I gotta give her a shout-out.

My editor, Kristine Swartz: Thank you for making this process so easy and also for occasionally posting pictures of your cat on Twitter. Thank you to everyone at Berkley, especially my Jessicas (Brock & Plummer), Megha Jain, and copy editor Angelina Krahn. Thank you to Vi-An Nguyen and Christopher Lin for the best cover I've ever seen (and I'm not at all biased).

There isn't enough I can say about my agent, Devin Ross. She's levelheaded and smart as hell and somehow always knows whether I need hand-holding or a kick in the pants. I'm both incredibly lucky and immensely grateful to have found her and the entire New Leaf team.

Jasmyne Hammonds convinced me to apply to Pitch Wars because the worst they could do was say no. They said yes to both of us. I can't wait to have a dedicated shelf for your books, J.

To everyone involved in running Pitch Wars: You have created something that truly changes lives and helps make dreams come true. Even now, after everything else that's happened, I still can't believe Farah Heron picked me as a mentee. Without her perspective and guidance, this book wouldn't be half what it is today.

Rosie & Ruby. I was worried about whose name I should put first, and then I realized in the next book I can just put Ruby first. I look forward to switching the order of your names in the acknowledgments for every book I write for the rest of my life. #TeamAllIn

Other people I have to mention: The Slackers can always make me laugh out loud when I shouldn't. Jen Deluca got me through a panic attack over edits without even trying. Zabe Doyle is my favorite person to brainstorm with. She can flail better than anyone I know. My third-grade teacher, Mrs. McBeath, told my parents to teach me to type so I could edit easily instead of erasing an entire page of work to add in a sentence, as I had been doing previously. One of my seventh-grade teachers, Ms. Dolinski, gave me space to write about things close to my heart. Numerous people, including strangers on the internet, helped make Emma's Judaism and Jo's Chinese American experience authentic. Thank you to Lauren, who let me take her out to coffee and ask her about her family's Hanukkah traditions. Thanks also to Addie, Julia, and Andi for their help with the Hollywood aspects of the book.

Thank you to my parents, who let me have an old brick of a laptop when I was just a kid. It only had Microsoft Word on it. I wrote tens of thousands of words of mostly bad fanfiction, but I know there was bad poetry on there, too. Thanks for giving me the opportunity to improve. And thanks in advance, Mom, for the dog and tattoo you promised to pay for when I got my first book published.

I don't know if Tash McAdam realized what they were getting into when they first shouted at me about fanfiction, but I'm so grateful that they did. They helped power me through the first draft of this thing, but more importantly, they got me through the Depressive Episode of 2017.

Christina Cheung let me steal her last name. She's also read this book more times than anyone else besides me. She reads every word I write, and reads them again no matter how few changes I make between drafts. She asks me questions about characters and plots long before I have answers for her. My writing is stronger because of her.

And of course, saving the best for last—my wife, Brooke. Every time I said, "Can you believe this is happening?", she said yes. Thank you for listening on every walk, every car ride, every time we waited for a meal at a restaurant, as I talked through trouble spots. Thank you for cooking and cleaning and reminding me to take breaks. Most of all, thank you for loving me—especially through copy edits.

SOMETHING
TO TALK ABOUT

Meryl Wilsner

DISCUSSION QUESTIONS

1. What effect did the rumors have on Jo and Emma's relationship? Do you think they would have developed feelings, or recognized those feelings, had the rumors never existed?

2. Jo was worried about taking advantage of Emma. Why is this? How did she ensure the power imbalance from their working relationship didn't make their personal relationship unhealthy?

3. How does the book portray sibling relationships? Compare and contrast Jo's relationship with Vincent and Emma's relationship with Avery.

4. What trade-offs do Jo and Emma have to consider when deciding to be in a relationship? How might their reputations and careers suffer? Do you think it's worth it?

5. Why wasn't Jo publicly out? What factors affected this decision?

6. Discuss Jo's relationship with her father and how it affects her and her decisions.

7. *Tikkun olam* is a Jewish concept regarding an individual's duty to improve or repair the world around them. How does tikkun olam influence Emma's behavior throughout the book, but especially in response to Barry Davis?

8. Why might Annabeth Pierce not have come forward about Barry Davis's behavior earlier? What factors affected her decisions, both to stay quiet, and to eventually come forward?

9. Why did the suits at the network suggest Jo be seen out with a man? How might they have reacted differently if the rumors involved Jo and a man instead of another woman?

Photo by Brooke Wilsner

MERYL WILSNER writes stories about queer women falling in love. Born in Michigan, Meryl lived in Portland, Oregon, and Jackson, Mississippi, before recently returning to the Mitten State. Some of Meryl's favorite things include: all four seasons, button-down shirts, the way giraffes run, and their wife.

Ready to find
your next great read?

Let us help.

Visit prh.com/nextread